Mrs. Campbell Praed

Madame Izan

A Tourist Story. Special Edition

Mrs. Campbell Praed

Madame Izan
A Tourist Story. Special Edition

ISBN/EAN: 9783337190026

Printed in Europe, USA, Canada, Australia, Japan

Cover: Foto ©Andreas Hilbeck / pixelio.de

More available books at **www.hansebooks.com**

MADAME IZÀN

A TOURIST STORY

BY

MRS. CAMPBELL PRAED

AUTHOR OF

'THE ROMANCE OF A STATION,' 'MRS. TREGASKISS,' ETC.

SPECIAL EDITION

For sale only in India and the British Colonies

LONDON

CHATTO & WINDUS

1899

MADAME IZÀN

CHAPTER I.

JOHN WINDEATT saw her for the first time in the lift of the big hotel at Hong Kong. That was an epoch in Windeatt's life, though he was not at the moment fully conscious of the fact. He did, however, feel vaguely that something rather out of the common had happened, though this was only that the most beautiful woman he had ever beheld suddenly stepped into the dim, fusty, steaming box which was conveying him and his sister to their recently-acquired rooms on the fifth story.

She entered with a little wavering movement, out of keeping with the Diana-like carriage of her head and bust. This was the suggestion she gave —that of a Greek goddess just descended from Olympus. She had the radiant, surprised expression which, under these circumstances, a goddess might be supposed to wear, and seemed to exhale, as it were, some celestial aroma of youth, and to

I

personify the freshest joy of existence. It was
not, however, a favourable opportunity for cata-
loguing features or for discriminating as to tones
of colour in the matter of hair and complexion.
He perceived that she was a brunette, that nose
and chin were of classic mould, and that about
the splendour of her dark eyes there could be
no manner of doubt. Another lady followed her,
smaller, insignificant, and distinctly more mature.

No other passenger appearing, the four went up
together. In speaking of the four, the Chinese
conductor is naturally not included. This person
leaned in the corner, his head on one side, an expression of weary resignation upon his stolid flat
face as he languidly fanned himself with one hand,
while the rope slithered softly through the other.
Never in tourist experience had that Chinaman
been known to speak, smile, or, indeed, vary the
blank, unintelligent stare with which he greeted
humanity as it presented itself at the entrance to
the lift. He smiled now, the feeblest ghost of a
smile, and he spoke, too, later, when the goddess
addressed him, with a pretty imperious air of
curiosity.

‘ How does the thing go ?’

‘ Has she but just touched earth ?’ Windeatt
asked himself, and reflected, being a person of old-
fashioned taste in literature, that in the days when

Zeus controlled the affairs of the world, eagle's feathers as a means of locomotion had been in vogue, and elevators had not been invented.

The Chinaman shook his head.

'How does it go?' repeated the goddess. 'There was no lift, Herminia, at Singapore?'

'No, there wasn't, dear,' assented the other lady.

'Nor in Colombo,' pursued the goddess. She bent forward and touched the rope and gearing with childlike interest. 'Is it steam that makes it go?' she asked.

'Oh dear no, Izo; lifts are mostly hydraulic!'

Izo did not seem much the wiser, but she sat silent till the last stage was reached, and the Chinaman and his pigtail slowly disappeared up a bamboo ladder and came down again, while the others waited, not being quite certain that they had arrived at their destination.

'What is that for?' demanded the goddess.

'Oh, Izo dear, it's nothing!' said the other lady.

'But I want to know!' exclaimed Izo.

Windeatt lingered at the lift-opening after his sister, Mrs. Eugarde, had passed along, and heard her add petulantly:

'You are always pulling me up, Herminia. And how am I ever to learn the East if I don't ask questions?'

'You could have learned lifts in Paris if we had stayed in a hotel,' replied Herminia. 'They're common enough everywhere.'

'Oh! are they? Well, I want to learn them here. What for, Chinaman?—Topside?—So?'

The enchanting smile and still more enchanting undulation of the goddess's arms, first towards the bamboo ladder and then in the direction of the rope, fascinated Windeatt, and he lingered on. The Chinaman was fascinated also, and the strings of his tongue became unloosed.

'That water. No water, topside—no lift. Mine ling-a-ling-ling '—touching the electric button— 'and mine no savey. No come.'

'Oh, well!'

The goddess didn't seem quite satisfied with this explanation, but her companion would not wait. Here was Windeatt's chance. In stepping out, the lady of his admiration stumbled again, and stretched forth her hand uncertainly. He extended his own to help her, and she touched it for a moment. Their eyes met; he bowed reverentially.

'Oh, thank you!' she said, and, turning down a side-corridor, caught up her friend.

John Windeatt followed his sister. From the end of the corridor two of their fellow-passengers on the steamer advanced to meet them.

'Here are Mr. Barradine and Captain Kelsey, Jack,' exclaimed Mrs. Eugarde.

'We've been to your rooms to look for you,' said Mr. Barradine, a thin, elderly gentleman dressed in gray alpaca, and speaking in a plaintive high-bred voice. 'I wanted to tell you, Mrs. Eugarde, that this won't do at all—oh dear no, not at all! There are five cases of plague in Hong Kong.'

'There are thousands in Canton, and I'm not afraid of them,' said the other man.

'Look here,' said Windeatt, thinking not at all of the plague: 'did you notice those two ladies who came up in the lift? Can you tell me who they are?'

Captain Kelsey, who was a big, dark Indian officer on furlough, making for sport in Alaska by way of Japan, gave a rough guffaw.

'What! another divinity?'

Mr. Barradine knew nothing about the divine lady—had not remarked her, and was far more deeply interested in the reports of the plague.

'I shall go back in the steam-launch, Mrs. Eugarde. I'm certainly not going to stay on shore to risk catching the plague, for if there *is* anything to be caught, *I* catch it. Mumps was the last thing—and at *my* age! No, I shall live on the boat.'

'And I,' said Captain Kelsey, 'am going to Canton. Follow my example, Windeatt: let the divinity rip, and see what you can. Don't be scared by the plague ; Europeans never take it.'

Whereupon Mr. Barradine produced an instance of a European who *had* taken the plague, and had died and been buried.

'It's all rot !' said Captain Kelsey. 'Come along, Windeatt, to Canton. We'll look out for a Mandarin chap—that's the correct thing, they tell me—to shepherd us.'

But here Mrs. Eugarde had something to say. She was a neat, rather impressive-looking woman of about forty, with a pince-nez and a kindly and sensible face. No, she was not going to be left lone and lorn in Hong Kong to hunt up copy for her weekly ' Round the World Jottings.' If Jack went to Canton, she would go too.

' Ah, dear Mrs. Eugarde !' protested Mr. Barradine, ' I assure you that Canton is quite impossible even with a Mandarin to look after you. People are dying in the streets, taking off all their clothes, which would be unpleasant for a lady, and grovelling to the great enemy. Do not be misled by Kelsey ; go back to the boat. One might make inquiries about the Peak, but I really think we should do better on the boat. This hotel is quite the worst I have set foot in yet, and

the dearest. I had a cup of gruel—I didn't
dare take anything else—and they charged me a
dollar.'

' I,' said Captain Kelsey, ' had oysters and iced
sauterne, which were reasonably cheap. They
don't understand gruel in the East.'

Mr. Barradine shuddered.

' Oysters ! Nothing would induce me to swallow
an Asiatic oyster. When I was in Bombay, seven
persons were poisoned by eating oysters.'

' I've eaten a good many scores of dozens in
Bombay and never had an ache,' declared Captain
Kelsey. ' And it wasn't because they were
Kurrachee oysters: you think you're safe if you
ask for a Kurrachee oyster at Green's. And they
get 'em from Kurrachee, and put 'em in Bombay
beds. But I know a fellow that *would* wash down
his oysters with pegs of whisky. Consequently
they turned to leather in his inside and gave him
indigestion ; and he swore ever afterwards that the
oysters had poisoned him. Whisky is fatal to
oysters. . . . Lord !' he continued, ' if you went
on Barradine's tack in India, you'd starve. There
are eleven men in a hundred that won't eat meat
out there, because they'd once been scared.
" Trust in Providence " is my motto, and thank
it for a good appetite. Otherwise, eat everything you fancy, and don't care a hang.'

'Excuse me,' cried Windeatt, whose eyes had been roving down the corridor. 'I quite forgot about some inquiries I wanted to make at the office. There's the lift again. Shall see you at tiffin, I dare say, Barradine. Will you come, Ju?'

'It's the goddess going down,' said Mrs. Eugarde, nodding pleasantly. 'Jack will never be satisfied till he has found out her name, and got someone to introduce him. You must really help me, Mr. Barradine. These divinities are becoming an embarrassment.'

Two figures in grass-cloth gowns and pith helmets, of which one towered a good five inches above the other, appeared from a side-passage, and showed in profile to the group.

'It's the tall one, I suppose!' said Captain Kelsey. 'By George! she's a ripping fine woman; which outspoken remark jarred upon Windeatt. He hurried on his sister, observing that he disliked that fellow Kelsey, a coarse brute, who didn't know how to talk about ladies. And when the Chinaman wanted to wait for those two gentlemen who came sauntering leisurely towards the lift, Jack wouldn't have it, but peremptorily bade the Chinaman start off, which seemed rather a base trick to play upon the gentle valetudinarian. He at least had said nothing to deserve it.

Again Windeatt was struck by that curious

hesitancy in the tall and beautiful lady's way of moving. She had a groping fashion of putting out her hands, as though she were uncertain of the actual distance of any object which might loom before her, and another slight stumble as she entered the lift gave him excuse anew for proffering assistance.

'Oh . . . thank you,' she said again.

Her manner of addressing him—certainly he was a stranger—was jerky and half frightened, yet not without a simple sort of dignity, and her voice was rich and musical. Jack's bow expressed all the homage which such a voice and a pair of eyes so lovely had it in their power to command. The other lady scrutinized him with her head at much the same angle as that of the Chinaman, and with something of the air of an inquisitive bird. From him she glanced at Mrs. Eugarde, and the impression appeared to be satisfactory, for she shed on brother and sister an impartial and grateful smile. She was rather an attractive person, not young, but still pretty, slightly freckled, with curly reddish hair and limpid blue eyes. She murmured something indistinct as to the general unpleasantness of lifts, and Windeatt, emboldened, inquired if she had been up to the Peak in the cable-car, and if she had found the ascent disagreeable.

'No,' the freckled lady informed him, 'they had not, so far, been able to make the ascent.'

And the goddess put in eagerly: 'But we want to very much; we thought of going this afternoon.'

'The view ought to be extremely fine,' said Windeatt.

'Do you know Hong Kong?' asked the freckled lady.

'Oh, not at all,' answered Mrs. Eugarde. 'We are only here since yesterday—waiting for the Japan boat.'

'Oh!' exclaimed the younger one in a tone of awakened interest, and appeared to wish to pursue the subject; but the freckled lady turned it off with the observation that there seemed a promise of a clear afternoon.

'Oh, I hope so!' exclaimed the goddess. 'It is so splendid to *see* everything all spread out before one.'

She laid an oddly pathetic accent on the 'see,' which reminded one somehow of a prisoner let loose. Now the lift stopped at the dining-room, and they all got out. There was a thin crowd streaming into the great pillared place, which was set about with many small tables, and the usual groupings of people that one sees in an Anglo-Eastern hotel—tourists, of course, of the different

types ; a few foreigners ; some English officials,
languidly imperious and indifferent, except to their
food ; men, evidently in the army, in drill suits
and cummerbunds ; and ladies in muslin blouses,
sallow and tired-looking, and with that indefinable
self-conscious smartness acquired by Englishwomen quartered in the East.   Among them all,
the Chinese boys stalked noiselessly—pigtails
hanging, blue gowns flapping with the swing of
the punkahs—always imperturbably remote.   The
freckled lady made for a table in a corner, swept
by the tail of a punkah, and began to fan herself.
She was the kind of woman to whom a fan at her
girdle appears the natural appendage.

Windeatt manœuvred his sister to the next table,
adroitly placing himself so as to get a good three-
quarter-face view of his divinity, and barely a
profile one of her friend.   No doubt he had
reflected that his full gaze might be disconcerting,
for it did not appear that his eyes wandered very
far from that next table, except when they were
bent upon his plate.   Mrs. Eugarde sat facing the
freckled lady's back, but had uninterrupted facilities
for studying the charms of Izo.

'Really, Jack,' she said, taking advantage of
the clatter made by a party of tourists not many
paces off, so that there should be no possibility of
her remarks being overheard by their object, 'I

don't think that I ever saw anyone quite so striking-looking.'

'No, isn't that so, now?' and he seemed charmed at her enthusiastic praise. 'That's exactly what I feel myself. She is more than just pretty or handsome. There's something altogether out of the common run about her—a kind of majesty, an unconsciousness, I don't know how to describe it—something, you know, Ju, that reminds one of a Greek goddess.'

'You couldn't have seen many Greek goddesses out in Australia, Jack.'

'No, I didn't,' he answered frankly; 'and I don't know that I had seen many before I went there. It's just an idea of mine—my fancy of how a Greek goddess ought to look: right over ordinary people's heads in a sort of surprised glory.'

'She may well look over some ordinary people's heads—mine, for example,' said Mrs. Eugarde. 'I should say that she can't be less than five feet nine in her heels.'

'She doesn't wear heels—not to speak of. I noticed that when she got out of the lift.'

'Well,' said Mrs. Eugarde, 'if there's any doubt about the glory, there's none about the surprise. Odd, wasn't it, that she should never have seen a lift before she came to Hong Kong?'

' Yes, it was certainly odd.'

Windeatt seemed to find no satisfactory solution of the problem, which was evidently perplexing him as he gazed abstractedly across to the table where the two ladies sat.

' I think she must be short-sighted,' he said. ' Did you see how she kept putting out her hands, as if to feel her way ?'

Mrs. Eugarde assented.

' But she doesn't look short-sighted.'

' Wonderful eyes, aren't they ? I'm so glad you agree with me, Ju, about her. You see, I'm not easily knocked over——'

' Oh no, indeed,' ironically cried Mrs. Eugarde. ' And what about the pretty girl from the Riverina country who went ashore at Albany, and disappeared? And who was it that insisted upon my scraping acquaintance—and getting snubbed—with the mamma of that golden-haired scion of the aristocracy at Kandy? And we have no recollection whatever, have we, of the charmer who coached you up in the history of the Ruanweli, and good King What's-his-name, and wanted you to chip a piece off the Buddha, who had been sitting since before Christ all alone in the jungle ?—no, I suppose the jungle had grown up round him afterwards, but that's a detail. She lived in Denver City, do you remember? Don't be rash, Jack. America is a

fine matrimonial market. . . . And, of course, you
have entirely forgotten how far things went with
the *fiancée* of the doctor at Singapore. Those
flirtations don't count, do they? Oh dear no!
you are not in the least impressionable—not in
the very least.'

'Don't chaff, Ju. You know quite well what
I mean. I'm not talking about common or garden
flirtations like those. Naturally, when a fellow
has been knocking about for years in the Bush, he
appreciates the society of ladies, and wants to make
the most of it—naturally! And there's nothing
common or garden about this one. I wish I could
remember what the statue is that she makes me
think of—just now, do you observe?—as she
holds her head back and stares in front of her
with that wondering kind of dignity. I've seen
the look in a startled heifer—never in a girl.'

'A Greek statue and a startled heifer! Gracious,
there's a comparison! But I think I do understand. How do you know, though, Jack, that
she is a girl?'

'Of course she is a girl. You don't tell me
that she is a married woman! She is a young girl,
fresh from school—or a convent. Did you remark
that she crossed herself? The freckled one is
chaperoning her. Probably she is an orphan and
an heiress.'

'Her clothes certainly suggest affluence,' replied Mrs. Eugarde, appraising the goddess's attire with a critical eye. 'That jacket is distinctly French, and not cheap French.'

'Wonder if she is staying in the hotel?' mused Windeatt.

'We can find out.'

'Well, yes, I rather think we shall find out. And suppose that she is waiting, like ourselves, for the boat to Japan! That would be—— Yes'—in a louder tone—'Barradine was right. I don't think much of this hotel. It's the worst curry I have tasted in the East. . . . Don't stare, Ju; she is looking this way.'

But the goddess's glance swept indifferently past the table. She appeared quite unconscious of Windeatt's admiration and of his sister's scrutiny. In fact, she was far too absorbed in studying the scene, and also in the viands placed before her. She ate with healthy gusto—not like Herminia, who merely pecked. A dish of fresh lichees seemed as great a novelty as the lift.

'Strawberries!' she exclaimed, with that uncertainty of gesture which had before struck Windeatt and his sister.

Picking one of the fruit—in appearance it is not unlike a yellowish-pink strawberry—she examined it at a little distance, and then drew it

close to her eyes. Mrs. Eugarde came now to
the conclusion that her dreamy, puzzled—what
Windeatt called her startled-heifer-goddess—look
must indeed be due to near-sightedness. The
freckled lady laughed as Izo put the lichee to the
bow of her lips and made a wry face at finding
hard rind instead of luscious pulp, and a small
passage of banter passed between them. Presently,
however, Herminia became sentimental, and
perched her head again at the lackadaisical angle.
Something was said about a 'burying-ground, and
its being a sacred duty,' which led the Australians
to suppose that one or other of the two had a
relative interred in Hong Kong.

The American manager behind the office
counter grinned knowingly when Windeatt asked
to see the visitors' list. He motioned to where
Captain Kelsey stood, his red face bent over its
contents, and as Windeatt addressed him, Kelsey
looked up, with his finger laid triumphantly upon
a recent entry.

'There,' he said, 'I guess what you are after,
and so does the office fellow. Some other gentlemen have been on the same business. I spotted
her at tiffin, and she is out-and-out the finest
woman I've seen this many a day. But she is
booked, my friend. You can't lawfully endow
her with your bit of the great Wee-Waa Mine—

just at present, anyhow. You'll have to try the
effect of cold steel on her husband first, or otherwise discreetly settle him. I bet my hat she is
going out to join the husband, most likely at
one of the Legations. From the name, I should
say the Russian Legation in Tokyo or Pekin.
See here.'

He pointed to two names bracketed, and in
the same round schoolgirlish handwriting, which
Windeatt assumed to be that of the more inver-
tebrate-looking Herminia, but which he afterwards
discovered to be verily the caligraphy of his
divinity :

> '*Madame Izàn* }
> *Mrs. Bax* } *from Marseilles.*'

'Marseilles! That don't tell much. And
which is Madame Izàn?' said Captain Kelsey.
'Sounds Russian, eh? I lay it's the tall one—
the beauty ;' and he went forward and interrogated the clerk, returning with information. 'It's
as I said: it is the beauty. And they can't tell
anything about her, except that she arrived yesterday in the French boat, and is going on to Kobe in
the *Makara*. Nationality unknown.'

'Herminia Bax is British!' exclaimed Mrs.
Eugarde. 'There can be no doubt as to Herminia.'

'Is that her name—Herminia?'

2

'The freckled one,' said Windeatt.

'You look depressed, old chap. Give it up, my boy. Madame Izàn can't be a widow; there's no sign of widowhood about her. Try Herminia : mauve necktie, chastened sorrow— that's more like it—and she's not bad-looking, either. Well, good-bye, Mrs. Eugarde. I've got hold of an obliging Mandarin, and I'm off to Canton.'

Inside the hotel were chairs and bearers, dignified and obtuse ; outside, rickshaws clamoured, equally obtuse, and a bit more amusing. It was evident that rickshaws, if dirty, offered a chance of wilder excitement than the stately sedan-chairs, and the Australians engaged them. So, upon the same reasoning apparently, had Madame Izàn and Mrs. Bax, for, turning a curve as they whirled along the flat road to Happy Valley, Windeatt and Mrs. Eugarde perceived the two ladies in front of them. Windeatt declared to Mrs. Eugarde that he had instructed the coolies to take them to the cable-car station, but he had omitted to say ' topside.' They had by this time learned that if you don't say ' topside ' in Hong Kong, and very often if you do—being a tourist, and thus recognisable—you are incontinently and invariably dragged to Happy Valley. Twice already that morning had these Australians been dragged to

Happy Valley. Under other circumstances Windeatt would have been angry ; he was now meekly pensive.

The rickshaw-coolies stopped with an air of finality before some open white gates, which had already admitted the two grass-cloth-clad ladies, and pointed within to a garden embellished by white pillars and pieces of statuary. When the visitors had walked as far as the fountain in the centre alley, they discovered that the garden was just the most beautiful cemetery there could be in the world—an ideal God's-acre, sloping backward up the hill, open below to ocean's breezes, and to the blueness of sea and sky and lovely land-locked harbour. Natural grottos and ravines furrowed the hill, and the whole was a strange blending of wildness and artificiality. All among the wildnesses lay grave-gardens, set about with carefully-tended shrubs and flowers, velvety grass-plats between, and dividing hedges of gorgeous tropical creepers and the overpoweringly sweet Chinese jessamine.

The statuary was of a mournful and religious character, and on the obelisks and tombstones 'Died young' and 'Died in the service of his country' were the legends mostly inscribed. Over one flat grave, which was shadowed by a slender palm tossing its broad fronds upon the scented air, there bent the forms of two women. Windeatt got a vague impression that one of the women was weeping, and hurried his sister down a side-alley.

'It's quite possible,' he said, 'that she was married straight out of a convent. You know, they do that sort of thing in France. And if she was an orphan to start with, why, naturally, she would have stayed always in the convent, and wouldn't have seen much of the world. Then it was most probable that her husband was in the navy—that seems to me a much more likely supposition than that he is now in a Legation—and he may have had to leave her at once, at the church door, perhaps, for it isn't only in you people's novels, Ju, that romantic things happen. Why, there might have been a hundred reasons. Then, of course, he was killed in the service of his country, or died of fever, and, with proper feeling, she has come out to see his grave. As for what Kelsey said about mourning,' he went on, 'why, how could you expect a beautiful young thing like that to trail widow's weeds after her, and in the tropics? Think of a black gown in the tropics! That, you may be certain, is the explanation.'

'But this is the Protestant cemetery, Jack.'

Windeatt had to own that the ground was not quite covered by his explanation.

'Mrs. Bax looks to me much more like the widow,' went on Mrs. Eugarde. 'She is older and more worn in the face, and the tilt of her head suggests somehow the possibility of her having worn a crown of sorrow at some period of her career. And then Mrs. Bax wasn't eating much at tiffin. Madame Izàn's robust appetite didn't strike me as altogether compatible with conjugal bereavement.'

Windeatt laughed, though he was jarred.

'By Jove! yes; she was hungry! And I don't see that that's anything to do with it. I like a woman to tackle her grub properly. How you do notice things, Ju, and draw inferences! Now, *I* never draw inferences; you're so apt to be wrong in your premises.'

'My dear boy, you've done nothing but draw inferences ever since we met Madame Izàn in the lift. And please to remember,' added Mrs. Eugarde with sententious utterance, 'that my observant faculties, allied to a certain facility in literary composition, have supplied me for many years with the luxuries, not to say the necessities, of civilized existence.'

'Oh, but that's all ended now, happily; I'm running this show,' said Windeatt.

'And you have got also to remember, you budding millionaire, that I had signed the contract for " Round the World Jottings " before your generous transference of Wee-Waa shares. I'm still a journalist on the scent for copy.'

' That's nonsense,' said John Windeatt. ' I won't have you make yourself out a mere literary hack.' But he did not pursue the subject further. Presently, after some aimless pacing and inspection of epitaphs, he said: ' We'll give them time to exhaust their grief, and then we'll sneak round and make sure whether the tombstone has been put up to the departed Bax or to the defunct Izàn.' Which they did.

The mourners had gone, but there was a cross of fresh lilies on the grave, and Mrs. Eugarde fancied that she had seen the identical tribute that morning in the window of the florist close by the clock-tower. Sure enough, the headstone set forth that the monument had been erected to the memory of Richard Bax, surgeon on board the P. and O. steamship *Lassa*, who had died of fever contracted in this town some ten years previously ; likewise that the monument was a memorial of affection, placed by his sorrowing widow, Herminia Bax.

' That settles the question,' said Mrs. Eugarde. ' It's Herminia Bax who is the bereaved one.'

As they turned away, that lady herself confronted them. She was hurrying back with a little bunch of white roses in her hand, and looked really pretty with the flush upon her freckled cheeks, and the tears shining in her blue eyes and darkening her reddish lashes. She was one of those who can cry becomingly. Windeatt and his sister exclaimed simultaneously with her :

' I beg your pardon !'

' Oh, I bought these,' Mrs. Bax explained confusedly—' I bought them from a Chinaman. Roses were *his* favourite flower. He always liked them better than lilies, but I couldn't find any in Hong Kong this morning. We were only married six months,' she added apologetically, evidently a little ashamed of her exuberant confidence, ' and then, as you see, he died.'

' It is very sad,' murmured Windeatt ; and Mrs. Eugarde also made an attempt to express her sympathy, retiring with her brother, and so leaving the widow to indulge unmolested in her very natural emotion. They were rewarded by a meeting with Madame Izàn, who was waiting for her friend. She leaned quite motionless against a granite obelisk, her eyes closed as though she were asleep. As Windeatt's footsteps crunched the gravel she gave a violent start, and with a little ejaculation opened her eyes bewilderedly, making involuntarily, as it were, that groping gesture with her hands while she moved uncertainly forward.

Windeatt took off his hat. 'I am so sorry. I am afraid that we frightened you.'

'Oh, I didn't know—it wasn't that. But I was shutting my eyes for a bit. They get so tired. I can't accustom myself.'

Accustom herself to what—to earth after Olympus? Jack Windeatt wondered, and Mrs. Eugarde hazarded the remark:

'To the glare of the East? It *is* trying.'

'I find such a difficulty in telling if things are close or far off,' said Madame Izàn. 'That's how it is.'

She had dropped her parasol and a bunch of flowers she was carrying ; now she peered down from her slim height, apparently measuring their distance from where she stood. Jack picked them up and handed them to her.

'Oh, thank you,' said Madame Izàn. 'I'm rather helpless without Herminia ; she finds things for me and pulls me along. But I'm getting better every day. I shall soon be quite like everybody else.'

There was a slight pause. Windeatt and Mrs. Eugarde wondered still more, when Madame Izàn cried out suddenly, 'Look!' and indicated with her parasol a faint dark object creeping into the Lymoon Pass. 'Isn't that a P. and O. steamer? I think I can tell the funnels: Herminia taught me. She, of course, knows all about the line.'

Certainly, Madame Izàn could not be short-sighted. The naked orbs of the Australians were quite unable to distinguish the marking of those funnels. Windeatt pulled out his glasses.

'Your eyes must be pretty sharp to make out the funnels at this distance,' he said. 'Yes, it is a P. and O. boat. The *Makara*, I suppose. She was expected in this afternoon.'

'Oh, it's only about the near things that I am so stupid,' said Madame Izàn. 'That's our boat,' she added.

'And ours,' said Mrs. Eugarde. 'You are going on to Japan?'

'Yes.'

'And probably, like ourselves,' put in Windeatt, 'returning home by the Canadian-Pacific?'

'Home!' She repeated the word with a plain-tive intonation. 'Oh, I don't know.'

'Well, anyhow,' said Windeatt, 'we shall be fellow-passengers as far as Kobe. 'That's as good a reason as any for an introduction, isn't it? If you will allow me, Madame Izàn. I have already heard your name.' John Windeatt made his fine bow, which he had not learned in the Bush. 'This is my sister, Mrs. Eugarde. And my name is Windeatt. I'm an Australian.'

'Oh, you are from Australia.' Her face glowed—it was like the face of a child in its quick changes of expression ; and her manner, which might have seemed offhand in anyone else, seemed to Mrs. Eugarde noble in its simplicity. 'Here is Herminia,' Madame Izàn exclaimed ; 'I must tell her. Herminia, you were quite right. You know, you said this gentleman was an Australian.'

Mrs. Bax looked archly embarrassed. She appeared to have left her melancholy with the last bunch of flowers she had placed upon her husband's tomb, and from the manner in which she glanced at Windeatt one might almost have conjectured that she, on her side, would not be averse to a flirtation.

'It isn't fair, Izo, to betray me like that,' she said. 'You see I recognised the type,' she added again, smiting Windeatt with her deprecatory and appealing glance.

'She says it is a magnificent type,' put in Madame Izàn calmly, as though she were merely stating a fact which had no personal application.

'Oh, Izo!' Herminia seemed abashed for a second. 'Well,' she retorted, smiling from Windeatt to her friend ; 'you yourself are a specimen, and so you needn't talk.'

'We do seem to be big,' said Madame Izàn.

'But you seem to be bigger in proportion than I am;' and she looked up at Jack, who stood six feet two in his stockings and had a frame to match, with well-developed muscles.

'There's not so much difference, considering you are a woman and he is a man,' said Mrs. Bax. 'One might call you a daughter of the gods, Izo, you know—mightn't one, now?'—they learned afterwards that Mrs. Bax had a tendency towards cheap sublimities—'divinely tall, but *not* divinely fair.'

'It is he who is divinely fair,' replied Madame Izàn in the same matter-of-fact manner, and Mrs. Eugarde began to think her one of the most outspoken young women she had ever met.

'*You* are not Australian, are you?' Izo went on, addressing Windeatt's sister.

'I suppose so—since he is my brother.'

'But you are little, and brown, and different;' and Izo took note of Mrs. Eugarde's features, much as Mrs. Eugarde had taken note of her—Izo's—clothes. 'That's not the Australian type, is it, Herminia?'

'Izo!'

'You said so yourself, Herminia.'

'Perhaps,' suggested Mrs. Eugarde, 'the variation in type may be accounted for geographically.

He went out young to the Bush : I have lived all my life in Europe.'

' Oh, so have I,' returned Madame Izàn.

' Izo,' remonstrated Mrs. Bax, ' it is not polite to make personal remarks.'

' I know it isn't. Never mind—*Maskee !* That's such a nice word, Mrs. Eugarde. I've learned it from a Chinaman, and I'm so proud of it. It means anything. I dare say among other things it means " I beg your pardon." I didn't want to be rude. Please makes allowances for me, because, you see, I'm not quite like everybody else.'

' Madame Izàn means that her life has been a very retired one, and that she has not had the usual social opportunities,' said Mrs. Bax, bridling with a prim little air of coquettish importance, which was intended to counteract informalities. ' Madame Izàn,' she continued, 'has seen very little of the world.'

' Oh yes, and now she is making up for that by going round the world,' fatuously observed Windeatt.

' Herminia,' said Madame Izàn, ' did you know —they are going to Japan.'

' Oh, really, indeed !'

' In the *Makara.* And the *Makara* has arrived ; and so at last you'll be travelling in a P. and O. boat. Mrs. Bax has been longing to get on to a P. and O. boat ever since she left England. It's been the dream of her life, hasn't it, Herminia?'

Herminia sighed. The dream was obviously connected with the late Richard Bax, and did not admit of intrusive comment.

'Herminia,' said Madame Izàn, 'I thought we had settled to go to the top of the mountain?'

'I expect we'd better wait now till to-morrow, Izo.'

'The dream of *my* life,' exclaimed Madame Izán, 'has been to see things from the tops of mountains ; I don't want to waste any more time among tombstones. Of course it's very nice and right-feeling of Herminia ; but there's all the rest of the world requiring attention : Herminia forgets that I've a hundred years to make up for.'

Neither she nor Mrs. Bax explained the statement, and the Australians did not like to ask questions. On reference to Windeatt's Murray, it was decided that the mountain had better, as Mrs. Bax said, be left till the next day ; and the discussion of the cable-car and Madame Izàn's interested questioning concerning its dangers and possibilities seemed an implied invitation to share them with her. Anyhow, Windeatt took it as such, and the four joined company and strolled

together back to the rickshaws. Mrs. Eugarde
could not contain her curiosity.

'What does Madame Izàn mean by saying that
she has a hundred years to make up?' she asked
Mrs. Bax, as they two fell behind the others.

'Oh, that was an exaggeration : she meant
twenty,' replied Mrs. Bax, and added with her
sentimental sigh, ' Madame Izàn is in a peculiar
position.'

Mrs. Eugarde waited for further enlightenment.

'She was totally blind for nearly twenty years
of her life,' continued Mrs. Bax.

'Ah ! that explains——'

'I see, you noticed. I thought you'd remark
little peculiarities in her way of saying things, and
of going about, and it seemed to me that I'd
better tell you, especially as we are going to be
fellow-passengers.'

Mrs. Bax had an air of holding facts in reserve.
Mrs. Eugarde inwardly made conjecture as to
what other circumstances, physical, moral, or social,
had combined to enhance the peculiarity of Madame
Izàn's position.

'Ah, well !' Again Mrs. Bax heaved an enigmatic sigh, and seemed about to divulge something, but checked herself. 'So naturally,' she
went on with sprightly ease, 'objects that are

quite commonplace to us seem to Izo new and extraordinary, for the reason that till a very few months ago the world was nothing but darkness to her. In fact, she is only now discovering life.'

'How extremely interesting!'

'But extremely painful as well. You can't imagine how painful it was just at first. I really think that sometimes Izo wished herself back into blindness. It was like a baby beginning to walk. I dare say you noticed that she is not ready at measuring distances.'

'I noticed—a hesitation.'

'And her outspokenness. That's like a child, too, isn't it? Occasionally people who are not—not nice-minded, misunderstand Izo. But I am sure that neither you nor your brother would do so.'

'No, certainly not. . . . But surely there is nothing to misunderstand in Madame Izàn's simple frankness and charm.'

'You feel her charm? Yes, it's quite remarkable. Often I am entirely carried away by her—beyond my judgment. It's her unlikeness to women in general, which comes from her long affliction. That always appealed to me so tremendously. For we are not related, you know, though I do stand to her in something of the position of a guardian. Poor Izo! There! See! Oh, Izo, do take care!'

Madame Izàn, in the eagerness of her talk, had well-nigh rushed into collision with a snapped pillar of porphyry—symbol of a life early broken. But Windeatt's quick intervention saved her.

'It's darker than the others,' said Mrs. Bax; 'and so she imagined it was further off. I like to be beside her for that reason. Though really now she is getting over her trouble, and I don't feel the same anxiety. At the beginning, when in a difficulty, she used to shut her eyes and *feel*. She used to say that she longed for night-time; everything in daylight was so bewildering and so unlike what she had imagined it.'

Mrs. Eugarde asked whether Madame Izàn had been blind from birth, and to what she owed the recovery of her lost sense.

'No, not from her birth. She became blind at five years old.'

Mrs. Eugarde made a mental calculation. Five to twenty, and a year added; Madame Izàn was therefore very much older than she looked.

'It was that great oculist at Wiesbaden who gave her back her sight,' continued Mrs. Bax. 'He performed an operation. There was a doubt at first as to whether it would be really successful. Circumstances which occurred just afterwards—

a severe family bereavement and other matters'
— Mrs. Bax sighed once more — ' retarded the
recovery, but I'm thankful to say that the cure
is now a certainty.   Still, as Madame Izàn said,
she has a great many years to make up for.'

CHAPTER II.

MADAME IZÀN showed a determination to take full advantage of her opportunities. She would waste no time in loitering, but was whirled away with her companion, both making the most of a limited vocabulary of pidgin English to impress speed and the wished-for destination upon their rickshaw-runners. The Celestial, however, is never disposed to hurry himself on a stretch, nor is he remarkable for quickness of comprehension when such intellectual effort demands extra bodily exertion. Consequently, when the Australians, following at a less vigorous pace, arrived at the Bund, they found the two ladies stationary, Madame Izàn laughing like a child and eating fruit, while Mrs. Bax, tearful and expostulatory, waved her parasol frantically townwards.

'There! Topside! Tram—hotel—shops! We want to do shopping : we want to have our tea. *Maskee*—home! *Anywhere*, if you'll only move. Oh, will somebody be so kind as to tell them that we don't intend to stop here all the afternoon? *Will* you go on, Chinamen?'

'My no savey;' and the two runners squatted and conversed. When a Chinaman says ' No savey,' there is nothing, short of violent measures, to be done. Windeatt adopted violent measures. A crowd threatened, whereupon he appealed to a withered-looking English resident, just then being borne past in a sedan-chair by three bearers in livery. The resident eyed the party with languid contempt till his glance was arrested by Madame Izàn. Then he took off his hat.

' You are very brave to go about in rickshaws,' he said. ' Most people here use chairs.' After which he talked what seemed gibberish in an imperious tone, and sent the Chinamen trotting once more.

' I see how it is,' said Windeatt. ' Madame Izàn, we are offending against social canons. The law of Hong Kong is not as the law of Colombo. Apparently, none—except a bounder—goes in rickshaws here. Let us return to the hotel and take chairs. It would be fatal to self-respect if we were not carried to do our shopping.'

But in the end it was long past tea-time when they did get back to the hotel. Madame Izàn could not tear herself away from contemplation of the many-hued and strangely-inscribed banners on

3—2

the outside of the stores, and of the brilliant stuffs and embroideries and screens and what not displayed within. She seemed to have a passion for gorgeous colouring, also—judging from the extent of her purchases—plenty of money to spend upon its gratification. Windeatt, too, flung about his dollars royally. One doesn't own three-fourths of a gold-mine to no purpose, as the flat-faced dealers soon found out. And, indeed, during the remainder of their stay, these same curio-vendors became to the Australians a pagan abomination and a cause of dire offence.

After they had been down the Queen's Road and up again, had encountered each other in a dozen stores, and had bargained together over snuff-bottles and silver spoons and hat-pins of hieroglyphic device—these meaning a benison in Chinese, which greatly delighted Mrs. Bax—after they had been well cheated, and had finally invested in Japanese dictionaries and phrase-books and beautiful little pictures of fan-persons on rice-paper, and all the other things one does get cheated over, and that one buys in Hong Kong, the four might have known each other intimately for as many years as there had been hours since tiffin. Going up again in the lift, they found that all were located on the same fifth floor, and that their rooms adjoined. So from the one balcony they

gazed down upon the Bund—a white line cutting
on to the blue water, with the rickshaws crawling
like fat beetles along it, and lazy bundles in blue
sacks hanging on to the parapet. To their right
lay the wide level of the quay, with its busy life
of boats and cargo-barges and steam-launches,
and of all the sampan-abiding population crowding
against the abutting piers ; while beyond spread
the harbour, dotted about with great ships and
bounded by bare brown humps of hills, tinged
with vermilion in the setting sun.

It was all very fairy-like and delightful, and
each one of the others seemed infected by Madame
Izàn's irresponsible gaiety. Mrs. Bax had cast
away from her the sentimental shadow of the
burial-ground. Mrs. Eugarde, who had a vein
of quiet humour, recounted Singapore experiences,
and Windeatt had never been in lighter vein.
Nothing would content Madame Izàn after dinner
but another rickshaw ride through the serpentine
street, which was like a big illuminated bazaar,
with its many lanterns and cabalistic sign-banners,
its glints of gilding and lacquer, of reds and blues
and gamboge yellows, and its glimpses of round-
headed, pig-tailed, grotesque forms in shapeless
garments, fanning themselves, or sleepily talking
or eating, or else industriously plying a trade.
Madame Izàn's rich soft laugh contrasted strangely

with the cries of the rickshaw-runners and chair-bearers as they jogged along, dispersing the lazy groups of Chinamen gathered in the roadway. She wanted to know the name of everything, wanted to buy everything, and could with difficulty be restrained from entering into places where, perhaps, European ladies might not have been very welcome. This eagerness for information and action obliged Windeatt to keep his rickshaw on a level with hers, for the other two had chosen to go in chairs. It was not surprising, as the lamps flashed upon the animated faces of this good-looking pair, while they bent to each other exchanging comments and bits of guide-book knowledge, that the bystanders stared and chuckled, and made remarks which the runners declined to interpret.

Clearly, the signs of the times pointed to a flirtation, more serious than those Windeatt had so far indulged in, between him and the fair mystery, and Mrs. Eugarde was not a little uneasy, and began to ponder upon the advisability of asking Mrs. Bax for some accurate statement concerning the absent or dead Izàn. On the whole, however, she decided to wait till events had further evolved themselves, and the party were established on board the *Makara*.

Then, after the expedition, there was the lounge

on the balcony at the beginning of that sleepless tropical night. Such a night! It would have been purest poetry but for the vile stench which floated up at intervals from the sampans. Truly, is it not a problem on a par with the origin of evil and the doctrine of election, this unnecessary and meaningless juxtaposition of the malodorous with the sublime as presented in the East? Madame Izàn was sensitive to smells, as she was also to contact with rough or jarring substance. She insisted upon her chair being pushed out so that there was no chance of its touching the stone, and she told them of her dislike to wearing woollen stuffs, and her predilection for grass-cloth and Oriental silk and every texture that was smooth to her fingers.

It was upon such trivialities—intimate, and yet befitting the limitations of a recent acquaintance-ship — that they discoursed, while from down below came the subdued hum of the Chinese people chattering together, where they might be descried sitting in sampans—sometimes a shower of tiny stars surrounding them when they shook out the sparks which had lighted their pipes—or as they squatted among the glow-worm lamps of the rickshaws that were drawn up against the parapet. Dark shapes of different craft lay outlined on the water, and here and there a white sail flitted across the harbour like a ghost. The twinkling reflections seemed to catch the froth of babbling talk. Sometimes they spread in long bars of wavering brightness from the electric lamps of the Bund, and sometimes were a mere glimmer from the lanterns of junks and sampans; while high above the dun line of hills opposite, which, too, were speckled with little flames, shone a full moon, putting to shame all the lesser illuminations.

That was how the first day passed, and how Windeatt plunged into friendly relations with Madame Izàn. All the rest came as a natural consequence of the meeting in the lift. It was only to be expected that the two forlorn ladies should take kindly to the notion of a male escort, for when you can't speak Chinese, and know scarcely anything of pidgin English, a man's more forcible mode of argument, even in an unknown tongue, is often efficacious.

Next morning they shopped again, acquiring a considerable quantity of miscellaneous rubbish, and devoted the afternoon to the Peak. As the cable-car went up, at an angle which is duly set forth in the guide-book, it was curious to watch Madame Izàn's gradual transition from pale alarm to excited delight. For she could not be made to believe either that there was not a defect in her own new-found vision, or that the houses were not really sliding down the hill, and that the tall Sikh guards at the gate of Government House had other than a slanting sort of perpendicularity. Windeatt and she, who were sitting next each other, made little jokes and talked softly during the ascent, while Mrs. Eugarde assiduously gleaned 'copy' for her 'Jottings' from a fellow-passenger, and Mrs. Bax, who had again waxed sentimental, gazed silently upon the diagonal landscape. This was for her another pious pilgrimage, awakening mournful memories; for it appeared that her deceased husband had once in a letter described to her a typhoon which had overtaken him on the Peak, and had obliged him, with other persons, to retire into a cellar from the fury of the elements.

'That's where everybody takes refuge here,' observed Mr. Barradine. 'In case of any such emergency, I have been down to see the cellar of the hotel where I am staying, and have satisfied myself that it will hold all the inhabitants of the building, and that there need be no unpleasant rush.'

Mr. Barradine, divided between the risks of catching the plague in the lower town and that of the smells in the harbour, had compromised on the Peak, and had taken himself and his invalid paraphernalia thither on the previous evening.

He was wearing a respirator, and explained that it was to protect him from the damp mist which frequently envelops the summit of this Asiatic health resort. They fell upon him at the car-station, and he was introduced to Madame Izàn and Mrs. Bax, with the latter of whom, on the strength of a sympathetic tendency to throat affections, he at once fraternized, so that they arranged to inspect together this particular cellar of the hotel, which it might be assumed had sheltered the late P. and O. surgeon.

'They build the cellars here like vaults, on iron piles, so as to afford security during typhoons to the entire population,' said Mr. Barradine sententiously. He enjoyed statistics in any way relating to human mortality. 'And the verandas have outer walls so that the damp may be shut out when there's a fog, which I understand to be the case for two-thirds of the year. And this is what they call their sanatorium! Hong Kong is a terrible place, Madame Izàn.'

Madame Izàn flashed upon him a brilliant blank look of wonder.

'Why, it's the most beautiful and glorious place I've ever seen!' she cried. 'And if the rest of the world is only like it, *I* shan't grumble, except that I think I should like it to be a tiny bit cooler.'

'Ah, dear lady,' moaned Mr. Barradine, 'what it is to be young, and to have a superb physique! Nevertheless, I think that before you go very much further you'll come to the conclusion I reached some short time ago. England is good enough for most civilized persons. Once I get back to London, I shall never leave it again. The risks to health in travelling are really too serious. Cholera at Port Said, leprosy at Colombo —I heard of a family who had caught it in their washed linen—the plague here. Then the fog. And besides that, a fever they call the Hong Kong dog, which is nearly as bad as the plague· And if the typhoons blow away bacilli, they do damage on their own account in an equally extensive fashion, two thousand bodies, they tell me, floating about on one occasion in the Lymoon Pass. Well, there remains for us only the terror of war in Japan, and I am informed that there is very great probability of our finding Kobe bombarded by the Russians. Ah! believe me, it is a mistake to go round the world. And now,' he added, 'as the mist has been very unkind to me, and I am afraid of staying out late, if Mrs. Bax is ready, we will go and visit the cellar.'

The mist, however, was kind that day to Madame Izàn, and the dream of her life, as she had called it, was amply fulfilled. From the high point of the observatory, as far as the horizon line, she beheld Asia and the sea spread out around and below her. It was a great map on which were painted, in all their glow and colour, bays, hills, islands, the far ocean, the near town— white and green and gray, with motley splashes in the native quarter, and colonnaded houses set in squares of foliage. Then the gleaming line of the Bund, with men and rickshaws and chairs like insects crawling upon it ; the clock-tower, the flag on Government House, the harbour on which were drawn the thin lines and blotches of the ships and men of war and junks. That was in front of her. When she turned there was the shorn face of the hill, furrowed in tiny valleys and little green cones, as though a Titanic plough had been going over it. And away beyond its brow the sea studded with strange shapes of islands, and further still the misty coast of China.

Madame Izàn's great dark eyes roved over the scene, drinking it in, as it were, with a deep and heart-felt happiness and surprise, those eyes which had awakened so lately to the glory and beauty of the universe. There was, Mrs. Eugarde thought, something very pathetic in the gladness of this fair creature, freed at last from the black dungeon in which she had been so many years imprisoned. Izo threw back her head like an animal revelling in breeze and sunlight ; her lips were parted, and her chest heaved in a breath of intense enjoyment, while she put out her slender, ungloved hands in that touching way of hers, as though she must try and feel with her fingers all that was unfolded to her before she could realize it with her other unaccustomed sense.

'Oh, it's splendid—it's splendid!' she murmured, and gave a little hysterical gasp, and Julia Eugarde could not help putting out her hand and taking Izo's in sympathy.

John Windeatt was watching Izo all the time, nervously pulling his fair moustache. Suddenly their eyes met, and a vivid blush overspread Madame Izàn's face. Julia, being a professional novelist, had a *flair* for such emotional indications, and in the present instance it did not add especially to her satisfaction. Embarrassingly quick work this : blushes and tender perturbations produced in less than two days, and a husband in the background, unless, indeed, that family bereavement at which Mrs. Bax hinted had freed the lady from her matrimonial obligations. But surely in a year it is hardly permissible that a widow should abandon all faint visible signs of mourning. Mrs. Bax had certainly stated that it was less than a year since the operation had taken place, and that a severe family bereavement had delayed Madame

Izàn's recovery. That fixed things as to date. But, of course, the bereavement might have been of quite a different nature, and, somehow, the theory of widowhood did not seem to fit. Julia glanced at Madame Izàn's left hand, which her own hand clasped, and there, for certain, was the gold circlet on its third finger. Horrible qualms beset her ; she sent Jack off immediately to hunt up the bearers.

Madame Izàn scandalized Hong Kong proprieties still further by coming on board the *Makara* in a sampan. The devoted Mrs. Bax accompanied her, though her insistence on chairs during their other excursions in the little island proved her to be a person of more conventional instincts. Their luggage, which was bulky and heterogeneous, arrived with Mr. Barradine and the other passengers in the company's steam-launch. For reasons connected with the pre-transfer of their rooms at the hotel, and not indirectly with the importunities of curio-mongers, which had laid Windeatt open to a charge of assault in the Hong Kong courts, these two Australians had come on board the *Makara* the previous evening, and were quite at home, their deck-chairs placed and their cabins arranged, when Mrs. Bax's freckled, appealing face appeared above the railing of the companion. Captain Hann, who looked down just then over the bulwarks, delivered a wrathful grunt and a volley of Chinese.

'I won't have sampans alongside my ship! Here, quartermaster, send them sharp about their business! Oh, it's passengers! Well!'

The vision of Madame Izàn, to whose assistance Windeatt rushed frantically as she made her impulsive, ill-calculated step upon the ladder, struck Captain Hann dumb. It has been observed that this was often the effect she produced upon shy men. The captain was very shy, and avoided ladies as far as was consistent with his duties and with the company's interests. He was big—unusually so for a sailor—loose-jointed, dark, and grim, and looked as though his size were rather a worry to him. Mrs. Bax halted, her hand extended, her pretty speech and deprecatory smile all ready.

'Have we done anything very dreadful? Oh yes, I know we have ; we ought to have come in the steam-launch, but Madame Izàn said she was tired of steam-launches. We asked the clerk at the bureau if there was no other way, and he said, " I guess you can go in the steam-launch for three dollars, or you can take a sampan." So we took a sampan. It wasn't the three dollars, but Madame Izàn thought the sampan was more picturesque ; but, I'm bound to say, it was very smelly.'

'I'm not particular,' said the captain, ' but I bar sampans. You never know what they'll bring, and ye wouldn't be surprised,' he added, turning to Mr. Barradine, who had drawn near in fascinated terror, ' if you could see the Chinese families—and a few over—that live on the sampans. You wouldn't want after that to make your home on a sampan. But ye don't see the family, because, when a passenger comes along, it hides in the locker. You can smell it, though, and that's a caution.'

'Well, I must say it was,' frankly admitted Mrs. Bax. 'I trust the family hadn't got the plague.'

'Oh dear,' murmured Mr. Barradine, 'I sincerely trust not.'

'How do you do, Mr. Barradine?' went on Mrs. Bax. 'I see you are afraid to shake hands with me, but I think we are all right this time. I did remonstrate with Madame Izàn, but she said she *must* go in a sampan, and when Madame Izàn says she *must* do a thing she generally does it.'

Mrs. Bax's smile was quite irresistible, and, when Madame Izàn's smile was added on to it, completely subjugated the captain, who took the ladies down himself to instruct the steward that their cabins should be on the right side of the ship for coolness. All the officers were in black gauze suits, and the punkahs were rigged, for it was indeed very hot ; but Madame Izàn, in her fresh grass-cloth and sailor-hat, glowing with the radiance of youth and pleasure, showed no signs of being discomposed by it.

There were not many passengers on board ; the only other lady was a missionary. She was travelling with a second-class ticket, but was put into the saloon because it is contrary to European notions of fitness that an Englishwoman should take her meals alone with Chinamen. She had a brown, massive face, sparkling dark eyes, a heavy jaw, and a quantity of iron-gray hair. In the mornings she wore a rusty-black satin dress with a Medicis collar worked in steel beads. On the whole she was impressive, and had the look and manner of one with a mission. She carried an accordion, on which she practised furtively but assiduously, also a Prayer-Book and a Japanese dictionary. Report said that she had little other luggage.

Besides the missionary, there was a German gentleman with a broad band of crape on his arm, who had lately buried his wife.

'It appears that the *dramatis personæ* of this

act are mostly widowed,' remarked Julia Eugarde, who had a way of looking at life from the professional point of view; but, as a matter of fact, the inconsolable gentleman had very little to do with the play. Then there were some tourist young men, two of whom had been passengers on their last steamer, an Indian officer or so—not including Captain Kelsey—and some Chinese merchants, returning after the war to their stores in Kobe and Yokohama.

Windeatt and Madame Izàn stood side by side on deck, and took romantic leave of fast-receding Hong Kong. The big white houses, with the cavernous arches of their colonnades, which stood along the Bund and climbed up the lower slope of the Peak, grew smaller and smaller; the gardens and zigzagging white roads faded into indistinctness; and at last nothing seemed left but the heavy gray cloud enwrapping the Peak, to which Mr. Barradine pointed in melancholy self-congratulation.

'See what we have escaped! One day longer and I should have been laid up with bronchitis. How thankful I am that the week is ended. What a climate! What unholy odours! And what atrocious food! Most assuredly, I have no pleasing memories of Hong Kong to carry away with me.'

It seemed to Julia that a glance full of subtle meaning was interchanged between Windeatt and Madame Izàn—a glance which signified, no doubt, that they considered themselves richer in this respect than the amiable hypochondriac. Julia did not like that look, and yearned still more earnestly for definite information in regard to Mr. Izàn. But Mrs. Bax was not just now susceptible to discreet pumping ; her particular memories of Hong Kong were for the moment too overpowering, and her eyes strained the distance for a farewell glimpse of the graveyard in Happy Valley. Julia felt certain also that Mrs. Bax was going to be sea-sick. Freckled people very often take the ocean badly.

Her foreboding was realized ; Mrs. Bax retired shortly to her cabin. The rest held out for a time, and the tourist young men, whose spirits were rampant, struck up ' Radoo,' and got through it in diminuendo, made a gallant attempt at ' Tommy Atkins,' but broke down, and the Irrepressible Boy, as they called him, ordered champagne and soda-water.

' You really shouldn't give yourself away like that,' said the doctor. ' Everybody knows what champagne and soda-water means.'

' Can't help it, doctor ; it's a fact. I'm bad, and so is the captain ' — indicating Kelsey —

'though he has been swaggering about, declaring he never was sea-sick in his life.'

By dinner-time a strange quietude had fallen upon the saloon, broken only by the plaintive calls of Mr. Barradine from his cabin, and a vigorous volley, half in English, half in Hindostanee, which consigned Captain Kelsey's Indian servant to speedy perdition. For three days very few of the company showed up. Poor Mrs. Bax was extremely ill. Madame Izàn came to ask if Mrs. Eugarde had any smelling-salts, as they had forgotten theirs in Hong Kong. This request gave Julia a pretext for breaking in upon the invalid's seclusion, and also allowed Madame Izàn greater freedom to remain on deck under the care of John Windeatt. There was no knowing what strides their intimacy made in those three days. She was a very good sailor, so was Windeatt. As for Julia Eugarde, she was just bad enough to shirk responsibilities, and to prefer being left alone in her deck-chair, or in a certain cushioned corner of the saloon which happened to be close to Mrs. Bax's cabin, so that, in her good-nature, she became available in case of requirements on the part of that vanquished lady. Julia felt that she really could not desert poor Herminia, as Madame Izàn seemed heartlessly inclined to do. She was sustained, too, by the hope that there might arise opportunities for confidential conversation. But for a little while the hope was vain. Mrs. Bax was far too limp to show concern when Julia informed her at intervals, and with intention, of Madame Izàn's doings. First, that she made a practice of walking for an hour every morning up and down the deck on Mr. Windeatt's arm—a practice with which the rough weather did not seem greatly to interfere. Secondly, that Windeatt was teaching her patience, halma and other games, which agreeably filled up odd hours. Thirdly, that Julia had been obliged to remonstrate with her brother for keeping Madame Izàn on deck after all, except the officers, had gone below. These operations, it may be stated, extended rather beyond the three days of storm, but Herminia appeared in no hurry to reassume her position of watchful guardian. On hearing of all this, Mrs. Bax only groaned :

'*I* can't help it. Of course, I know that Izo does lay herself open, but what can I do?'

'You might explain to her, don't you think?'

'Oh, she wouldn't understand. You don't know Izo. She is like a baby about some things—but *as* pig-headed. I really can't always cope with Izo.' Then, cheerfully : 'But your brother is all right. He's a gentleman, and he'll not take advantage.'

The inference was clear that Izo had already

occasioned Mrs. Bax uneasiness in regard to persons who had not been gentlemen, technically speaking, and who had 'taken advantage.'

'Of course my brother would not take advantage—I don't quite know what you mean,' said Mrs. Eugarde in a doubting manner. 'But doesn't it strike you that——'

The suggestion was a delicate one.

'What?' asked Mrs. Bax.

'Well, you see, it isn't as if Madame Izàn were an ordinary unmarried woman. You said she was in a peculiar position. I hope you will not think it impertinent of me to make the remark.'

'Oh dear no,' said Mrs. Bax, looking uncomfortable, which look gave Julia courage.

'Possibly Mr. Izàn — I suppose there is a Mr. Izàn—though, if she's a widow——'

'Oh, she's not a widow,' said Mrs. Bax.

'Well, doesn't it seem to you that possibly Mr. Izàn might prefer that she should choose to walk and sit on deck and play patience with—an older person than my brother—Mr. Barradine, for instance.'

'Oh, Mr. Izàn!' began Mrs. Bax helplessly, and added : 'There wouldn't be any sympathy between Izo and Mr. Barradine. She is quite different from me ; she is so splendidly healthy.'

'If I were in Mr. Izàn's place——' ventured Julia.

'Oh, that's all right,' answered Mrs. Bax. 'Mr. Izàn won't know anything about it.'

'Still, that mightn't mend matters. It's no business of mine, but I was going to say that if I were in Mr. Izàn's place—supposing he were on board—I should be inclined to assert myself.'

'Oh, he'll never assert himself,' declared Mrs. Bax—'at least, not at present.' There was a brief pause. 'I'll speak to the doctor about it,' Mrs. Bax went on. 'It's the doctor who seems to manage everything on this steamer. He's a person of great tact and determination. I'll get him to advise Madame Izàn that the night air is injurious, though I don't know if that considera-tion would weigh much, she's so healthy. But the doctor will think of something. Anyhow,' she added, as if that settled matters, 'Mr. Barradine wouldn't sit on deck in the evenings ; and so it comes to the same thing.'

'If the doctor's influence is sufficiently power-ful with Madame Izàn,' Julia assented distrustfully.

'Oh, you don't know Dr. Duppo,' answered Mrs. Bax. 'He's very powerful. I've seen a good deal of him in here. I'm sure he would know how to tackle Izo. He can make *me* do anything.'

' But then you are sick.'

' And Izo is never sick,' replied Mrs. Bax regretfully. ' It's such a pity. If she were sick, she would be much less trouble. It won't last very long now,' she remarked, with an air of mystery. ' You'll see. When we get to Japan, things will settle themselves.'

' Perhaps Mr. Izàn will meet his wife in Japan,' Julia hinted.

Again Mrs. Bax looked uncomfortable, and took refuge in her prim little dignity.

' Nothing is decided yet,' she said. ' We shall know when we get to Japan.' She was silent for a minute, during which Mrs. Eugarde took off her pince-nez and cleaned it. ' You understood from me that Madame Izàn's position was a peculiar one,' Mrs. Bax said, abandoning the dignified attitude, but keeping the primness. ' I don't know whether I am justified in talking about Madame Izàn's private affairs, but I don't mind telling you that her blindness has complicated matters considerably ; it has complicated her marriage relations. The fact is,' she added in a burst of unpremeditated confidence, ' Madame Izàn has never *seen* her husband.'

The fog was clearing.

' Oh dear, I hope he won't disappoint her !' Mrs. Eugarde exclaimed ; and she could not help

making a mental comparison between the splendid
Australian Apollo on deck and the hypothetical
picture of a disagreeable Calmuck. Somehow, it
had become a generally accepted belief that Mr.
Izàn was a Russian.

' I hope not—oh, I do hope not !' Mrs. Bax
exclaimed fervently. ' Or, if he does——' She
did not finish the sentence.

' I see,' said Mrs. Eugarde, after another short
pause, leaving Mrs. Bax to infer what she did see.
' I assure you that I have no intention of being
intrusive.

' Oh no, not at all. It was quite natural.'

' I was thinking of my brother, who, as you
must have noticed, seems greatly attracted by
your charming friend. And I don't mind telling
you, on my part, that I am extremely anxious to
see him happily married ; for he has got the
notion in his mind, and it's bound to happen
pretty soon. In fact, I believe that he left
Australia with the intention of seeking a wife in
Europe. Thus, you see, the fire is all ready laid
for the match.'

' Yes,' I see,' said Herminia in her turn. ' Men
are like that.' And Mrs. Bax sighed, doubtless
in affectionate reminiscence of the departed Bax.

' They are much more weak-minded than
women in affairs of the heart,' said Julia, ' and a

great deal more susceptible. Now, it would be very sad, wouldn't it? for him if further complications arose through a misguided attachment on his part. But if I have your authority for stating that there is a Mr. Izàn in existence whom Madame Izàn expects shortly to join——'

'Oh, I didn't say that,' hastily interposed Mrs. Bax; 'I have no authority. But, of course, there *is* a Mr. Izàn—at least, there was, not very long ago.'

'That's quite enough to check any ill-founded hopes he may be cherishing. You know, we were neither of us sure, and especially as you had spoken of a bereavement from which Madame Izàn had suffered.'

'Oh, that wasn't her husband; it was her uncle. He died about a year ago, just after the operation, and he left Madame Izàn a good deal of money. That's how we come to be travelling round. Well, I'll do anything that I can, Mrs. Eugarde. But Izo is very difficult, and she'd fly out at me if I even suggested that she was encouraging your brother. She has no idea of flirting; she's very innocent.'

'At any rate, the information you have given me puts things on a safer footing,' replied Julia Eugarde, 'and I'm deeply obliged to you. I shall take the first opportunity of telling my brother that Madame Izàn is not a widow, as he may have supposed, and that he mustn't be so wrong and ridiculous as to fall in love with her.'

'People can't help that sometimes,' said Herminia sentimentally.

'Under certain conditions, the law of England obliges them to help it,' said Mrs. Eugarde rather sharply. Although she was a professional story-writer, she was not greatly given to sentiment.

'Oh, well, I'll do anything I can,' repeated Herminia.

And just then there was a tap at the door of the cabin, and the doctor came in to see after his patient.

CHAPTER III.

JULIA had not paid much attention to Dr. Duppo, not having been ill enough to require his services, and sitting away from him at the captain's end of the dinner-table. He was a square-set, clean-shaven, ugly man, with a downright way of talking.

'You've got to get up,' was his preliminary address to Mrs. Bax.

'Oh, you haven't asked me how I feel, doctor.'

'I can see that without asking. You're much better.'

In fact, Herminia was looking well and quite delicately pretty in her much - beribboned pink dressing-gown, with a flush to match on her cheeks, and her eyes shining in soft sympathy over the possibility of a tragic muddle arising from Windeatt's attraction to Madame Izàn.

'I'm feeling very weak, doctor; I couldn't possibly get up. I've tasted nothing but champagne and ship's biscuits for ever so many days. I couldn't possibly touch anything else.'

'You'll have some more, then. But you've got to get up; you've got to lie on deck.'

'I couldn't walk up the stairs, doctor.'

'I'll carry you'—stretching out his arms; 'I have got good muscle.'

'But I'm not dressed.'

'Mrs. Eugarde will put a blanket round you.

'And my hair isn't done.'

'What's wrong with your hair? I'm going along to get you champagne and biscuits, and you'll please to be ready, by the time I come back, for me to carry you up on deck.'

Mrs. Bax looked at Julia, and laughed with triumphant satisfaction. 'Didn't I tell you? Can't he make one do *anything?*'

The doctor came back, poured out the champagne, and produced a chicken sandwich, which Herminia ate with relish. He did not exactly carry her like a baby, but supported her up the companion and along the deck, where her reappearance made a sympathetic commotion among the passengers. Most of them were assembled there. The missionary woman, looking very bilious and huddled up in a plaid shawl, for the weather had become suddenly cooler, was settled by the skylight with her Prayer-Book and Japanese vocabulary before her, from which she was reading in an undertone. Mr. Barradine, with a woollen comforter round his neck, tottered up on the arm of the Irrepressible Young Man, and Captain Kelsey and two of the Indian officers were playing nap. Windeatt and Madame Izàn stood together contemplating the coast of China : a barren shore ; red sandhills ; a walled town dimly visible in the midst of a desert plain. The sea heaved greenish-gray. A little fleet of sampans tossed upon its swell, as they tried to make for a line of nets fastened to stakes not far within the steamer's course. The captain had his glass upon them, and now handed it to Madame Izàn.

'They're giving it up as a bad job,' he said. 'I never knew a Chinaman anything but a duffer on the water. It isn't a pretty shore, Madame——' The captain never quite accomplished the 'Izàn.' He had confided to Windeatt that his prejudices went against Russians. 'There's nothing grown along here but sweet potatoes and fish.'

'Feesh !' repeated the German with the crape round his arm, pausing in his tramp—'feesh is goot. Every kind of feesh is goot—the boil, the roast, the fry. In Eetaly feesh is beautiful ; the religion obliges the people to eat feesh ; they must be very particular in the cookings of their feesh. In England the feesh is boil, always boil. In Eetaly it is roast, in Germany it is stew——'

'And in Japan it is raw, and sometimes rotten,'

put in the captain. 'I've known a whole Japanese village poisoned through feasting on a big fish that had been cast up by the waves—in an advanced stage of decomposition.'

Mr. Barradine shuddered. 'You would not advise me to eat fish, then, in Japan, captain?'

'Yet it is goot—feesh-food,' said the German.

Windeatt looked a little conscious when Mrs. Bax called fretfully from among her cushions:

'Izo, I think it is too bad of Mr. Windeatt to monopolize you. I haven't seen you at all. Come and talk to me, Izo.'

'Why, I saw you this morning, Herminia.'

Madame Izàn went towards her friend, fretfully rubbing her fingers against the cloth of her blue dress. She looked even more handsome, if less like a goddess, in this semi-nautical costume, which suited her better than the grass-cloth, and was equally a Parisian product. Her eyes and cheeks were glowing, and she wore a rakish little English fore and aft, set upon the dark-brown waves of her hair.

'I told you I should never be able to endure it, Herminia;' and she held up her thin, sensitive hands. 'Every time I touch the stuff, I shudder.'

'That's curious,' said the captain. 'Is it the feel of the serge that makes you shudder, madame?'

'It's the first time I ever had a dress like this,'

said Madame Izàn, 'and I dislike it. You see,
my fingers used to be my eyes, and all my nerves
went into them.'

'It wasn't that I was thinking,' said the
captain ; 'but that Mr. Windeatt must have felt
uncomfortable with your shudderings, the times
when you've walked up and down with your hand
on his coat-sleeve. You should be getting used
to it by now, madame ; ye've had some practice.'

Madame Izàn was not at all abashed.

'It was perfectly horrid,' she answered ; 'but
Mr. Windeatt said I should fall, and so I should
if he hadn't held me. I'm sure he must be as
glad as I am that it's smoother weather, and that
I can get along without him.'

'There can't be a doubt about that,' said the
captain.

Windeatt looked cross, Izo a little puzzled,
at the laugh with which the captain left them.

'Are you better, Herminia ?' she asked.

'I want you to come and sit with me, Izo.'

'I'll come by-and-by. Now I'm going to play
quoits with Mr. Windeatt,' said Izo.

The two went round to the lee side, where a
band of spectators gathered round them watching,
Captain Kelsey taking upon himself the super-
intending of Madame Izàn's performance as soon
as he had finished his own game.

'I was certain that it wouldn't be of the least use, my trying to do anything,' murmured Herminia despondently. 'Izo never *will* see.'

Mrs. Eugarde's observations of the pair convinced her that she had better lose no time in tackling her brother. Later on, she managed to get hold of him, the doctor, rehearsing his own part in the comedy, having taken Madame Izàn, whose thirst for knowledge was even more insatiable than her apparent liking for flirtation, to inspect the engines down below.

'Jack,' began Julia Eugarde, 'you are not behaving at all nicely towards Madame Izàn.'

'I—not behaving nicely towards Madame Izàn?'

'In less than five days you have made her the talk of the ship.'

'Oh, but that's nonsense, Ju!'

'Not in the least. You are never apart ; you sit up on deck to all hours ; you live in her pocket. Everybody is remarking it. The missionary lady—her name, by the way, is Theodosia Gotch—asked me last night if you had travelled by the same steamer to Hong Kong, and if you were engaged.'

'Theodosia Gotch should mind her own mission, and leave people outside it alone. All the same, we may be.'

'Engaged !'

'Well?'

'Jack, she is a married woman.'

'*Was.*'

'*Is.*'

Mrs. Eugarde stamped her small foot emphatically.

'You are mistaken,' said he. 'Yesterday she told me herself that she is her own mistress, and responsible to nobody in the world. So where does the husband come in?'

'He does come in, though. I have it on Mrs. Bax's authority that Mr. Izàn is alive.'

'She is free,' persisted John Windeatt. 'She has told me so.'

'Perhaps,' suggested Mrs. Eugarde cruelly, 'her husband has divorced her. She is twenty-five—I have found that out, though she looks seventeen. It's quite possible, though even twenty-five is young to have irretrievably disgraced one's self.'

'Ju!' Windeatt's voice rang out, sternly reproving. 'You know that it's quite impossible, and you are only saying it to aggravate me. She is as innocent as a baby.'

'Read me the riddle, then. She says that she is free. Her bosom friend declares that she is bound, and that her husband is alive. Perhaps it's a judicial separation.'

'I don't believe it's anything whatever.'

'Well, I have good reason to conclude that matrimonially she is unattainable.'

'We shall see,' returned Windeatt darkly.

'You don't mean, really, Jack that you would marry her if you could.'

'I think that's pretty well what I do mean, Ju. The instant I set eyes upon her in the lift at Hong Kong, I said to myself, " There's no need for me to skoot round the world any further. I've found my wife." '

Julia was shocked beyond expression. Though she ought to have known that it was John Windeatt's way to make love, as he made money, at double-quick pace, she had not imagined that things had gone as far as this.

'I must say,' she said in a tone of mild exasperation, 'that you Australians seem to know how to make up your minds.'

'The exigencies of social conditions out West,' he replied, 'oblige us to be prompt in our decisions.'

The brother and sister looked at each other straight. Then both laughed.

'But if she is married already, Jack?' said Mrs. Eugarde.

'I can't help that, Ju. I shall have a try, all the same.'

'Jack, do you expect me to aid and abet you in defying the proprieties?'

'Certainly not, Ju, if you have any objection. You can always take the Empress boat straight across to Vancouver.'

'Oh, Jack!'

'Oh, Ju! Don't be stupid, dear. I'm only chaffing.'

'But not about your being in love?'

'No, indeed, not about my being in love. There I'm deadly earnest.'

'Has she told you anything about her life, Jack?'

'Not a word, except that she was blind. She is the oddest mixture of out-spokenness and reticence that I ever met. And she has a straight high way of looking at a fellow that effectually checks caddish questioning.'

'And how are you going to find out?'

'I shall wait till we get to Japan. Then, when opportunity occurs, I shall ask her.'

'Why not ask her at once?'

'Because, as I said, that would be acting like a cad. I should be putting her into an unpleasant position. You see, she can't get away from me on board this steamer. She can get away from me in Japan if she wants to, though I don't mean to let her unless she very much wants to. No, it would be playing it rather low down on her, poor little thing! to force her into a corner and make her tell me what perhaps she has her own good reasons for keeping to herself.'

'Poor little thing!' repeated Mrs. Eugarde with a certain tender derision.

'Well, poor big thing! if you like that better.'

'I can't see that there's anything caddish in trying to ascertain a fact which ought to have been made clear from the beginning. She is either free to receive honourable addresses or she is not,' objected Mrs. Eugarde.

'Lord! what a grand way you literary people have of putting things! Honourable addresses! As if—— It's simply a question of whether I pop the question on sea or on land. And don't you understand that my attacking the subject implies a motive? And the motive means—popping the question. Then there's the boiler bursting, and only deep ocean to jump into to escape being scalded.'

'And in the meanwhile?'

'Well, in the meanwhile?'

'Suppose you fall hopelessly and dangerously in love?'

'Oh, I told you—I've done that already.'

'And what if she does it, too?'

'Perhaps so much the better, perhaps so much the worse. But you needn't be afraid of that, not for the present, at any rate. I suppose it's her having been blind nearly all her life that makes her so different from everybody else. I don't think she has a notion of what falling in love means ; she is far too much taken up with seeing the world and enjoying it. That's her idea : to *see* all she can, and to *feel* as little as she can. She has done enough of feeling—through her fingers ; the word doesn't appeal to her in any other sense. My impression is that she is a sort of Undine, and has got to find her soul through love.'

'If that's the case, what made her marry Izàn?'

'Don't ask me ; *I* haven't the clue. Perhaps he made her. I'd stake the Wee-Waa that she was never in love with him. And I'd almost stake the Wee-Waa, too,' he went on deliberately, 'that Mrs. Bax invented that marriage and the name and the wedding-ring. One *has* heard of such romantic expedients. Wasn't there a book written about a certain non-existent Mr. Null?'

This was a new view of the matter, which, from the professional point of view, commended itself to Julia Eugarde as having some aspects of probability. She felt sure, on subtle indications, that Mrs. Bax was romantic enough for anything. You had only to look at the books she chose out of the ship's library, thought Mrs. Eugarde, to be certain of that.

'It's nothing short of mental dram-drinking,' Dr. Duppo had said. 'You're just ruining your intellectual constitution.'

Whereat Herminia, who was singularly amenable to the doctor's admonitions, put back her novel— harmless enough, but beneath the lowest literary standard—and during two whole days lugubriously perused Bacon's 'Moral Essays,' till the doctor, taking pity on her, stalked up one morning to her deck-chair and laid a volume of superior fiction upon her lap, with the remark that delirium tremens frequently supervened upon the too sudden cutting off of drams. As for Madame Izàn, she never looked into a book. This was, perhaps, not surprising, since she had for so long read through her fingers, and had hardly yet grown accustomed to using her eyes ; yet, considering her disabilities, she must have had a good capacity for assimilating knowledge. She was by no means ill-informed, and of history in especial knew a surprising amount, while she could recite long passages from Pope's translation of the 'Iliad' and 'Odyssey.' Julia Eugarde asked her how she had acquired her classical taste. She hesitated for a moment, her face clouded oddly, and the manner in which she replied, 'A man who was a student helped me,' was no encouragement to further questioning. It came out, however, that a certain scrappy acquaintance she had with modern authors was due to the good-nature and industry of Mrs. Bax.

Julia gleaned from sundry piecemeal information that Madame Izàn had not always been rich and cared for, but had passed a lonely and neglected girlhood, shut up in her darkness under the charge of an uncongenial relative. Herminia, it appeared, had been a lodger in the house of Izo's relative, or in an adjoining abode—-this point Mrs. Eugarde did not get clear—and, moved by compassion for the girl's sad state, had employed some of her own leisure hours in printing, according to the raised method for the blind, part of the contents of a miscellany of varied merit, called 'Gems from the Literature of To-day.' Mrs. Bax had also been in the habit of reading aloud to Izo for a short time every day.

The 'Gems' had supplied poor Madame Izàn with mental sustenance of a fairly satisfying kind, and the readings aloud, which, judging from Mrs. Bax's present literary taste, must have lain in the fields of penny fiction, had no doubt been the inspiration of day-dreams and romantic fancies, to which the poor blind Izo had owed all the joy of those dreary times. On these slight founda-tions Julia Eugarde made up a sketchy plot, which she burned with curiosity to verify; but the stray confidences which, in funny little outbursts of frankness, the two ladies made, were, it seemed, invariably repented of, and were often haltingly withdrawn or explained on some commonplace interpretation, too evidently an artless afterthought on the part of Mrs. Bax. For some inexplicable reason, it was certain that a rule of reticence had been decreed in regard to Izo's antecedents.

It was all rather puzzling—the more so, Mrs. Eugarde thought, because, as Windeatt had observed, Madame Izàn was, for a married woman—assuming her to be really married—curiously immature and ignorant in the matter of feminine worldly wisdom ; indeed, she seemed to shrink with a kind of terror from probing below the surface of things. It was as though she were afraid of making some discovery which might destroy her illusions and put an end to the butterfly existence she now enjoyed. She gave the impression of one who had deliberately chosen not to look realities in the face, knowing that sooner or later she must learn some unpleasant truths, and wishing to put off the disenchanting hour as long as possible.

Her delight in the veriest trifles of Nature was almost pathetic. The flight of a sea-bird, the iridescence on a fish's scales, some effect of sunlight or storm, the frothy arabesques on the wave-crests—such things as these seemed to stir her to quiet ecstasy. To the human side of life she seemed impassive, looking upon it as a mere play or picture. Apparently she did not or would not understand the possibility of deep emotions. As Windeatt had said, like Undine, she had yet to find her soul.

And truly this gliding through the Yellow Sea towards the Land of the Rising Sun was for all of them a basking and idyllic sort of existence. After the first few days of knocking about by rough winds, nothing could have been more perfect than the weather. The tropical heat had been left behind at Hong Kong, though it was still warm enough for luxurious deck-loungings and open-air music in the evenings. Dr. Duppo turned out to be an accomplished pianist. In this respect he and Mrs. Bax, who was gifted with a tender little warble, found sympathies in common, as they had also with Mr. Barradine. Poor Mr. Barradine suffered excruciating agony from the noisy breakdowns of the tourist gentlemen, headed by the Irrepressible Young Man.

'My greatest drawbacks through life have been a sensitive ear and a too susceptible palate,' he sorrowfully affirmed ; 'I might also add a disastrous tendency to attract disease germs. Captain, please wait a moment : I have been wishing to tell you that the missionary lady's accordion is a torture which I can no longer support with dignified patience. She has established herself on a portion of the second deck which immediately adjoins my cabin. There she conscientiously practises scales, vocal and instrumental, at the hour of my siesta. I wish to make a complaint before my reputation as a gentleman is irretrievably ruined. This afternoon I shouted " Damn !" and she heard me, and sent in to inquire if I were in pain.'

' Bribe a Chinaman to stick a pin through the blowers,' suggested Captain Kelsey. ' He'd do it gladly for a dollar, and we'll all contribute to defray expenses.'

' But she has a good face,' added the captain thoughtfully ; ' and she means well. Gentlemen, the complaint shall be attended to. Next time the accordion strikes up, send the quarter-master for me, and I'll discuss the question with Miss Gotch.'

The missionary lady had a queer fascination for Madame Izàn. In the evening, when the gentlemen were in the smoking-room, and there was nobody to play games or otherwise amuse her, Izo would hover round the saloon table where Miss Gotch usually sat poring over her Bible and Japanese dictionary, and would listen silently to the experiences Theodosia was always ready to

pour forth in the ears of an interested inter-
locutor—reminiscences mainly of East End work
in London, which were plentifully besprinkled
with allusions to sundry bishops and archdeacons,
and other clerical dignitaries in connection with
what she called the C.M.S. It was generally
Mrs. Eugarde who turned the tap on for Madame
Izàn's benefit, for while keenly observant and
ruminative, Madame Izàn seldom asked a question, and her air seemed to imply a half-conscious
dread of that dark social sphere in which Theodosia Gotch did battle for her sex.

Izo came down to the saloon the evening of
the day after Mrs. Eugarde's conversations with
Mrs. Bax, and later with her brother, on the
subject of Mr. Izàn. Julia had a suspicion that
Herminia must have repeated what she had said,
for Madame Izàn wore a puzzled defiant expression, had markedly avoided Windeatt, and
in her intercourse with Mrs. Eugarde was like a
child hesitating on the threshold of a stranger's
room, partly tempted, partly repelled, and waiting
for advances to be made. Julia was more inclined to wait for advances herself than to make
them on her own account, and so lay herself open
to the imputation of impertinent meddling. The
missionary lady, as usual, was engaged in her studies.
Izo seated herself at the end of the table and

leaned over with her elbows upon it and her chin resting upon her nervously-interlaced fingers, while her eyes roved from Julia's embroidery to Miss Gotch's dictionary. Then, contrary to her wont, she began with uncompromising directness :

' I should like to know why you fancy that you can teach the Japanese?'

The missionary lady raised her sparkling dark eyes from her exercise-book, and her rather coarse lips relaxed into a friendly smile.

' Well, Japan is considered a promising field,' she replied. ' There are now forty thousand Christians among a population of forty millions, and the native ordained preachers are thought to be reliable.'

' And you?' asked Madame Izàn. ' What are *you* going to do ?'

' First I have to learn the Japanese language, which I am now endeavouring to do,' answered Miss Gotch. ' They give one eighteen months for that. Then it will depend upon what the Bishop thinks I am fit for. I trust,' she continued with modest self-confidence, ' that he will take my previous training among the lost women of London into account. I must say that I feel a vocation towards that line of work amongst grown-up persons. I shouldn't say that I had any vocation for teaching children. Under God's help I should like to try and convert the grown-up Japanese to the Christian faith, and especially the poor abandoned women of the tea-houses.'

'Why are they abandoned?' asked Madame Izàn. 'Who abandons them?'

Miss Gotch regarded her with a perplexed expression. Madame Izàn's brown eyes were as limpidly uncomprehending as those of a child.

'Why—of course——' began the missionary lady, and stopped. . . . 'That's why I'm learning the accordion,' she said, turning to Mrs. Eugarde. 'I'm very sorry that Mr. Barradine objects to it. I should have liked to put my reasons before him, but the captain assured me that he would not find them convincing, and that it was of no use to attempt it. Still, I should have liked to try, for you could hardly believe the number of men I've been enabled to influence—young Guardsmen and men of that sort, who have sought me out. . . . They say that if one can sit down outside a Japanese tea-house and play a tune or sing a hymn, a crowd will shortly be attracted ; and there's your opening straight away for laying the Divine truth before them. I'm too old to learn to sing in any elaborate way, but I'm practising my sol-fa-do. They tell me the Japanese are fond of music, and that even this I shall find a help.'

Madame Izàn appeared deficient in a sense of

humour ; at any rate, she remained perfectly grave. But Julia Eugarde's aberrant fancy conjured up a vision of the missionary lady in her shiny black satin and Medicis collar against a kakemono background, manipulating the accordion and preaching the Scriptures to an assemblage of unconverted Japs—a picture which seemed to her sufficiently comical.

'I have been attracted to the East as a field of labour,' Miss Gotch went on with portentous earnestness, 'mainly through one or two cases of real and fictitious marriages between Europeans and Eurasians and Japanese, which have come within my experience. I may say that, under Providence, I was instrumental in obtaining her rights for a poor girl who had believed herself deluded by an illegal ceremony. I consulted one of the ladies of the League, the wife of a great barrister, and she laid the matter before her husband, with the result that the marriage was ultimately proved to be binding. It is a much more difficult thing than most people imagine to break a marriage contracted with an Eastern, according to the forms of his or her country— that is, if it ever comes into a court of law. Most of them do not.'

Madame Izàn rose abruptly.

'What do you know about it?' she exclaimed

with a vehemence that surprised both the missionary lady and Julia. 'A marriage like that is an injustice and a cruelty towards the one who is most ignorant. If that one wishes it broken, it ought to be broken, no matter what the law may be. I don't understand about your abandoned women and your false marriages. Marriage is a cruel mistake, and no one would ever marry if they knew what they were doing—signing their whole lives away, and putting themselves in prison for ever and ever. I don't want to hear any more about such horrible things.'

She swept down the saloon on to her cabin, and shut the door. The missionary lady looked at Mrs. Eugarde distressed and astonished.

'What did *I* say? What extraordinary opinions to hold! Is it possible that she is herself married to an Eastern, and wants the marriage broken? I can tell her that she won't find that such an easy thing to do.'

With the missionary lady's speech a light flashed upon Julia. Here seemed a terribly probable explanation of the whole mystery. And if so, what fate might not be in store for John Windeatt, if he should take the same view of the matter as Madame Izàn?

From deck burst down the strains of 'Tommy Atkins' again, and then the Irrepressible Young

Man called out, ' " Old Black Joe," that's a ripper! Let us have " Old Black Joe," ' which followed— pathetic, almost solemnizing. After that the young man sang ' Juanita ' in falsetto, and the whole of them, including Mrs. Bax, joined in the chorus of ' Dem Golden Slippers.' Mr. Barradine, haggard and harassed, descended the companion, and, tragically divesting himself of his comforter, commanded the Chinese boy to bring him a lemon squash. By-and-by Mrs. Bax fluttered down, also calling ' Izo !' But Izo was obdurate to Herminia's rappings at the cabin door.

'Go away, Herminia,' she cried out ; ' I'm sleepy !' But the tone of her voice suggested suppressed sobs.

Julia Eugarde went to her berth and greatly wondered.

CHAPTER IV.

As the coasts of Japan came in sight, it seemed to Mrs. Eugarde that Madame Izàn wore an air of repressed, almost tragic, excitement. She and Mrs. Bax held themselves apart, talking in a manner apparently so confidential that Windeatt and his sister hesitated to approach them. In John Windeatt, too, were signs of inward perturbation, not to say jealousy.

Madame Izàn had during the last few days, ever since the incident with the missionary lady, developed a violent interest in photography, and the Irrepressible Young Man had been teaching her how to use a Kodak. Consequently, she had been able to think of nothing else, and had given up her deck-walks and games of patience, somewhat to Windeatt's discomfiture. Mrs. Eugarde suspected some more subtle reason for the change, and was well pleased. She had not held any further conversation with her brother on the subject of Madame Izàn's marriage, supposititious or actual, as might turn out. When the episode with the missionary lady had been mentioned, he had positively refused to discuss Julia's suspicions.

'I shall ask her myself when the time is ripe,' he had declared. 'In the meantime, I don't want to hear anything about the matter ; and you would raise yourself considerably in my estimation, Ju, if you would not encourage Mrs. Bax to betray her friend's confidence.'

Julia was hurt at the rebuke, which she considered uncalled for. She took the line of total indifference to her brother's private concerns, and informed him scathingly that he, on his side, was at perfect liberty to encourage Madame Izàn in committing bigamy without let or hindrance on her part. After this a certain reserve had crept into their intercourse.

But, in spite of all, this was Japan—that wavy outline of peaks and cones tossed up against the silvery blue, and those queer, humped shapes of islets and peninsulas rising sheer from the level streaks of sunlight upon the bluer sea, and those fairy-sailed sampans and the decked junks, with the high prows and perforated bulwarks, and the gray villages scrambling up in the hollows between the hills, so overshadowed by trees that only patches of fantastically-curved eaves and dark roof-copings could be distinguished. How was it possible to cherish stupid British ill-humours when all around was so sweetly and poetically gay? Land, sky, sea; the dreamy sound of the water rushing from the vessel's bow as she steamed along, sails set as well; the tender sough of the wind which made music in the rigging; the frolicsome breeze, blowing in wanton puffs—everything contributed to this dangerous sense of irresponsibility.

And now they were in the harbour, where among the native craft and merchantmen were French and English and American men-of-war and a fierce Russian battleship, which looked as though it could, with its big guns, gobble up, as easily as the wolf gobbled up Red Ridinghood, pretty, harmless Nagasaki, lying so peacefully at the foot of her green hills.

It was a relief to Mr. Barradine when the three small brown health-officers in smart serge suits and peaked caps passed the *Makara* without making inconvenient difficulties on the score of those five cases of plague at Hong Kong. And here came the coal-barges, manned by dainty little women in dark-blue kimonos, with light-blue handkerchiefs bound round their elaborately-dressed heads, who beamed and smiled ecstatically upon the ship's crew, and turned even the prosaic process of coaling into a joy. Everyone in Nagasaki smiled and beamed welcome on the new-comers, from the rickshaw-coolies crowding the

Bund, laughing and gesticulating and bowing at
an acute angle from their waists, while they
pointed to the cabalistic lettering on their mushroom hats, to the oblique-eyed babies slung at
their mothers' backs.

The brown grigs between the rickshaw shafts
bent forwards their mushroom hats on a level
with their shoulders, the muscles of their bare legs
swelled into knots, and whirled the party over an
arched bridge away from the dull European
quarter into a doll-town of sights and wonders—
a town of queer small brown houses, which had
sliding fronts and magic panels and unexpected
windows, pushed apart suddenly, to show rosy flat
faces with painted lips and sleekly tired heads
bristling with coloured pins ; a town of lanterns
and banners and inflated fish flying from the
house-tops, and of persons who seemed to have
stepped out of fans, tripping along on wooden
clogs—clack, clack—over the stones, with kimonos
narrowed round their feet, and huge butterfly
sashes if they were young maidens, and big flowered
silk knapsacks if they were matured women, in
the middle of their backs ; a town of umbrellas,
and kites, and pagodas, and dragons, and porcelain
monsters, and temples, and much tea.

And Madame Izàn's depression vanished as mist
vanishes in sunshine. She gazed at each bowing

person and smiling passer-by at first, Julia fancied, with vague alarm, then with unfeigned delight and amusement.

'Herminia,' Julia heard her say petulantly in answer to some remark of Mrs. Bax's, ' oh, do let us be happy, and forget that this is anything but Japan.' (' Why, what else could it be?' thought Julia.) ' I want to *see*, Herminia, not to think. I did quite enough of thinking when I was in the dark. Now, Herminia, I declare solemnly that if you make me think of what I want to forget, I shall leave you behind, and you may travel along by yourself. I have absolutely made up my mind that I will *not* think till I'm obliged to, when we get to Tokyo.'

Clearly, then, Tokyo was the goal of Madame Izàn's Eastern pilgrimage, and there doubtless the mystery would unravel itself, unless, as Julia grimly foreboded, Windeatt's lover-like impetuosity should provoke some untoward explosion before that, which would force Madame Izàn, in spite of herself, to think, and perhaps also to feel.

As though to emphasize her declaration of irresponsibility, Madame Izàn turned now to Windeatt with her old radiant smile, which had been dimmed these last days, and the little helpless swaying of her arms that always brought him to her side on the instant.

'Madame Izàn, you had really better take my arm now that you've got out of your rickshaw. For you'll tumble over a dragon or a bowing gentleman to a dead certainty, if you don't. You see your eyes have got to learn Japan, haven't they? Poor baby eyes! You mustn't give them too much to do just all at once. Do please take my arm.'

Which she did ; and that was how they walked along the Kago-machi. No wonder that the four-feet-nothing Japanese looked up in astonishment at the splendid stature of these two fine specimens of man and woman. So tall were they that they could scarcely help knocking their heads against the ceilings of the curio shops, and yet so mag-nificently proportioned that in an ordinary way one would hardly have been impressed by the fact that they towered above the rest of their kind.

Well, if there's one experience in the world—in a small way, of course—that one would like to dream over again o' nights, it is one's first expedi-tion in the Kago-machi. Ah, those curio shops! But for Dr. Duppo, John Windeatt and Madame Izàn would have bought them up entirely, straight off, including the fan-person who, as the strangers entered, would glide forward through a sliding paper screen, and with his two hands upon his knees would butt deferentially from his haunches till his forehead touched the matting.   Three times thus would he butt.

'Oh hairi nasai !'

'Honourably deign to enter,' translated the doctor.   'Konnichi-wa !' politely returned the doctor.   And then the bargaining would begin.

'Ikura? [How much ?]   No, Madame Izàn ; it's against my principles to see unprotected ladies taken advantage of.   Three yen !   Don't you believe it.   One yen—not a sen more.'

Then the fan-person would grimace in respectful deprecation and bow once again, profoundly murmuring something about old Satsuma.

'Old Satsuma !   Rubbish !   There's not a bit of old Satsuma to be bought in Japan.   It's Kioto Satsuma.   One yen.'

'Nikko Satsuma !' submitted the fan-person, his head touching the ground.   'One yen fifty, then.'

And so it would go on.   The fan-person would consult a sort of magician's book inscribed with strange letters on rice paper, and mournfully shake his head.   Whereon the doctor would wheel round, followed by that son of Anak, Windeatt, and would make a feint of departing.   Then the fan-person would snatch up the article in question, gaze at it lovingly, passionately wrap it in more cabalistically-stamped paper, thrust it into a box as mournfully as though he were burying his last hope, and deliver it into the hands of the doctor, prostrating himself many times in farewell ; and amid 'Sayonaras' and 'Arigatos' they would proceed on their way again in proud possession of tortoiseshell rikisha, dragon - spouted teapot, bronze saki-cup, and what not, till another rickshaw had to be engaged to carry the spoils.

Then there came tea and jam-rolls in the balcony of the Bellevue, looking over the harbour and down upon a little garden with contorted trees and doll lakes and play-box bridges and rhododendron and orange trees in bloom. Julia Eugarde and Mrs. Bax objected to the tea served in cups with handles, and to the jam-rolls ; they had wanted real Japanese tea and some of the pretty pink cakes they had seen in the Kago-machi.

'Very well,' said the doctor, ' you shall have a second tea at the Tea-house of the Frogs, and the very same cakes that Madame Chrysanthème used to order ; and you may have some raw carp and vermicelli and sugar and soy, if you wish to be strictly Japanese ; and I warn you that you'll be quite content to remain English in future—anyhow, in the matter of your victuals.'

Only Julia Eugarde, the literary one of the party, knew anything about little ' Kiku-san,' and the doctor promised to give Mrs. Bax a treat, and buy her a copy to read going through the Inland

Sea. Presently they were all whirling off again, though you must please understand that in Japan there is never any hurry, and that whirling is only a figure of speech, and applies to nothing but rickshaw locomotion, for it wouldn't mean whirling anywhere else. Here were strange barbaric arches, the like of which no one except the doctor had ever before seen—great naked pillars with curved architraves, that they were to become familiar enough with before long. And below and above and between the gateways, flight upon flight of stone steps and funny little courtyards set about with grotesque monsters and big bronze tubs and fountains, with many paper banners and fluttering white scrolls, which were the prayers of the devout. For it was the Suwa Temple on the hill, and these were the steps up which Loti and Yves dragged Madame Chrysanthème. Now crowds of men and women and mousmés, with sashes spread out like dragon-flies' wings, were tripping up and down, and the air was thick with the clack-clack of the wooden pattens. Men and boys were flying kites, and some were holding umbrellas, and others were carrying gay lanterns to light them home in the evening : these were they who meant to dine in the Tea-house of the Frogs. It was as though a swarm of odd-shaped and brilliant-hued insects had alighted and were clustering round the low

brown buildings of the temple, so quaint with
their turned-up roofs and heavy bronze copings—
a swarm that dispersed by batches among the dark-
green firs which almost hid the temple and the
tea-house, and hid the human dragon-flies, too, so
that one only heard the sound of their elfish
laughter.

The doctor had his jest, and there were wry
faces over the cakes and the concoctions in lacquer
doll-bowls. But what did that matter? Those
were real fan-figures which set down the thimble-
cups and all the queer paraphernalia of a Japanese
feast ; and this was the land of bloom and pastime
—Japan, dreamy, delicious, languorously stimulating. And did it not seem to both Julia and
Windeatt that Madame Izàn was already affected
by its strange spell, since her perverse mood had
left her, and verily Undine was finding her soul!
For upon her face, amid all its smiles, there was
something pensive and womanly which neither
had observed in it before ; and her laugh, that had
been silvery and unemotional as a bell, had now a
tender ring. Windeatt longed to ask her the
reason of her previous humour and of her shunning
airs, but dared not, lest the humour should return.
Perhaps it was the surest sign of deepening intimacy
that, though they were alone, they talked less
freely than at the beginning. The company had

divided. Mrs. Bax and the doctor were watching the kite-flying from the head of the stairway in an abstracted and somewhat melancholy manner, Mrs. Bax looking sentimental and the doctor grim ; while Julia Eugarde had pulled out her note-book and was seated among the pilgrims' banners, with pince-nez adjusted and alert eyes taking in everything, adding to her weekly instalment of ' Round the World Jottings.'

Captain Hann was in a bad temper. A steamer belonging to another line had come in before him, had bought up the fresh milk and green vegetables, and secured the first lot of passengers to Kobe and Yokohama. But not even this prosaic note could mar the dreamy exhilaration of that party of five—including Dr. Duppo, for it would appear that he also had private reasons for feeling exhilarated—who went ashore for that first time at Nagasaki.

It was like piercing into the heart of an un-known fairy kingdom to glide along between the peaked hills, through the narrow, blue passage which leads towards the Inland Sea. There were quaint villages scrambling about the feet of the hills, and the slopes showed broad bars of pale green— the green of young corn—alternating with sharply drawn stretches of darker vegetation—all in straight lines, which sometimes took a zigzag course, giving the effect of a gigantic stairway. There was a hint of gnome-life about the queer-shaped rocks, and of some sort of Nature-god in the weird-looking firs. There was one, the only growing thing upon an upheaved rock, which lay like an antediluvian beast upon the face of the water. The tree spread out deformed arms, as though imploring notice in its solitude. Elsewhere a still stranger old pine would lift itself from the roof, as it were, of some gray pagoda. It shadowed the temple with its blobs of horizontal foliage, just as in the landscapes on lacquer boxes and tea-trays, so that Julia Eugarde made a note to the purport that these things, which she had imagined grotesque creations of fancy, were in fact absolute realism.

The sun was near its setting, and gradually lowered till the distant mountains were rosy and the near ones deepest green, with black shadows in their dents and furrows; while in the fore-ground, here and there against the line of hills, there showed the gray perforated hulk of a junk, standing out spectrally, its tall stern and pointed prow and tattered sails wobbling on the swell of the steamer's course, and reminding one somehow of old engravings to the ' Ancient Mariner.' . . . And before long all the hills together melted into a roseate mist, and from that became soft violet blots upon the sky. And soon all the lights came out—irregular lines of fiery dots, and more brilliant flames at wide spaces apart, of buoy and lighthouse. . . . And that was the last of Nagasaki.

At daylight the next morning Julia Eugarde awoke with a start, for the stewardess had touched her on the shoulder.

'It is for you to go on deck. There is something you ought to see.'

Julia huddled on her clothes, and mounted. The decks were swimming, and the further world was wrapped in a mantle of gray haze, through which gleamed opal tints, and, faintly discernible, the bizarre outlines of peaks and islands. Round about, near the steamer, lay scattered a fleet of junks and fishing-boats, some of the sails making dark squares on the gray haze—for they were ancient and weather-stained—and others freshly white as seagulls' wings.

It was very beautiful ; and there was something ethereal in these long level lines of pale illumination streaking the tender indefinite blue. And now, for a quarter of an hour, the sun shone out, lightening the mist, and gave a clearer view of the green ranges and the gray villages at their base.

Then suddenly the fog fell, a dense curtain of white velvet, shutting out everything.

The fog-horn wailed eerily, and sometimes the engines stopped altogether. Mrs. Bax, who certainly had less sympathy with the eccentricities of Nature than with the vagaries of human emotion, shivered and went down below. So did also Captain Kelsey and an Indian officer, and the tourist young men, who had stolen up in pyjamas and overcoats; and Mrs. Eugarde could hear them talking over their tea and toast and morning fruit. Captain Kelsey was telling a story of how by stratagem he had decoyed a boatload of a savage enemy close enough for his men to fire with effect. 'Raked 'em through, just below the belt,' he was declaring with gusto, and Julia never liked him afterwards.

It seemed as though three persons and some ghosts of sailors now had the deck all to themselves. The three were John Windeatt, Madame Izàn and Mrs. Eugarde, who, shrouded in her heavy cloak and lost in professional reverie, was scarcely distinguished by, and almost oblivious to, the pair a few paces from where she sat.

Windeatt had insisted upon Madame Izàn taking his arm as he moved about the deck. It was customary with both on such occasions to make some friendly little jokes over her dislike to the feel of his frieze coat. She had not put on her gloves this morning, and his eyes travelled tenderly downward to the sensitive fingers which rested above his wrist.

'Are you getting accustomed to me?' he said, with an odd intonation in his voice.

But Madame Izàn took him quite literally.

'I suppose that I am,' she answered. 'I don't seem to mind nearly as much as I used. But, then,' she added, 'I'm getting accustomed to everything.'

'To everything!' he repeated, a little disappointed—'to all the rest of the world, and to me as a part of it?'

'Yes,' she answered simply, and went on: 'For, you see, I haven't had so very long to get accustomed to things, and, of course, for the first month or two, when I began to go about like other people, it was as if one had been a kitten with one's eyes just opened. But there's one thing I should never get accustomed to,' she said brightly, 'and that is the wonder and the glory of the sight we saw this morning when the fog lifted. Oh, this beautiful world! And to think it has been here always—always!'

'Always!' he echoed.

'And I didn't know it, in my dark times.

'Ah yes, I understand. What did you feel like,' he asked abruptly, 'when you were blind?'

She gave a little shudder.

'Don't talk of it, if you'd rather not!' he exclaimed, smitten with compunction. 'I oughtn't to have reminded you of those bad times. They must have been very bad times.'

'Yes, they were very bad.'

'Sit here,' he said, pulling up a deck-chair against the shelter of the captain's cabin. 'You don't want to go down, do you? There's an hour till breakfast, and it's very pleasant here, though we can't see anything, except ourselves. But the fog may lift at any moment, and you wouldn't like to miss that.'

She let him put her in the deck-chair, and folded her cloak tighter round her.

'You ought to have a rug to keep the damp from your feet,' he said. 'Do let me fetch my 'possum rug.'

And before she could say yes or no he had run down the companion-way. Presently he reappeared, carrying a splendid dark rug of Tasmanian opossum, which he tucked in over her.

'You don't know,' he said, 'what a satisfactory thing a 'possum rug is.'

'Oh, but I do know,' she answered. 'I've got one in my cabin. No, it's in my big box in the hold. Uncle O'Halloran gave it to me. He brought it to England with him from Australia.'

' O'Halloran !' he repeated in a surprised tone.
' I wonder if it could be the same. I used to
know an O'Halloran—Redmond O'Halloran—
out on the Doondi River—not very far, that is,
from the Wee-Waa—and he struck gold before
the Wee-Waa rush, and started the Doondi
Diggings. Yes, I wonder if it could be the same.
How curious that would be, wouldn't it? He
made his fortune and went Home.'

' That must certainly have been my uncle !'
cried Madame Izàn. ' His name was Redmond.
And do you know that *I* have got a claim on the
Doondi Diggings? How odd it seems—to be a
poor blind pauper nearly all one's life, and then
suddenly to find one's self a *seeing* girl, and rich,
with a share in a gold-mine !'

' It can't seem odder to you than it does
to me,' said Windeatt gravely. ' That's my
experience, too. I was a pauper one day—only
I wasn't blind——' The deep note of sympathy
in his voice made Madame Izàn look up at him
with a grateful wonder in her eyes. ' A ruined
squatter,' he went on, 'and the bank down upon
me. Then, in less than a year, I had got hold of
the Wee-Waa. And—here I am.'

' The Wee-Waa !' she said, a little puzzled.

' The Wee - Waa Gold-mine—shortly to be
floated on the English market as a limited

liability company ; and that's what I'm going Home for—that and other things.'

He became reflective. Madame Izàn, reflective too, stroked the fur rug wrong way up, and made a pretty grimace ; then right way down, caressingly.

'Your 'possum skin makes me think of the only friend I had for a long time, except Herminia Bax, though it was before I knew Herminia,' she said.

'And was your friend a woman?' asked Windeatt.

'No,' she answered ; 'it was a cat—a tabby cat. They told me it was a tabby,' she added ; 'I never saw it. The cat was the cause of my knowing Herminia.'

'Oh, how was that?' inquired Windeatt eagerly.

'Well, you see, Herminia lived in the next house to us, and there were ' — she seemed to hesitate for a word—'there were other lodgers in the house, and one of them was not at all a good young man ; at least, Herminia said he was not at all good, and that it was he who poisoned my cat.'

'So the cat was poisoned?'

'And Herminia came to break the news to me,' went on Madame Izàn. 'Herminia knew I was fond of the cat, for she had watched me nursing it outside in the back-garden—we had a little strip of garden to each house. Herminia used to sit at

7—2

her window sewing, and she has told me how
sorry she used to feel for me, being lonely herself,
and fancying that I was lonely and neglected.
Because Aunt Sophia found me rather a trouble,
you know, and would have liked to keep me
always at the school.'

' A school for the blind ?' he asked.

' Yes. My mother sent me there before she
died ; and it was all right as long as she lived,
but afterwards—there was only Aunt Sophia. I
liked the school much better than Aunt Sophia's
house. It was unfortunate that they wouldn't
keep me beyond the age of nineteen. . . . But I was
going to tell you about Herminia Bax. She took
the opportunity of the cat's death to make friends
with me. Wasn't it nice of her? You really
wouldn't believe how much I owe Herminia,
though I am ill - tempered and perverse, and
sometimes threaten to leave her when she worries
me. Of course, though, I should never leave
Herminia, if it was only because of the cat. Well,
she used to get me up to her room, where I would
sit with her while she sewed : and she would read
to me—stories mostly ; or she would talk romantic-
ally about Mr. Bax, and marrying, and love and all
that. Herminia was very romantic then—more
romantic even than she is now. I suppose it was
because of her having been in love with Mr. Bax,

and his dying. That's why she is so fond of the
P. and O. and of Dr. Duppo. He was a doctor
on a P. and O. steamer—of course you know all
about that : you saw his grave at Hong Kong. I
wouldn't look at it ; I don't like graves. I don't
like anything disagreeable ; and graves are disagreeable, don't you think ?'

'Yes,' assented Windeatt; 'at least, it depends.
I suppose if one loved anyone very much, one
would like to tend her, or his, grave.'

'Oh, I don't like graves!' repeated Madame
Izàn.

'It's excessively interesting,' said Windeatt—
'your story, I mean. My heart aches, to think
of that lonely blind girlhood. And so Mrs. Bax
took the place of the cat. Or perhaps you got
another cat ?'

'She—that is—someone—wanted to give me
another cat,' answered Madame Izàn, again
hesitatingly. 'But Aunt Sophia wouldn't let me
have it. She had always disliked my cat —
However, then——'

Madame Izàn seemed to be pulled back upon
herself, as it were, by some not too agreeable
memory, for she gave her shoulders a little shake
and her brows drew together in a frown, while she
fell into a sudden silence.

'Oh, please tell me more,' said Windeatt, with

tender persuasion, 'if you don't think it impertinent of me wanting to know. I love to hear
about your girlhood. And, you see, I am not at
all a stranger, having met your uncle O'Halloran
— I — I was great friends with your uncle
O'Halloran,' he added mendaciously. 'Why, you
and I might have been friends for years. For
what would have been more natural than that you
should have come out to your uncle at Doondi,
supposing he hadn't come Home to you? And I
might have known you out there in the Bush,
where people don't stand on ceremony and formal
introductions, and all that sort of nonsense—
known you as Miss—Miss O'Halloran?'

He pronounced the name in tentative interroga-
tion.

She nodded. 'Yes, I was Miss O'Halloran, I
suppose.'

'Izo O'Halloran,' he went on, taking pleasure
in the slight familiarity. 'I've heard Mrs. Bax
call you Izo, and I've wondered what it stood
for. Izobel, I fancy—or the Scotch Izobel.'

'My mother was Scotch,' she answered—'Izobel
Carmichael. That's much prettier than Izobel
O'Halloran.'

'Is it? I don't know. But it's not prettier
than Izobel Izàn, which is a most peculiar and
effective combination.'

He spoke shyly, greatly daring ; but Madame Izàn moved uneasily in her chair.

'I don't think I want to talk any more about my name or my girl-life,' she said, with her child-like directness, which was at once an appeal and a rebuke: for he flushed, and made some incoherent apology. 'I don't want to talk about my dark time. I'd like to forget—to forget—to forget!' she repeated, with a tragic intensity which startled him, as well as that, so far, unthinking listener, Julia Eugarde. 'Now I'm going down!' exclaimed Madame Izàn abruptly, and got up, shaking off the opossum rug.

Windeatt was deeply distressed.

'Oh, why?' he cried. 'Please—please forgive me! I was carried away by my—my interest in you. And don't you know that I wouldn't willingly cause you a moment's pain or uneasiness —not if——'

He, too, paused. For there came a sudden calling and scurrying on deck, and the captain's voice ringing out imperatively from the bridge, and another voice answering from behind the white velvet curtain. There was a ringing of bells and a shrieking of the fog-horn and a queer scraping sensation of reversed engines.

'What is it?' cried both Madame Izàn and Julia Eugarde. But to Windeatt's shame, he took

no notice of his sister.   Indeed, he had not
realized her nearness.

' A collision,' he answered quite calmly.

Just at that moment a shapeless black mass
loomed diagonally out of the mist, which it could
be seen in a moment or two was another great
steamer, with men and women on deck, and so
close that it seemed as though hands stretched
out from bulwark to bulwark could have clasped
fingers.   Windeatt flung his arm round Madame
Izàn, drawing her protectingly to his breast.

' Don't be frightened, Izo,' he said.   ' We're
together, anyhow, and that's enough for me. . . .
No ; it's all right now, dear.'

The bows just barely grazed : there was hardly
a tremor.   And then the white mist swallowed up
that black monster again, and the *Makara* was
gliding on as if nothing had happened.   But it
was several seconds before Windeatt released
Madame Izàn from this wild embrace in which
their two hearts had thumped one upon the
other and he had kissed her lips.   She gave a
frightened gasp and looked bewilderedly into his
face, reading the confession too plainly written in
his eyes.   Then she broke away from him and
would have fallen upon the slippery deck, had not
Mrs. Eugarde, against whom she brushed, caught
her arm and steadied her to the companion.

'Jack!' Julia cried in reproachful indignation.
'Oh, Jack!'

At breakfast no one thought—except two,
maybe—or talked of anything but the narrow
escape they had had of a collision; which was well,
perhaps, for that particular two—Windeatt and
Madame Izàn. They sat as usual in opposite
places, a little below the captain, and their efforts
to avoid meeting each other's eyes might otherwise
have awakened comment.

'That was the ship I had a grudge against for
taking our fresh milk and our passengers at
Nagasaki,' said Captain Hann. 'It was her fault.
She had no business to be anchored just in the
track, and to take it for granted that everybody
else would see fit to anchor likewise. She should
have answered our signals. But I know how it is.
Her bell is over the captain's cabin, and he don't
like to be disturbed by it. Well, I have given
him a scare!' added the captain with a grim
chuckle, 'and he's a man that's easily scared.'

Now quite suddenly the fog lifted, leaving only
a faint, poetic haze. The sun shone out, and the
blue waters seemed alive with strange great fish
and couchant beasts; some almost submerged, with
only the jagged end of a rock fin or snout showing above the surface, and not a ripple round it.

One might have fancied them primeval seals and
walruses, if, indeed, one could imagine walruses in
these Eastern summer seas.   Others gave the
rugged profile, as it were, of some benevolent
monster of old, and with what might be a heraldic
dragon's tail twisting upward—a travesty of a
tail, which was, in fact, one of the queer, weird,
knobbed, blobbed and uncouthly gnarled, tea-tray
firs.   Those monsters were some of the tiny
thousand islets of the Inland Sea.   But there were
bigger, more natural islands with shorn protuber-
ances and stairways of crops, for that was the
effect which the alternation of dark and light gave.
This one had a square top, upon which a line of
firs made a topsy-turvy fringe against the sky,
with the pattern of its plantation set grotesquely
in a vandyke, upside down.

A straggling village, pagoda-roofed, and with a
sampan-strewed beach, made a broad gray streak,
into which the points of the vandyke merged.
How sweetly, tenderly, thought Windeatt, life
might flow in such a fairyland hamlet, in company
of the lady of his love!   How happy, surely, he
and the divinity might be, living Japanese fashion!
And though she was almost twice as tall as the
ordinary Japanese woman, yet would not the
clinging kimono lend new grace to the lithe lines
of Madame Izàn's form, and the fantastic head-

tiring fresh glory to those waves of dark brown hair? Yes; a butterfly existence like that of Loti and Madame Chrysanthème, but beautified and ennobled, as theirs was not, by the holier emotions of a higher love. And he asked himself, could he be content with such an idyllic dream, or would he sigh again for the world of men?

Alas! Madame Izàn would not respond by the most fleeting glance to those signals of penitence and beseeching that from time to time he cast towards her. She was an impregnable fortress, entrenched on one side by Mrs. Bax, on the other by Julia Eugarde, and it was only a pretence she made of reading Loti's novel which the doctor had bought; yet it served as an effective shield, whenever a breach was made in the line of fortification, by the temporary absence of one or other of her warders.

For sometimes Dr. Duppo would turn, attracted by Mrs. Bax's pleading blue eyes, and the two would stroll off together to the further end of the deck, or Julia would be beguiled from her post. Or else the Irrepressible Young Man would come along with his Kodak, in which on this particular morning Madame Izàn was showing a new and revived interest. Windeatt wondered to himself, in bitterness of spirit, how those negatives would turn out, which had been the occasion for so much laughter as well as for so much earnest manipulation and discussion.

Then at luncheon Madame Izàn came in late ; and no doubt it was by reason of a wicked and elaborate plot devised among the three women that, instead of occupying her usual place close up by the captain, Madame Izàn was moved three down, and sat between the Young Man and Mr. Barradine, quite beyond the range of Windeatt's attentions, so that he had not even the poor satisfaction of handing her the salt or pepper.

CHAPTER V.

THERE was a great bustle on board, when soon after sunrise the steamer anchored at Kobe : for it was there that most of the passengers were to disembark. The mission lady placed herself betimes at the bulwarks, with an anxious yet ecstatic expression, as of one to whom Destiny was about to reveal herself. She—not Destiny, but Miss Gotch —waited the arrival of the missionaries who were to welcome her to her new sphere of work, and could not be persuaded to quit her post, even for breakfast. Nevertheless, when breakfast was over, and all the rest were dispersing about their business on shore, the missionaries had not arrived. This did not, however, discomfit Miss Gotch. Her big sun-burned face, with its full-moulded lips and benevolent smile, beamed with kindly satisfaction. The bag holding her accordion was by her side, and the large Prayer-Book and Japanese dictionary on her lap : she was armed at all points. The two Australians and Mrs. Bax bade her good-bye.

Theodosia then stepped out to Madame Izàn, who had not advanced with the others.

'I want to say something to you,' said Miss Gotch. 'I want you to take this;' and she thrust a card between Madame Izàn's fingers. 'No, I know you don't like me. But the time may come —you can never tell—when you might be glad to feel that you had an English friend in Japan. And there I shall be—backed by the whole strength of the C.M.S., which is saying a good deal— ready to help you.'

Madame Izàn thanked her coldly and put the card into her reticule.

'Now, mind,' said Miss Gotch, 'if you are ever in any trouble and want advice which Mrs. Bax, maybe, hasn't had experience enough to give, apply to me.'

And just then the captain came up, and with him a Japanese gentleman, who might almost have been a gentleman straight from Bond Street, so well was he tailored, and so little was there distinctively Japanese in his gait and manner. He did not bow as though a string had been pulled in his middle, but removed his hat and glove in the English style—the last a mechanical act, for he could have had no expectation of shaking hands with the ladies, and stood at attention with an air of respectful reserve. Indeed, small as he was—

and though he was taller than most of his compatriots, Windeatt was a giant to him, and Madame Izàn topped him considerably—his extreme impassiveness gave him a certain dignity, which not even a pair of blue goggles that entirely covered his eye-orbits could mar. The goggles made it difficult to judge of his face, but it had power, was Bismarckian after a miniature fashion—square-jawed, high-cheekboned and determined-looking. He was clean-shaven except for a heavy moustache, and might have been any age, for though his dark skin was but little lined, his hair was quite gray.

'Madame Izàn and Mrs. Bax,' said the captain. 'This is——' And he looked at the Japanese gentleman.

'Kencho Hiro - Kahachi,' said the Japanese gentleman, delivering a card, which the captain passed on to Madame Izàn. And, oddly enough, Mrs. Eugarde noticed, she glanced at it timorously, as though dreading something it might reveal; also she had become extremely pale.

'Of the Imperial Association of Guides,' added the Japanese gentleman.

'Oh!' said Mrs. Bax, a disappointed note in her voice. The man had the appearance of at least an important official. 'Now I understand. This is the courier Dr. Duppo advised us to telegraph for.' She took the card out of Madame Izàn's fingers, and spelled out with difficulty : ' Kencho —Hiro—— Oh, we really couldn't say all that : we couldn't, *really*.'

' It is not at all necessary,' said the Japanese gentleman, who spoke excellent English. 'Kencho will do very well.'

' Oh, thank you !' fluttered Mrs. Bax. ' I am surprised that you speak such good English.'

The guide bowed without answering.

' Well, he'll take you on shore and put an end to all your difficulties,' said the captain. ' He'll see after your luggage, pass you through the Customs, and settle you in the hotel. He'll even unpack your dresses for you if you like. They're extraordinarily handy men, these guides. And now, as I've got to go into the town, I'll leave you in his charge. So good-bye, ladies, and I hope I may have the pleasure of taking you back again.'

The guide made no comment upon the captain's jocose encomium. Julia Eugarde fancied that he might be offended, he looked so very much of a gentleman. Perhaps, she thought, he was a Japanese nobleman who had fallen upon evil days. He stood there perfectly silent, and seemed to be in a sort of dream. To break the awkward pause, she asked if he knew anything of the guide she and her brother had likewise telegraphed for.

'He is here, he is waiting your orders,' replied Kencho, and gave a signal to someone behind, who pressed forward, his clogs making so much noise on the deck that he stopped deliberately and took them off. This was a very small Japanese man in a blue kimono and sailor hat, the ugliest man upon whom Mrs. Eugarde's eyes had ever rested, with his narrow shoulders, his unhealthy yellow face, the obliquely-fixed beads of eyes, and the cavern of a mouth, from which protruded two enormous yellow tusks. He took off his sailor hat, displaying a shock of black hair that stood up like the bristles on a scrubbing-brush, placed his hat and his two hands on his knees, and made the customary butt three times, after which he handed out a soiled card and presented it to Windeatt.

'I Yamasaki, guide,' he announced.

'Then Yamasaki, guide,' said Windeatt, 'we will make over to you ourselves and our belongings.' Whereupon ensued some practical explanations, prolonged during the space of Dr. Duppo's leave-takings—he, too, had to go on shore—and some whispered talk, apparently of a pathetic nature, took place between him and Mrs. Bax. Madame Izàn and Kencho, the guide, stood apart meanwhile, both abstracted and indifferent to outside occurrences.

But presently Windeatt cut short the instructions.

8

'Come along,' he said, seeing that the others of the party were descending the companion ; and poor Windeatt was terribly afraid that they might be whirled off—who could tell where?—perhaps to Kioto that afternoon, and no chance be given him of explaining and atoning for that rash kiss on the deck in the fog.

When their small packages had been counted and consigned to Yamasaki's care, Windeatt still would not depart, but insisted that Julia should wait till Madame Izàn emerged from her cabin, where Mrs. Bax's shrill little voice could be heard recounting to Kencho the tale of their various pieces of baggage, and making irrelevant personal communications. The goddess did not seem to be saying a word. Presently pecuniary details were entered upon, which showed that, though on pleasure bent, Mrs. Bax, like Mrs. Gilpin, had a frugal mind. The guide's deep, rather husky voice chimed in at intervals, mostly in acquiescence. Was the fee to include his food and lodging? Yes. And travelling expenses? But surely no. And was he a married man, and had he testimonials?

'I am a married man, madam,' was the guide's answer. 'And as for testimonials, the fact of my being employed by the Guides' Association is a voucher for my respectability, as, no doubt, the captain would tell you. But if it would give you any satisfaction, I shall be happy to show you a letter from an official of high position in Tokio, which declares me to be a man of honour and integrity.'

There was the rustle of rice-paper, and Windeatt could hear Mrs. Bax's rather simpering laugh.

'Oh dear me! But I should want it translated. And how very decorative the Japanese character is! Well, I'm sure it must be all right; for here is the stamp of the office—Ministry of Justice, is it?—oh, that is quite satisfactory. Mr. —ah, Kencho—I suppose that we may regard you in the light of a courier?'

'Certainly.'

'It is always so much better to define a position at the beginning,' said Mrs. Bax. 'Really, you seem so much more English than Japanese. I should think you must have been some years in our country.'

'I have lived in England, but not lately.'

'Oh, that is very nice; you'll understand our ways, and we shall feel so much more comfortable. You see, when two ladies are travelling alone they are obliged to be very careful; and you must excuse my having made such a point of testimonials. And now this box. You will never give it up to guards or porters, if you please; it contains jewels and other valuables.'

8—2

At this instant Madame Izàn came out of the cabin. Windeatt made an imperative sign to Mrs. Eugarde, who was in like manner directing Yamasaki from the door of her cabin—a sign which she interpreted as an injunction to stay where she was and not interfere. Then Windeatt went straight up to Madame Izàn ; for this was the very first opportunity he had had of speaking to her alone since that wild moment of the threatened collision. He had never seen her so pale, and he had not before noticed that half-frightened, half-resolved expression upon her face. She seemed lost in her own thoughts, and for a moment he was vain enough to imagine that he himself was perhaps the subject of her reverie.

' Madame Izàn,' he said in a moved voice, ' I have been so wanting to say something to you all these last days, but you have seemed to avoid me, and, perhaps—well, perhaps I have deserved it. But you must know that there's one thing which would cut me to the heart, and it is your fancying that I had failed any way in respect to you. I couldn't bear that. And you *must* know—oh ! surely you *do* know—*that* couldn't be true.'

The startled way in which she looked at him, as though recalled from some quite foreign and engrossing train of thought, rebuked him for his presumption in imagining himself so much to her as to have been the cause of her present moodiness.

'I—I didn't think that,' she said.

'But you'll admit that there were excuses for me,' he went on impetuously. 'I had meant to be so careful not to shock or annoy you by showing the feelings which have grown so tremendously —I can't tell how or why, unless it's just the doing of Fate — in this short time that we've been together. I'm not going to say anything about those feelings now,' he added. 'No, no! don't be afraid, I shall not bore you with them now.' For she had shrunk back, as it seemed, in terror.

'Oh no, you mustn't—indeed you mustn't,' she exclaimed.

'Very well. I am not going to say anything about them,' he repeated. 'If I can't be anything else, I want to be your friend while we're here in Japan, anyhow.'

'Oh yes,' she replied, and an expression of relief came over her face. 'Of course, that's what you can be. How could you have dreamed of anything else? Why should anybody ever dream of anything else? The rest is all nonsense, terrible nonsense— only fit for the stories Herminia used to be so fond of, and that she would read to me for hours when I was blind. I didn't know any better then. I know ever so much better now, and so do you,

Mr. Windeatt.   And if I wanted to think, I should have a great deal that is more important to think about than quarrelling with you about a nothing —a nothing at all.'

It was nothing to her, then—that mad kiss, which had been heaven for the second it had lasted to poor Windeatt.

' But I don't want to think—about that or about anything that has to do only with our two selves. When there's all the world outside one, how silly it is to be shutting one's self up in a kind of prison ! —which is the case if one keeps worrying over one's own thoughts and feelings.   You should do as I do : put them away till you are forced to consider them,' her face darkened, ' because you have got to make some important decision.'

' That's all very well for you, who don't care two-pence for a fellow,' he said bitterly.   ' It's easy enough for you, perhaps, to put them away.   But suppose I can't do that ?'

Her gray eyes met his with a child's unblenching perplexity.

' I don't understand why you should make so much fuss, when we have settled things quite nicely.   I am very pleased to be your friend.'

He pulled himself up.

' Thank you.   That's a comfort, at any rate.'

' Now, I'm glad you feel about it as I do.

Only '—she paused and lowered her eyes in some embarrassment—' only, Mr. Windeatt, you mustn't show your friendship just in *that* way.'

' I was a cad !' he cried. ' Forgive me.'

' Oh, of course,' she went on hurriedly ; ' I never thought about it, except that as we were in danger, or fancied we were, you wanted me to know that you'd take care of me. And I'm very thankful indeed, Mr. Windeatt, that you didn't have the chance, and that we hadn't to buffet about together in the waves of the Inland Sea. So now there's no need to think of that again.'

Thus she dismissed the episode. Windeatt was chilled. This was not what he had hoped for— expected, even—this air of entire satisfaction with conventional limitations.

' What I wanted to ask you,' he said stiffly, ' was whether you had any objection to our going —Ju and I — to the same hotel as you and Mrs. Bax. You see, it would be so much more pleasant and friendly. And perhaps—we might do things together sometimes: make excursions, and get a lot more out of Japan than if we were pottering along each party by itself ; for we are all strangers and pilgrims, so to speak, in an unknown country.' Windeatt could not help echoing her laugh, serious as the situation was to him, at this pathetic picture that he drew of the

new Innocents abroad. 'It's just a little lonely
for Ju,' he went on ; 'and naturally she takes so
much pleasure in your—and Mrs. Bax's—company.
It would be a great pity, don't you think, on her
account, if we were to drift apart ?'

'Oh dear no ! we mustn't do that,' she answered
brightly. 'Why, of course, we mustn't do that.
And why should we, since we are going to be real
friends? I'm so glad it is settled in so satisfactory
a way. Herminia'—to that lady, who now emerged
from the cabin, followed by the impassive Kencho.
He carried the leather case containing, presumably,
the jewels of Madame Izàn, for Herminia had not
given indications of the possession of such valuables.
'What are we going to do next, Herminia ?
Mr. Windeatt wants to know which hotel we are
going to.'

Then Kencho—or, rather, Yamasaki—came
into the conclave. Yamasaki's chatter seemed to
quench the interest Kencho might have been
supposed to take in the movements of the party
under his charge. After all, it was a very simple
matter to decide ; there is no great choice of hotels
in Kobe.

So it happened that the whole six of them went
ashore together, and the four were passed through
the Customs with no difficulty whatever ; for
Windeatt noticed that a few quiet words from

Kencho and the exhibition of a certain document
—perhaps it was the letter from the State official
which he had shown to Mrs. Bax—was a kind of
'open sesame' as far as Japan was concerned, and
procured them a respect and consideration which
heightened Mrs. Eugarde's opinion of the courtesy
of that smiling nation into whose midst they had
entered. Then they and their belongings were
taken possession of by a covey of little brown
men, who put themselves between the shafts of
the rickshaws and whisked them to the hotel first,
and afterwards to the Consulate, where Mr. Barradine and the Irrepressible Young Man were making
application for passports.

'It's splendid!' cried the Young Man. 'It's
like a fairy tale : you've only got to clap your
hands, and there's a slave of the lamp ready to do
anything you want. I want to be tattooed—there's
a wonderful tattooer in Kioto ; he tattoos all the
people who come here. I'm going to Kioto, and
I want to shoot the Rapids, and to see the Dai—
what-do-you-call-'em ?—Colossus of Rhodes sort
of thing. I want to go to an Imperial garden-
party, and to eat a real Japanese dinner, and to have
all my negatives developed ; and then I shall be
ready for sport in Alaska.'

'Oh dear me!' moaned Mr. Barradine. 'I have
already had enough of Japan. I don't think that

I shall stay. The hotel is full of dreadful Cook's tourists, and the food is most unwholesome.'

'Two dollars to pay. Call again to-morrow morning,' said the clerk of the Consulate, or the Consul himself—how should they know? And after that they were trotted off again—to the bank, the post-office, the photographers' shops, and all the other initiatory shrines of tourists. Somehow, it seemed that it was Yamasaki who took the lead, and not the superior Kencho, who, in spite of his grand testimonial and his admirable English, appeared distrait, and was neither so practical nor so enthusiastic as his compatriot in the matter of sights and diversions. He merely acquiesced now with an abstracted air in Yamasaki's suggestion that they should go 'where Japanese make sport with fish.' Mrs. Bax confided to Julia that she could not feel quite comfortable with Kencho, and she wasn't certain whether she ought to call him plain 'Kencho' or 'Mr. Kencho.' He didn't seem like a common courier person, any way, and he wasn't what she called sympathetic. On the whole, she didn't feel sure that she wouldn't have preferred Yamasaki ; but she concluded that, owing to Dr. Duppo's insistence in the telegram upon unimpeachable steadiness as a qualification of the guide required, the management had sent the grandest on their list. Of course, it was a comfort

to know that Kencho had a testimonial from a
Minister of State—though for her, she said, the
letter might as well have been written in Greek
as Japanese, since she didn't understand either
language.

Yamasaki, to Julia's intense appreciation, proved
himself also a man of a delicate consideration and
the higher chivalry.   It was in keeping with the
fine Japanese instinct that he should sign to the
coolies to halt before a shop in the main street, a
grocery and wine shop of hybrid nationality, with
a bottle of Hennessy's brandy and some tins of
Brand's Essence and sundry specimens of Lea and
Perrin's manufactures taking the place of honour
in the window among a variety of products strictly
Japanese.

'One leetle sit still, if ladies please, or get down
see my shop,' said Yamasaki, flourishing his sailor
hat.   'I haf my wife, and I haf my leetle chil'.
But now the chil' is walk.'

Whereupon the ladies graciously descended, and
Madame Yamasaki, in a soft gray kimono and
knapsack obi, advanced and saluted, Japanese
fashion, with much grace and dignity.   And having
shown incontrovertibly that he was a man of
substance and of the domestic virtues, Yamasaki
wasted no more time on sentiment, and they trotted
on once more.

Madame Izàn had been a little depressed and
pensive, but, as at Nagasaki, it seemed as though
the magic of Japan restored her vitality and zest
for enjoyment, and dispersed the vague shadow
which had haunted her on arrival. She lost her
look of timid alarm ; her gray eyes darted hither
and thither at every new sight and sound, till in
laughing bewilderment she put her hands over
them, and said she must be dark for a minute to
take the whole in.

How odd and full of charm it all was !—the
cardboard houses, the floating banners, the strings
of lanterns, the boat bridge, the tripping tea-tray
figures, the piles of clogs and umbrellas at the
entrance to tea-house and temple, the waterless
river of sand with its shadowing trees and many
booths and imp-like, naked children diving into its
dusty bosom ; and, joy of joys ! the tea-pavilion on
the top of the tower, where respectable fathers and
mothers drank saffron tea, and smoked lilliputian
pipes, and shovelled strange brown and white messes
with chopsticks down their throats ; where sweet
mousmés fluttered and ogled and played—but only
played—with tea and pipes and vermicelli in baby
bowls, and whispered to each other ' Yuroshi !' at
sight of the beautiful European lady who was so
frankly interested in their proceedings. How
unreal and topsy-turvy it seemed !—the pagoda-

roofs, the decorative mountains—all looking as
though they had been 'placed' by a landscape
gardener—the screen-trees and the queer people,
with their draperies narrowed at the shoulders and
the ankles, and bulging in the middle, and their
heads and fans at irresponsible angles. Yet they
were real trees and bridges and mountains and real
people, whom each one of the party, except poor
blind Madame Izàn, had known from the beginning
of life, and had never believed in.

They went to a fair on their way home, and
bought quantities of beautiful-looking doll-cakes,
which were excessively nasty when they began to
eat them, and yards of variegated ribbon, and pins
and trifles by the score. The drums and gongs
were beating, and there was a theatrical performance
going on—fan-tableaux of figures in grotesque
attitudes, with gold devils embroidered on their
black kimonos, and fiercely accentuated eyebrows
and portentous wigs.

Madame Izàn was so fascinated that they could
hardly draw her away. Indeed, Kencho made no
attempt to do so, though Yamasaki protested :

'No good store Kobe ; plenty good store Kioto.
No buy Kobe.'

But Kencho made no effort to guide the exuber-
ance of Madame Izàn's instinct for the acquiring
of rubbish. He stood riveted, as it were, by her

vivacity and brilliant beauty, gazing at her through his blue goggles in a posture of silent melancholy. Julia Eugarde, professionally alert, began to suspect that his English visit had left behind it tragic memories of a misplaced attachment. They would not have got away in time for *table d'hôte*, but for Yamasaki and a temple whither he was bent on taking them.

There was the prehistoric survival of a gateway, as at the O-Suwa, but this temple was only the tomb of a holy man and the shrine of a degenerate Buddha. A straw rope, with a cracked brass bell at the end of it, hung at the gateway.

' You pull, call the god,' explained Yamasaki ; and Madame Izan set the bell jangling. And then came up a pious Jap and pulled too, making his ducking obeisance and clapping three times, after which he muttered a prayer and departed with another obeisance. Yamasaki lingered behind to perform his own particular act of devotion, which raised him still more in Mrs. Bax's estimation ; and she could not help again regretting that Fate had not apportioned to her the cheerful, communicative and simply human Yamasaki instead of dignified, apathetic Kencho.

It was Yamasaki who explained the flying carps on the house-tops, which had excited Madame Izan's wonder

'That son. . . . . Suppose new son, put up fish. Very old custom. Country people keep up old custom—Government no care. That want new European custom. Plenty old custom go, but plenty, too, stop.'

Perhaps it was the attraction of Yamasaki, perhaps a feeling of loneliness without the grim but ever constant attentions of Dr. Duppo, that caused Herminia to accept the joint travelling arrangement without the demur which Mrs. Eugarde had expected—nay, even hoped for. There seemed little enough prospect of a divergence in different directions. Windeatt and Madame Izàn spent the evening poring over Murray and planning expeditions, so that everything was cut and dried before the two guides appeared for the morrow's orders. Telegrams engaging rooms at Yaami's Hotel in Kioto were sent ; and it appeared certain that during the next three weeks or more Windeatt and Madame Izàn would spend very few hours of the day apart. Julia Eugarde was extremely uneasy. Windeatt took the tone to her of an armed neutrality, tacitly established between them on the subject of Madame Izàn. Julia, in her perplexity, ventured upon a renewal of her previous remonstrance with Mrs. Bax. To no effect, however.

'She has refused him,' declared Herminia.

'Refused him!' Julia echoed, at once relieved, wounded by her brother's reticence, and yet highly incredulous. 'I don't see how that is possible. They seem such very good friends.'

''That's just it,' said Mrs. Bax, 'Izo told him the other thing was all nonsense, and they settled to be friends.'

Julia suspected a lover's stratagem on her brother's part—on Izo's an evasion of fact.

'Do you mean that he has actually asked her already to marry him?' she said.

'Well, I'm not sure that it went *actually* as far as that,' answered Mrs. Bax ; 'but it meant the same thing. I know something rather definite happened. Izo confessed so much last night. I believe it was in the Inland Sea. Izo wouldn't tell me what occurred, but one can guess that it was the usual thing.'

'The usual thing!' repeated Mrs. Eugarde in quiet derision. 'No doubt you are more versed in such matters than I am.'

'Perhaps I am,' complacently simpered Mrs. Bax ; 'I'm younger, you see. It's very curious,' she went on reflectively, 'that men always go the same way to work when they begin to make love, no matter how different they may be in other respects. I've observed it over and over again ;

and Dr. Duppo was saying only the other day'
—Mrs. Bax sighed—'that you can follow the
stages just as you might an attack of measles.
Seems a kind of universal law, like religion, and
fetiches, and the immortality of the soul, and all
that.'

Julia received Herminia Bax's profundities with
an impatient gesture.

'What I should like to know,' she said, 'is
whether Madame Izàn told Jack the truth.'

'The truth !'

'About her being a married woman with a live
husband. That's all that concerns me, and I take
the fact on your authority.'   .

'Oh, I told you I had no authority!' cried
Mrs. Bax in trepidation ; 'Izo would never
forgive me if I assumed an authority. And,
besides, I don't know that it is the truth.'

'I should think,' replied Mrs. Eugarde severely,
'that, even if you don't know, Madame Izàn
must surely be aware whether she is married or
not.'

'But she isn't. She says she isn't—married, I
mean. There ! I have been telling more than I
ought. Really, I promised Izo, Mrs. Eugarde,
that I wouldn't allude to the subject again till we
got to Tokyo, and you'll agree that I'm bound to
keep my promise. Izo said that if I mentioned

9

it to her or to anybody else she would travel on and leave me ; and she has got all the money, you know, and is quite capable of doing it. She'd go on with you and Yamasaki, and I should be left with Kencho ; and,' concluded Herminia piteously, 'what good would that do to any of us? And it wouldn't be respectable, besides, for me. I really couldn't travel round with Kencho, Mrs. Eugarde : he's too much of a gentleman. I don't care for Kencho ; he never says a word to me if he can help it, and he won't look me in the face ; though, of course, with those horrid blue glasses, it is not easy to see whether he *is* looking at you when he does look you in the face.'

'Then,' said Mrs. Eugarde, 'there's nothing more to be said, and I ·can only apologize for intruding upon your private affairs. I assure you, Mrs. Bax, that I shouldn't trouble myself in the least degree about your feelings towards Kencho, or your obligations to Madame Izàn, if it were not that my brother's happiness is in question, and that this might be destroyed for ever by his continuing to delude himself with false hopes.'

'Well, that's his look-out, isn't it ?' said Mrs. Bax ruefully. 'I'm dreadfully sorry for Mr. Windeatt. I'm always intensely sympathetic with men who are in love—I can't help it ; and my sympathy *does* seem to produce a sort of affinity, you know, so many have come to me for advice in their difficulties, and for help and consolation. I shouldn't wonder if Mr. Windeatt did, too, and then I might be able to say a word, and if I *could* conscientiously further his cause—— But, oh dear, what am I saying? I mean, if it were to turn out that she isn't married, or that he isn't married—Izàn, you know—why, then——'

'Dear me, you seem to be giving forth very shifty and immoral sentiments,' grimly observed Mrs. Eugarde; 'and after what you have told me about your promise to Madame Izàn, I can't presume to ask any further questions, unless it would be no breach of confidence in you to tell me whether since your conversation with Madame Izàn about the—the recent occurrence, you feel any uneasiness on the score of *her* feelings.'

'Oh dear no!' briskly replied Mrs. Bax, delighted to be eased from the burden of her involuntary revelation. 'I put it to Izo that way, and she assured me there was no cause for uneasiness whatever; in fact, the last thing she wants or thinks about is falling in love or getting married. It's my solemn conviction, Mrs. Eugarde, that dear Izo is incapable of being in love; she hasn't got the ordinary feelings of a woman. If you

knew her as well as I do, you'd understand what
I mean. Supposing——'

Mrs. Bax's blue eyes wandered round the landscape in search of a simile, and found it suggested
by the roof of a pagoda.

'Supposing that the Grand Llama of Thibet
were to go down on his knees to her, she'd only
look at him like a baby and wonder what he could
possibly be doing it for.'

It was while walking up and down the platform
of the railway-station that Mrs. Bax thus delivered
herself. They had arrived betimes at the station,
which was no doubt owing to Yamasaki's desire
for an affectionate and prolonged farewell to his
family. He now appeared accompanied by
Madame Yamasaki, leading his offspring, and
followed by a retainer in a blue kimono, with
white lettering on its lapels, who carried his
master's luggage. This consisted of an English
carpet-bag, having a pattern of huge green leaves
and gigantic roses and brilliant steel clasps. There
was also a compressible Japanese basket. Of
Yamasaki the Japanese, however, nothing now
remained except his teeth — the most notable
object in his little brown face—and his sailor hat,
which was not Japanese. For he had discarded
his kimono and clogs, and to-day was dressed in
the neatest of blue serge coats and gray trousers.

A courier's bag was slung across his shoulder, and he wore shiny patent-leather boots and tan gloves, and carried a cane.

In his excitement and emotion he moved as upon wires, and was an odd contrast to the stately and impassive Kencho, who, in charge of the jewel-box, walked close behind Madame Izàn and Windeatt. How strange it seemed to be starting on a railway journey in Japan! It would have seemed more natural, thought Julia Eugarde, to be borne aloft on the backs of winged dragons. And what a monstrous incongruity were those common pasteboard railway tickets, printed though they might be in hieroglyphic characters, while the Japanese lettering, which Mrs. Bax declared to be 'so decorative'—she had imbibed art phrases from an Impressionist fellow-lodger in West Kensington —did not counteract the jar of seeing 'Booking Office,' 'First-class,' and so on, printed in crude English beneath it.

Mrs. Bax was aggrieved because, shortly before the train started, Kencho disappeared, and allowed Yamasaki to perform his duty of ushering her and Madame Izàn into their seats. Herminia's dislike to Kencho was becoming a definite emotion. She complained that he was never at hand when she wanted him, that he gave himself airs and ignored her observations ; and what, she plaintively exclaimed, was the use of paying two dollars a day for a courier if no one could see that you had got one ?

There was a good deal of bustle on the platform. Two Japanese Generals recently returned from Port Arthur were travelling in the train, and all the railway officials drawn up in line were tendering deferential homage to the victorious heroes. They were fine-looking men ; these Generals made impressive figures in their heavily gilt uniforms and the array of medals on their breasts, and Windeatt could not help admiring the mechanical dignity of the military salutes with which they acknowledged the obeisances from the platform. In the carriage with the Australians and Mrs. Bax were two younger officers. These wore moustache and imperial, looked well groomed, and had very white teeth and a pleasant smile, while one opened the window for Madame Izàn with an unexaggerated courtesy which was distinctly of European origin. Windeatt and his sister were struck by the expression of Madame Izàn's face as she furtively watched the two Japanese men. It showed at once relief, puzzlement, and a vague pain, and both brother and sister wondered within themselves what could be the cause of her undoubted perturbation. Mrs. Eugarde, however, reflected very justly that Madame Izàn's was a face upon which every passing feeling wrote itself in large letters. No doubt she, like some others of the party, was beginning to realize the necessity for reconstructing preconceived notions on things and persons Japanese.

CHAPTER VI.

'Ho, ho!' shouted the runners as the file of six rickshaws scampered through the streets of Kioto up towards the Maruyama hill on which Yaami's Hotel stands.

It was dusk, and in front of, and above, and around the little brown houses soft red and pink lanterns glowed and swayed in the gentle breeze. A mousmé, peeping out from a fretwork house-front as the rickshaws clattered by, waved a hand in smiling salutation as Madame Izàn looked up and met her eyes, and Windeatt thought he had never seen any gesture so pretty and appropriate as that with which Izo kissed her hand in return. The mousmé's tinkling laugh floated after them, and Izo turned delightedly.

'Now I have had a real welcome to Japan!' she exclaimed, and blushed and averted her face as she perceived that it was not Windeatt she was addressing, but Kencho the guide, whose rickshaw had somehow crept up beside hers and displaced that of the Australian. She was too gracious not to try and repair the slight act of discourtesy, and turned again. 'Is that a Japanese custom—one of the old customs Yamasaki talks about—this of greeting strangers so prettily?' she asked, and wondered a little at the hesitation he showed in replying to so simple a question. But he spoke with an unexpected gallantry, 'When they are strangers such as you, madame,' and added, with, as Julia Eugarde noticed, a tremble in his voice, 'You seemed pleased. I hope that you like my country.'

'I don't know yet,' she answered. 'I have not thought about it. I want to see everything first, and I shall think afterwards.'

'What a singular creature it is!' thought Julia to herself, 'and what an objection she seems to have to mental processes! I wonder whether they will read me the riddle at Tokyo.'

And now they were toiling up a steep road, the coolies panting and grunting good-humouredly, and bursting into grateful laughs, as other coolies, of whom it was no concern at all, stepped amiably forward to help their brethren of the shafts by pushing beside and behind. Windeatt, who could not reconcile himself to the dragging of his bulk and inches by his own kind, had long ere this got down, but it had not seemed to occur to either Kencho or Yamasaki that they might do likewise.

There was a temple gateway with an ornate arch at the end of the road, and a garden beyond, and zigzag paths leading to the quaintest cluster of gray-roofed buildings at different levels, joined together by bridges and balconies and promiscuous outer stairways, the whole making one rambling edifice—a cross between a temple and a bunch of Swiss châlets. Well, they learned afterwards that the hotel had once been a monastery in the times when Yaami's and English globe-trotters were not.

And now, what was this great sonorous hammer-stroke which smote the air, and that wonderful reverberation, lingering, as it seemed, for minutes—that deep, glorious bell, so rich, so pure, so altogether heavenly?

'That temple bell,' said Yamasaki in his queer English. 'Many temple all over. This sacred hill.'

And there was another sound, too, which fell fresh upon their ears as they sipped pale tea on the balcony outside their rooms. For almost facing the balcony there was a Japanese bath-house fronting a stair street, up and down which pattens clacked, and umbrellas bobbed, and lanterns moved like fat glow-worms—a bath-house with many lanterns, too, and banners and balconies and sliding doors, in and out of which strange figures flitted. That was where that eerie twanging came from—the music of the samisen.

Were the strange happenings of that day never to cease? The ladies had bidden Windeatt good-night, and the three of them were together in Julia Eugarde's room—their chambers adjoined—gossiping as women do at bedtime in dressing-gowns and curling-pins—which last item suggests a libel on Madame Izàn, for her wavy brown locks needed no artificial crimping — when a slowly repeated knock sounded. Julia rose to answer it, and as she did so the door softly opened, and in the opening there appeared a brown man in a kimono, whose head was on a level with his knees, and with a great yellow bundle, which he carried on his shoulders. He prostrated himself lower still, with his forehead on the matting, then crawled a little further, and again knocked his forehead ; on again, till he had reached the centre of the chamber. And, lo! behind him were other crouch-ing forms, who also made obeisance, to the number of five, each one bearing a yellow bundle, which he deliberately removed and placed upon the floor ; after which they all five stood upon their feet. Then the first handed Herminia a card, and the others held out their cards also.

' I Curios,' said Number One. 'Shioda Curios,' said Number Two, and ' Kwambi—Curios ' was Number Three. Nobody got any further, as at this point Julia Eugarde protested—courteously, it must be stated ; for how is it possible to address even an intrusive vendor in any but the language of courts in a land where abuse is couched in such terms as ' O yoshi nasai ' (Honourably abstaining deign), and a gentleman conveys that he is hungry by stating that his honourable inside has become empty ?

' My friends, this haste is unseemly. We are tired ; we wish to go to sleep,' said Julia. And Mrs. Bax made a sympathetic pantomime with her eyes closed and her arms extended towards the bed, and Madame Izàn tragically ejaculated :

' Oh, Herminia, I *did* say that I'd wait till to-morrow, when Yamasaki said he'd show us first-class store !'

It was of no use protesting, so beguiling were the Curios, so heavenly were their smiles, so artlessly enthusiastic was their speech.

' One—only one.' Kwambi was holding up a cloisonné vase. ' I myself make. Fifteen days I make. I come show you. I very cheap Curio.'

And then Shioda Curios, breathlessly displaying a gold-embroidered kimono :

' I bring show you. Very good kimono. Once belong Daimio. Give present Japanese lady husband. Japanese lady buy European dress. Must money. I sell.'

And so it was that frail womanhood succumbed

to temptation. From out the yellow wrapping came little square boxes, and from out the boxes bags of costly silk, and from out the bags ivories and cloisonné and Satsuma and the like. And when at last the ' I Curios ' wheeled round and retired backwards, their faces to the ground, they had good reason to adore the Number One Daimio lady who had bought so liberally of their wares.

And if Windeatt could have beheld Madame Izàn clad in the kimono—which was a very gorgeous affair of red crape with gold-embroidered Shogun's crests and Imperial chrysanthemums, and with a long wadded train that made it fall not amiss on Izo's tall form—he would have been amply satisfied in the fulfilment of his speculations concerning her appearance in such garb.

Then it was decided among the ladies that the costume should be completed in all its accessories, and that on the morrow Yamasaki should be consulted as to local tailors. And so it was that the great temple bell boomed out its call to the first morning orison before these three alien heads— pepper and salt and flaxen and glossy—were pillowed in their Japanese beds.

The sun was shining, the birds were singing, and the grasshoppers whirring, when Julia Eugarde came out dressed upon her balcony to take her first real view of that jewel of cities, the sacred capital Kioto. There it lay, almost like a lake, broken by rocks and green islets, all gray and misty, the night vapours still clinging round it, with a faintly yellowing streak of wheat-fields making the lake's shore, and all round the great plain mountains of shadowy purple.

Close below spread the Yaami gardens, a landscape in itself : rocks, and bridges, and miniature caves, and old stone lanterns, and deformities of trees, and masses of azalea bloom. From outside the ornate gateway floated up the chattering of the rickshaw-runners as they waited, with their perambulators drawn up, for the hotel to be astir. Then through all the little clatter and burr boomed out the sweet, stupendous bell note, making the whole air one vast and melodious vibration. It came from the gray temple on the right, just showing among the dense foliage of a grove of trees. Was ever any sound more solemnizing? Slowly the resonant waves died away, and following upon them came a woman's laugh. Horror of horrors to Julia Lugarde! She knew that silvery tinkle, and she knew also the manly voice, with its touch of acquired Australian drawl, which replied to it. Here already were Windeatt and Madame Izàn pursuing their nefarious flirtation.

Mrs. Eugarde leaned over the balcony, and sure enough there beneath her were the two, with 'I Curios' in waiting, his precious embroideries spread out upon the gravel at their feet. He must have slept in the veranda, prepared to pounce at any moment upon his easy prey. No Mrs. Bax was visible. As a matter of fact, Herminia still slept, and dreamed rosy dreams, perhaps, of the lost P. and O. surgeon, or possibly of Dr. Duppo, now arriving in Yokohama. Julia observed, however, with satisfaction, officially speaking, that Madame Izàn was not entirely unchaperoned. Kencho the guide, who might not unnaturally have imbibed some English notions of propriety, stood a little back from the two. He was leaning against a pillar something in the attitude of a villain in a melodrama, one arm folded below the other, his right hand nursing his moustache, his hat pushed slightly forward upon his head, while his eyes, obscured by their blue goggles, were fixed upon Madame Izàn. His air was moodily alert, and it seemed almost to Julia that he was trying to overhear what her brother and the lady were saying. There could have been no mystery about that, at any rate, for as the thought crossed Julia's mind Windeatt, becoming aware of the guide's presence, called out 'Kencho!'

The Australian, with no intention whatever of

giving offence, had rather an autocratic way of
speaking to those he considered beneath him, the
result, probably, of dealing with obdurate black-
boys and shearers in branding-yards and wool-
sheds, and obtuse Mongolians. It was quite
apparent to Julia above that the curt summons
had jarred upon the sensitive Japanese. She could
tell this by the slight angry shake Kencho gave to
his shoulders, and his obstinate immovability when
Windeatt repeated his name. Clearly, he did not
recognise the Australian as his master. Mrs.
Eugarde left the balcony, and ran down the outer
stair. She had no mind to leave her brother any
longer exposed to Madame Izàn's dangerous fasci-
nations, and, moreover, she intended to give him
a hint of a discovery she had made by her own
intuition: that Kencho Hiro-Kahachi was assuredly
no lowborn servant, but a gentleman, probably of
as good lineage as Windeatt himself, and maybe
better.

Very likely the same thought had occurred to
Madame Izàn—women are quicker than men in
such matters—for she had advanced to the guide,
a piece of embroidery in her hand, and, with that
half-hesitating, jerky manner which was withal so
pleasant and girl-like, said :

'Will you tell me, please : Do you think that
this is really from an old temple?'

In a second Kencho was transformed. He had taken off his hat and made such a bow to Madame Izàn as he might have made to the Queen or to his own Emperor, supposing it were consistent with the traditional reverence exacted by that august personage to receive a bow from an ordinary subject. All the man's fierce surliness had vanished ; he looked shy, overwhelmed.

'What is the witchery of the creature,' said Julia inwardly, 'that it can strike an emotional chord in the breast even of Kencho ?'

The guide took the piece of embroidery from Madame Izàn, examined it deferentially, and almost shrinking in his humility when she, coming a little nearer him, laid her finger also on the silk tissue. Finally he pronounced it an imitation, and delivered a little lecture on Japanese needlework, ancient and modern, to which 'I Curios,' catching its drift, listened with no approval.

'Thank you so much,' said Madame Izàn.

It was characteristic of this young woman that she was more womanly and gentle in her way with those who might be supposed beneath her than with such as stood upon a social equality. It was as though she had some special sympathy with these persons, as though she had herselt known what it was to be oppressed and looked down upon, and was therefore determined that no one should suffer through her in like fashion.

'I wish I had asked your advice,' she went on, 'before buying all the things I bought last night. I'm afraid that I have been very foolish ; but I hope that you will be kind enough to help me in future.'

And Kencho seemed so overcome by this graciousness on the part of the beautiful lady as to be hardly capable of replying in suitable terms. Julia Eugarde felt certain that the tenderest gratitude would have beamed from his eyes had not the blue goggles effectually dimmed them.

'I shall be—— Oh, of course, you know it will give me the greatest pleasure,' he stammered, and added, pulling himself as it were together, 'It is only my duty, madame.'

'Oh, but "one's duty"!' she returned with a pettish shrug. 'If the world were all duty—well, one wouldn't want to have one's self turned into a peg for having dutiful actions hung upon. Duty is a bore, Mr. Kencho, and I like kindly feeling much better, and a love of art better still. You understand about these things—art and the rest. Not that I am artistic — oh, I am not like Mrs. Bax—but I should hate to be laughed at as having made mistakes. You don't talk much, but I can see that you understand.'

'And how can you have discovered that, madame?'

'I watched you yesterday, when Yamasaki was telling us about the different shops in Kioto, and the kind of things we ought to buy. You did not want to hurt Yamasaki's feelings—I observe that you Japanese are very careful not to hurt people's feelings; oh, you didn't want to hurt him at all, or to seem to know better. And, besides, I dare say you thought, for a set of mere ignorant tourists, what did it matter? But—I am certain that you are an artist, Mr. Kencho, while Yamasaki is just a showman.'

'Madame,' said Kencho—and his voice seemed huskier even than usual—'for a mere tourist, as you call yourself, you are exceedingly observant.'

She looked at him with her clear, straight look, in which there was an expression plaintive and childlike. 'If you had lost your eyes for twenty years, and had been led, through having no eyes, into errors and wrong ideas about life,' she said, 'you would, when your eyes were given back to you—well, you would be observant, too, of things —and men.'

Kencho's aspect and demeanour struck Julia as in keeping with all that she had heard of Japanese delicacy. He stood silent, but from every feature there radiated a sympathy and a respectful compassion, more eloquent than words. It was not for him to ask a question, to presume upon her artless confidence, but—well, Julia fancied to herself that if any designing ' 1 Curios ' attempted in future to impose on the innocence of Madame Izàn, he would find his match in Kencho Hiro-Kahachi.

At the present moment he went up to ' I Curios,' who was malevolently regarding him, restored the rejected embroidery, and said a few words in Japanese, with the result that 'I Curios' shouldered his yellow bundle at once, and, after the customary prostration, departed to seek other prey.

Windeatt was cross over the episode. What right had Kencho to send the man away? He was an ill-conditioned fellow, that guide, and Madame Izàn's condescension had turned his head.

But Izo only laughed.

' I think I am going to like Kencho,' she said. ' I feel as if I knew how horrid it must be for him, having to trot round about and show off his country to a set of stupid foreigners. He is obliged to tolerate us. I sympathize with him.'

' He is paid for his toleration,' said Mrs. Eugarde.

' Two dollars a day,' put in Herminia, ' and travelling expenses.'

'And, after all,' said Madame Izàn, 'it doesn't make any difference to you, Mr. Windeatt, does it? For you've always got Yamasaki.'

Which remark did not tend to soothe poor Windeatt's irritation. Nor was he altogether pleased—though it was to the profit of his sister and himself—at the greater consideration accorded to Kencho by those high officials whom Yamasaki approached in vain for permission to enter certain Imperial and holy precincts, not usually profaned by tourist feet. Yet it appeared that Kencho carried with him a talisman, some document with no doubt a potent signature appended, before which custodians at the gates and the little gentlemen with chrysanthemum badges in their caps, who demanded passports at every corner, and even Buddhist and Shinto priests and dignitaries in all abodes of light and learning, were bland and subservient. Anyhow, these four foreign persons passed through palace apartments closed to the herd, inspected art treasures the like of which are not often exhibited, entered shrines where sat Buddhas unknown of the multitude, witnessed dances sacred, rare, and altogether distinctive, were initiated into the most esoteric rites of Cha-no-yu, and were granted many a privilege such as does not fall to the lot of less favoured travellers.

It was clear that Madame Izàn's intuition with

regard to Kencho had not been at fault. He was a man of knowledge and of artistic perception, cultivated far beyond the ordinary standard. There was about him, too, though showing quite unconsciously—for he was singularly reserved—an unexpected idealism and an elevation above the usual levels of thought, which appealed oddly to Madame Izàn. It sometimes struck Julia Eugarde, who was apt to ponder upon these things, that Izo's very shrinking from the psychological side of life proved rather a timid attraction on her part towards it. Kencho on his part had no such shrinking, and had evidently meditated deeply upon problems touching his country's welfare. He held the ancient customs and superstitions in tenderest respect, and when he related some grotesque Japanese legend would invest it with a certain poetic value—unlike Yamasaki, whose contemptuous patronage of his country's traditions jarred considerably upon Julia Eugarde. She, however, charitably excused this on the suspicion that it might arise from an exquisite politeness.

But Kencho was very different. He knew all about the old history and the old religion and the old inner philosophy—at least, so it seemed to Madame Izàn, for it was she who, with her simple knack of questioning, would lead him on to talk. And very soon it became evident to the sore and jealous Windeatt—though it was of course absurd, he admitted, to feel jealous of a mere guide—that Kencho did not care in the very least what he thought about the matter, if only he might bring the dreamy light into Madame Izàn's eyes, and the little interested pucker between her brows. Yes, Kencho was an artist in his thinkings. He seemed to regard the whole art-evolution process from a point outside chronological and geographical limitations. He was fond of drawing parallels between Occident and Orient, and would declare that the same spirit animated alike the early Florentines and the Japanese Hokusai. He had fixed ideas as to an Asiatic-European renascence, by which the whole world should be lifted higher along an evolutionary spiral. He had theories, too, in regard to the religious development of Japan, and would speculate upon the future place she should take in the procession of nations.

It was his belief that the seclusion of Nippon for all her two thousand years had been no mere accident of national temperament, but had been inspired by Divine command, in prevision of the destiny that awaited her. To him the badge of the rising sun was a truth, a symbol of future glory, and emblematic of the dawn of a new civilization in which East and West should blend art and religion. ' All faiths,' he said, 'come from the One, and to the One they shall go back again. In all are the same truths expressed in different language ; and creeds are but as vestures to be changed according to climate and geographical conditions. So our Kwannon, Goddess of Pity, is no other than your own Lady of Intercession ; and see, what great difference can you find between the ceremonial of the Hongwanji here, and High Mass in your Oratory at Brompton ?'

This was when they were visiting the great temple. They had wandered through open pillared courts, with their wonderful ornamentation of pediment, eave, and cornice, and through presence-chambers gorgeous with grotesque paintings on gold leaf, with lacquer and damascening ; and now they found themselves in that part of the building where a Buddhist service was going on. The chancel was a splendid confusion of gold tracery, of brilliant arabesques, of bronzes, gilded lotuses, incense - burners, flowers, and lighted candles. The incense rose in clouds ; the priests, in brocade vestments, moved with impressive gestures, chanting musical prayers ; the bell rang, the golden shrine was opened, and every knee was bent and every head bowed to the soft clink of rosaries, as the invocation went up—' Nam-ami-dabutzu '—in one long, gentle wail.

Madame Izàn, being a Catholic, made involuntary reverence, and, when she raised her head, perceived that Kencho had kneeled down by her side. The others were somehow withdrawn into the background. These two lingered for several minutes, and then passed out in silence. Presently she reminded him of what he had said, and remarked :

'No, there is no great difference.'

Then he seemed to forget for the moment that he was merely the guide, and began to talk to her after the manner of a scholar and a friend, telling her of Nichiren of the New Dispensation, of Sontok the peasant saint, of Toju the teacher in Omi, so humble that he would scarce accept the title of Master from that samurai who, searching Japan for a saint, and having found the way to Toju's dwelling, waited three days and nights on the threshold in silent supplication to be received as a disciple. Yet so proud was this same saint that he would keep the greatest of the Daimios unanswered at his door, rather than interrupt a lesson to the village children.

Madame Izàn was deeply interested. Her imagination took fire at the picture he drew of the old times, when, even in feudal Japan, sacerdotalism had corrupted faith, and there had been need of a new teacher of the type of the Fisher of Galilee to bring the Gospel of holiness to the land.

'And are there no teachers now in the temples?' she asked.

Kencho hesitated for a moment before he replied.

'Madame,' he answered, 'you must not judge of Japan by what tourists tell you, and by what you read in pretty story-books of the nation of dolls and good children. There are great masters in the temples still, and the Keepers of Wisdom are always ready to give forth of their stores to the humble and sincere ; but they wait to be sought, they do not come out and court the crowd.'

Whether by accident or design—and this would be hard to decide, for certainly Kencho had a much better acquaintance than Yamasaki with the inner courts of the temple—the two guides separated, and Kencho and Madame Izàn, having lost the rest of the party, found themselves alone together. It was upon this occasion that Madame Izàn first realized the extent and variety of Kencho's intellectual resources. He took her to the temple library, and afterwards to a sort of inner library, where he introduced her to a most dignified and sweet-voiced old man in priest's dress, who spoke English perfectly and was evidently an intimate friend of Kencho's. Indeed, Madame Izàn learned that Kencho had been his pupil, and she wondered whether he could be one of the masters of whom the guide had spoken.

The old priest smiled benevolently on the beautiful Australian girl, and seemed to take a personal pleasure in drawing out her ideas and experiences and impressions of this new people. Oh yes, certainly, she thought to herself, the Japan of the priest and of Kencho Hiro-Kahachi was not the frivolous pleasure-land of the tourists. The priest, too, was enthusiastic as to the future greatness of his country—'the Asiatic Greece,' he called it, which should leave such an impress on ages to come as Greece had left on ages past.

Thinking over his talk afterwards, Izo remembered that he had been quite aware of her long blindness, and wondered if she had herself unconsciously told him, or if it had been Kencho who had given him particulars of her history. It was all odd, she thought, and vaguely exciting ; and afterwards, pondering things over, she remained for a long time pensive and perplexed ; for, indeed, as Kencho had said, this Japan, which he was now making known to her, was not the Japan her uncle had derided to her—not the Japan, even, of fans and comic operas. It was a country and a people to be taken seriously, and she was beginning, in fact, to take them seriously—more seriously than any of the party had the least notion.

John Windeatt and Mrs. Bax were both in a bad humour when, after having waited for a considerable time among the clogs and umbrellas outside the Hongwanji, they at last saw Madame Izàn on the topmost step of the great flight, with Kencho on his knees before her, untying the blue socks she had worn in the temple. More than once during their various excursions had Windeatt envied the guide his agreeable task of covering and uncovering those shapely feet. Mrs. Eugarde, looking up from her ' Jottings,' appeared, on the contrary, whimsically jubilant. She had begun to see daylight through the emotional complications, and her brother's discomfiture was not at all unpleasing to her.

' Really, Izo, it's too bad of you. We have been here for hours,' fretfully exclaimed Herminia ; and Windeatt vented his annoyance on Kencho.

'Did you not understand that we were all to keep together? You should be more careful. When you saw that Madame Izàn was separated from her party, you should have waited or come back to look for us.'

' Pardon me,' replied Kencho, 'I received no orders to that effect from Madame Izàn.'

Windeatt bit his moustache in anger, but said no more. He turned to Madame Izàn.

'It was of you I was thinking, and of how tired you must be with that aimless wandering. I don't know how the blunder could have occurred. It does not say much,' he added in a lower tone, 'for your guide's efficiency.'

'But *where* were you, Izo?' asked Herminia. 'We have been *everywhere* searching for you. We have seen the tree that squirts water when the temple is on fire ; and I am quite disgusted with Yamasaki, for he turns up his nose, and says, " That only Japanese story." We've seen Hideyoshi's garden ; we've seen the library.'

'It's a pity you missed that,' said Mrs. Eugarde.

'But I didn't,' returned Madame Izàn ; 'we've been there all the time.'

'Impossible!' cried Windeatt. 'I was watching the door. I poked into every corner.'

'Not into my corner. I've been specially favoured.'

And then she stopped for some unaccountable reason ; perhaps she found Kencho's eyes fixed upon her, and she never said a word to the others about the old priest, which one might naturally have supposed she would do.

CHAPTER VII.

At Kioto, in the month of May, life passes after a story-land fashion. One awakes in the morning to glorified spring, and with the certainty that whatever one may see or feel or do is bound to be very good, and that, in any case, mere existence in one of the balconies at Yaami's must be more or less beatitude. The crickets whir merrily ; there is a gentle murmuring of cicadæ, and the rustling of wings and chaffering of small birds.

Just below the balcony the azaleas were in full bloom, and a gardener in a mushroom straw hat trimmed the hedge or tended the dwarf plants on the border of the miniature lake. Beyond the garden were the groves of camphor and cryptomeria, among which were set the pagoda roofs and great gateways of the temples along the Maruyama slope. There was a strange dreaminess in the air, and the faint blue haze floating over gray town and green wheatfields and blue mountains seemed to wrap all things moral and physical in a veil of

poetry. Nothing jarred ; all was soothing to the
nerves and grateful to the senses, and it sometimes
seemed to Julia Eugarde as though one were
taking minute doses of opium with no baneful
after-effects.

There were dream-days on which these four
new-comers and their guides would start forth in
jinrikishas, two runners apiece, and were whirled
through what indeed seemed like a landscape in a
story-book. Between the gray-coped walls of
temple enclosures they would go, past fields of
yellowing corn, of blooming poppies and young
rice-blades ; past little gray villages embedded in
cherry-orchards, by red temple gateways with their
barbaric turned-up architraves, by lacquer pagodas
and picture farmhouses, and along hill-slopes that
were vivid green and pinky mauve with young maple
and flowering azalea. Yes, dream-days these, in
which the air shed drowsy delight and had in it a
sort of mystic hush, through which the cries and
calls and chirpings, the temple drums, the monotonous samisen, and the rich reverberation of the
great bronze bells, came muffled as from a long
way off.

' Oi ! Oi !' the jinrikisha-runners would shout
continuously while they trotted briskly along—
nice merry-faced brown humans who, every now
and then, would fling back a laugh at each other

as though the whole affair were an excellent joke
Even when, at mid-day, the perspiration streamed
down their faces, and they would stop to take
off their hieroglyphically - marked blouses and
wipe themselves dry with queer blue cotton
handkerchiefs, they would still laugh, and never
slacken or grow weary. And now they would
clatter down the narrow street of some quite big
town—all brown houses, doll interiors and bright-
sashed moving figures—Otsu it might be, or perhaps another ancient capital. There are so many
ancient capitals and sacred cities in Japan.

It was almost always Kencho who planned these
dream-excursions. And might not this have been
because he had observed that in the temples and
shops and fairs and shows Madame Izàn sometimes seemed perplexed and a little dazed and
world-tired, whereas out in the open the free,
frank, 'goddess' look would come back to her
face, and she would be once more the irresponsible
Nature-joying creature, whose every glance and
smile suggested triumphant revolt against the
commonplace burdens of existence?

A curious difference might have been noticed
between the two guides in their several tendencies
towards places of tourist resort. The temples
Yamasaki evidently regarded as a patriotic duty,
a solemn obligation, which he discharged, neverthe-

less, in a somewhat perfunctory manner. To Yamasaki, on these occasions, Kencho usually left the guide-book business, while he himself, as has been seen, indulged Madame Izàn in scraps of more recondite information and in access to secret shrines, apparently beyond the range of Yamasaki's influence. And no one could openly resent this, as it was quite impossible to say whether or not his evasions of the rest of the party were deliberately planned—more especially as they appeared to give Madame Izàn, for whose benefit they were contrived, perfect satisfaction.

After the temples and palaces, the curio stores came next on Yamasaki's programme, or the workshops of Tashimura and Namigawa, and such eminent purveyors of embroideries and cloisonné, of cut velvet, and porcelain and cherry-wood cabinets and other fascinating products of Japan. And here Yamasaki was genuinely enthusiastic, taking the deepest interest in Windeatt's purchases and proffering much worldly advice in the matter of their selection. The beauties of Nature, on the other hand, awakened no enthusiasm in Yamasaki's breast, and he scorned the traditions of his country, which were not saleable. He was, in his way, an exponent of Marquis Ito's masterly policy, which aims at the supplanting of Orientalism by the amenities of European civilization, and

Yamasaki would drag forward his convictions that 'English fashion very much number one best' with a polite insistence that became at times oppressive. It was not clear to Yamasaki why Europeans, who had finer examples at home, should want to come and gaze at Japanese mountains and lakes and study old-fashioned village customs, and he and Kencho had words occasionally on the subject of those dream-day expeditions. Windeatt explained Yamasaki's want of appreciation in regard to landscape and social ways on the ground that mountains and lakes and farm-labourers paid no commission. But Yamasaki had no doubt whatever as to the superiority of Japanese curios. That was the one branch in which, according to him, his country stood unrivalled. For it was not long before he discovered that, in spite of their not being 'Legation people,' the Australians had long purses, and were without subtlety in the making of bargains; and many a grudge did he owe Kencho for interfering with his little plans and preventing him from taking full advantage of these peculiarities.

Kencho did not, however, throw obstacles in the way of Madame Izàn's equipment as a Japanese lady. She might not have the long sleeves, he explained, as she was no longer an unmarried girl; and at this bald statement of fact, which he delivered with a certain deliberateness, his spectacles fixed on her at the time, poor Madame Izàn blushed deeply, and for several minutes said nothing. Fortunately, however, the Shogun's chrysanthemum kimono had been the ceremonial garment of a matron. But in the matter of the obi Kencho took infinite pains, and the gold-threaded strip of brocade was a marvel of beauty in colour and design. Then there was the white silk under-kimono to be considered, and the further one of delicate crape and the crimson crape skirt, and the lacquered clogs and white socks—not such an easy matter, these last, to provide, for, slender and well-formed as were Madame Izàn's feet, they were considerably larger than those of Japanese women.

This was a dress rehearsal of the part: and there she stood, a quaint vision of loveliness, which made Windeatt's heart throb, and must have cost Kencho also an emotion, for his hand trembled visibly when at Izo's artless request he adjusted the loops of the famous obi. The nezans, who had arranged her hair, bubbled over with laughter and delighted admiration. They touched her face with an infantile gesture. 'Verai—nice,' they stammered. 'White . . . ichi-ban! Japanese not white—like this!' and they stroked the brown chair first and then their own cheeks, and pouted in amused seltdepreciation. After the essaying of this ceremonial robe, nothing would content Madame Izàn but the possession of a complete everyday costume— the soft gray-blue kimono and dainty obi and delicate neckfolds, which Windeatt thought suited her better even than the crimson vesture gorgeous with gold.

'And is that all I need?' she asked, turning to Kencho. 'Are there any other costumes which a Japanese lady wears?'

'There is the Court costume,' he answered, 'which is the most beautiful of all, and which, though it is no longer worn at Court, madame may see exhibited at the noble girls' school at Tokyo.'

'Oh dear!' put in Herminia Bax ; 'I suppose that, to wear that, one must be at least a " Legation person." '

Kencho smiled. Herminia was also attired in a kimono, a splendid sky-blue affair, and she had risen superior to national etiquette in the question of hanging sleeves. But the dress did not go well with her fair, freckled face and blue eyes and flaxen hair.

'In feudal days, madame, and according to the sumptuary laws of Japan, only the Court circle might wear the Court costume—the wives and daughters of nobles,' he replied.

'Mr. Kencho,' said Madame Izàn to him later,

'I can tell by the tone of your voice, when you speak of the feudal lords, that you attach great importance to being of noble birth. Do you wish that you had been born of a Daimio family? But, perhaps,' she added, 'you do belong to some great Japanese family, and I was wrong to say that. I have often wondered about you—whether——'

She stopped in her pretty, hesitating way.

'What have you often wondered—about me, madame?'

Kencho spoke with a catch in his deep voice, which struck upon Madame Izàn's ear, and made her glance at him from the camera she was handling. She saw that his lip trembled, and that he was bending towards her with an evident anxiety as to what she should answer—an anxiety which caused her a qualm of uneasiness. She evaded the question.

'I don't think I shall take any more photographs to-day,' she said irrelevantly. 'Let us sit down and watch the pilgrims.'

They were in the court of the Chionin Temple —they two alone, for Windeatt, to his chagrin, had been carried off bodily by his sister and Mrs. Bax to decide upon an ivory carving Julia wished him to buy, now at the Fine Arts Exhibition which was being held in Kioto. At the last moment Madame Izàn had declined to accompany him.

She had not felt in the mood for exhibitions, or for the shopping and bargaining which she knew would follow, since Yamasaki was in command of the forces. In her present mood there was something peculiarly soothing in the atmosphere of these gray old temple courts shadowed by the great camphor-trees, and with scarcely any sounds to break their dreaminess but the beat of the gongs within, and the clack of clogs upon the line of paving-stones which led between sentinel rows of lanterns to the broad flight of steps at the entrance, where worshippers were coming and going and prostrating themselves.

Kencho repeated his question, as they placed themselves upon a stone platform at the foot of one of the outer shrines. 'I wish I knew what it is that you wonder about me,' he said.

'I wonder,' she replied, 'that you, being what you are, should do the kind of work that you do. Now, can you understand?'

'Yes ; I suppose that I understand. You think that I might be something better than a guide to English tourists. But perhaps I have a good reason for acting in the capacity in which you find me, a reason that you will know some day.'

'Mr. Kencho,' she exclaimed impulsively, 'if I were as romantic as my friend Mrs. Bax, I should jump to the conclusion that you are a sort of dethroned Prince—some dispossessed Daimio, and not in the very least what you seem to be.'

'Oh no!' he replied with melancholy derision, 'It is much more reasonable for you to accept what you see, as plain matter-of-fact, and to believe that I am just everything I seem to be, which is certainly nothing remarkable or romantic. Yet why,' he added, ' should you so scorn the idea of romance?'

' Perhaps,' she said in a very low voice, ' because I have suffered from it.'

He took no notice of her interruption, but went on:

'And why should not Japan have her romances as well as any other country? I assure you that in the Guides' Association there are a great many well-born men forced to earn a livelihood, and glad to find such a pleasant and easy way of doing it. No, Madame Izàn, my grandfather was not a Daimio ; but it is true, nevertheless, that he clung to the old feudal traditions he had inherited, and re-sisted the Restoration, as it is called. Old man as he was, he joined the Tokugawa party, fought at Fushima, and later on was in the confidence of the great rebel Saigo. As you can understand, there was no favour for him under the new Constitution.'

Madame Izàn had learned enough about Japanese history to follow the explanation.

'And is it from your grandfather that you got all your feudal ideas?' she asked.

'I admired and reverenced my grandfather,' Kencho answered, 'and he stands out the most prominent figure in my boyhood. It is not so very long since he died. I can see him now in his simple dress of Satsuma cotton-stuff, with his calico obi and wooden clogs, which would be laughed at as the costume of a gentleman in these days. Many of his noble sayings have remained with me, and comforted me in hours of sadness. His living was low, but his thinking was high. He had great ideals. On himself in his richer days he spent nothing; for the good of his people he would cheerfully have given all that he had. The great Lord Yozan of Yonezawa was his model, and he copied him in all his ways.'

'Tell me about the great Lord of Yonezawa,' said Madame Izàn with the simplicity of a child eager for a story.

Then, as they sat in the court of the temple, Kencho related to Madame Izàn tales of the old-time Daimio—the poorest of the Daimios—who, nevertheless, by his self-sacrifice and wisdom and industry, made his people the noblest and his land the richest of all the peoples and lands in Japan ; who was indeed 'tender to his people,' after the vow he had made in boyhood, 'as to a wound in his own flesh.' Kencho told her of Yozan's splendid engineering works; of his foresight and the broadness of his schemes; of his plantings of mulberry and lacquer trees; of his administration of justice in his wonderful institution of the Companies of Fives and Tens, so that — and Kencho quoted from the great lord's own words— if there was one among them who was old and had no child, or young and without parents, or poor and unable to adopt sons, or widowed, or a cripple, or sick, or dead and left without burial, then should he be succoured by his company of five families; and if these were not able to support him, then should the company of ten families come to their assistance. Kencho told, too, how the Lord Yozan had by the law of Love suppressed vice and abolished theft from the land, so that on the wayside were stalls with labelled goods and no custodian, from which the people took, laying down the money, and robbed not. And he told, too, how, when the Lord of Yonezawa died, the nation mourned, and how to this day the silks of Yonezawa are famous, and its people known as most honest and truest in Japan.

Kencho's deep voice seemed to change from its habitual huskiness, and to become soft and ringing, as he talked on, forgetting himself in his enthusiasm. But he was called back by a sudden low exclamation from Madame Izàn, and, as he turned, was startled himself by the bewildered, almost frightened, expression he beheld on her face. He checked his eager speech and drew back, constrained and ill at ease.

'What is it?' he asked, and his voice sounded deep and harsh again.

'I don't know,' she answered, still looking dazed. 'I did not mean anything. It was only as you talked I was carried back — I seemed to have heard something of the same kind before — and yet not like it, either. Perhaps it was your voice which reminded me of' — she faltered a little — 'of somebody I knew long ago, who cared too for Japan.'

'Was that person in the least like me?' said Kencho deliberately, and he seemed to put himself forward, as though challenging comparison.

'How can I tell?' she said, 'and why should he be like you? No, of course not. He was young, I believe. . . . But I never saw him.'

'Ah!' There was again a catch in Kencho's breath. Any allusion to her blindness always affected him oddly. A silence followed. He sat immovable, all his eloquence quenched. The great bronze bell of the Chionin, the magic bell, boomed forth its glorious note.

'Go on,' said Madame Izàn presently. 'I am

sorry I interrupted.   I like hearing you.   Tell
me more — about the Daimios and about your
country.   Do you remember how the old priest
talked that day at the Hongwanji temple?'

'Yes, I remember.   You were impressed by
that priest?'

'It seems to me that you echo him.   I think
he, too, must be like your Lord of Yonezawa.
Yes, he interested me, and he made me feel that
we people over there have very false ideas about
you all here.   It is just what he said.   Nobody
takes you seriously.   He made me believe a little,
while he spoke, in the mission of Japan.'

'And what did he say was the mission of
Japan?'

'Don't you recollect?   Why, I can almost
repeat his words.   He said that Japan's mission
in the history of the world was to reconcile the
East and the West, morally, and intellectually, and
religiously.   Yes, I remember his saying—because
it was quite a new idea to me, and it seized me —
that when civilization started, at the beginning of
all things, in Central Asia, there were two currents,
one flowing west, by Babylon and Greece and
Rome, and culminating in England and America,
and the other east, through India and Thibet, and
ending in China.   Now, am I reporting him rightly,
Mr. Kencho?'

'Yes,' he answered, his whole face beaming with pleasure. 'I had never expected that you would grasp and appreciate the idea so fully.'

'I've thought of it more than I wanted to,' she said. 'It took hold of me, somehow, that notion of a magnetic circuit—that was how he put it—of which Japan is to join the two poles. I think of it when I see your electric light, and your railways and telephones, and all your other Western reforms, and I think of it when I see the Mass going on in the Hongwanji—I mean your Mass—and compare your Kwannon—as you said, the Lady of Mercy—with our Virgin Mary. Well, that priest's ideas are what you believe in, aren't they?'

'Yes, that is what I believe in,' he answered dreamily—' the mission of Japan among nations. It is we who will guard the sacred East by marrying her to the West; it is *our* rising sun which shall illumine both hemispheres. Japan will make the completion of the circuit, and become the central point of civilization. But first she must unite within herself the Lord Yozan's law of love and Marquis Ito's policy of progression. And this work,' Kencho went on, making a little fervid gesture, ' will be accomplished by us, the new generation of Japanese, who have imbibed the feudal instincts with our mothers' milk, but who have gone to school in the utilitarian West. That is the mission of this, our younger generation, which in Japan, too, as your Ibsen says, is "knocking at the door."'

Madame Izàn's gray eyes glowed, and then rested on Kencho's silver hair and young-old face, and a faint shade of disappointment crossed her features.

'But you,' she said—'are you of the younger generation, Mr. Kencho? Is this your mission, too?'

'Yes,' he said; 'I, too, wish to be a unit among the growing numbers, and to add my strength to the new force which shall lift my people higher.'

Again there was a pause. After a minute or two Kencho resumed :

'And you also, Madame Izàn. Now that you are beginning to get a glimpse of my country as it really is for such men as my master and friend, the priest of the Hongwanji, and not as the frivolous playground of your idle, pleasure-seeking English and Americans—well, does it not strike you——' He hesitated, his voice giving.

'Well,' she repeated, 'how? What is it that should strike me?'

'Does it not seem to you that it might be no unworthy destiny for a Western woman to stand by her Eastern husband's side, stimulating him to patriotic endeavour, quickening his faculties by her own intellectual appreciation and feminine intuition, helping him to realize his ideal of a world-spreading empire, forming in her own person the ideal towards which Japanese women should strive, and the link in the home between those two magnetic currents of which the priest spoke? Ah, do you not think——'

'No, no!' she cried, half rising, deeply agitated. 'I don't want to think! I will not think! What do you mean? Why should you say this to me? You don't know anything about me, about my——' She stopped, with an almost angry movement of her head. 'Why should you worry, disturb me, by speaking of such things? You have no right to do so, Mr. Kencho.'

He had risen, too, and they stood facing each other, and she fancied that even through the blue spectacles she could see the gleam of his eyes.

'No,' he said, 'certainly I have no right. Allow me to say that I am sorry for having annoyed you, and that I will not offend in this way again. For the moment I thought of myself as a Japanese gentleman, and forgot that I am Kencho, of the Guides' Association.'

He took up her camera, and with a low bow waited, his hat in hand, till she passed before him towards the temple gateway.

They went in silence up the stony street leading
to Yaami's, till they had reached that particular
photographer's shop among the line of little houses
on their left, as they mounted, where Madame
Izàn had established friendly relations, and where
her negatives were developed. Here she made an
involuntary halt, but evidently hesitated to express
her wishes, and Kencho, now the impassive guide,
and nothing more, anticipating these, stepped
forward, and asked in his usual manner if she
would not like to go in and leave the plates, and
get those she had given to be developed the day
before. It was a peculiarity of Madame Izàn's
childlike nature that a pleasant impression would
speedily efface one that had been disagreeably
upsetting, and in her excitement over the photographs, which had turned out exceptionally well,
she threw off the embarrassment of the temple
episode, and was her smiling, sunny self again.

'You see,' she cried triumphantly, pointing to a
print of one she had taken of the Yasuka Pagoda,
and of which she felt extremely proud, 'it is not
over-exposed after all. You said it would be,
and it is not. It is quite perfect, Mr. Kencho.'

'Yes,' he replied, smiling good-humouredly too,
'it *is* quite perfect, and I congratulate you. This
one is far better than those you took of Nagasaki
from the steamer.'

'Oh, of course !' she answered. 'The steamer was the steamer, you see, and this is Japan, and in Japan everything *must* go beautifully.' Then she remembered and reddened and seemed uncomfortable for a moment. But when they had got within the gateway of Yaami's she turned upon the guide with her straight gaze, kindly compunction and bashful courage showing on her face.

'Mr. Kencho, I am afraid . . . I think I spoke a little crossly just now. Naturally, you could not have meant anything personal, and it was my stupidity in taking things so. Please forget what I said.'

He bowed silently in his ceremonious fashion.

'And I hope,' she said, 'that you'll go on telling me your delightful stories still—all about your ideas, and the new generation, and the rest that the old priest was talking about. It interests me—indeed, it interests me very much. I hope you will tell me more about the feudal times, Mr. Kencho.'

'Certainly ! It will be the greatest pleasure to me to do so,' he answered. 'And again I ask you to pardon me for what was an involuntary impertinence, and for presuming upon your kindness so far as to forget my position towards you.'

'Oh, please,' she cried—'please, Mr. Kencho,

don't talk about positions. Your grandfather wouldn't have thought of anything so petty as positions. And I am sure that is not in the manner of your model, the great Lord Yozan.'

And she laughed her soft girlish laugh as she tripped up the steep stairway to Yaami's veranda, where Herminia and Windeatt, outside the reading-room, were awaiting her. And she did not notice — how should she, indeed? — the glance of despairing devotion which Kencho Hiro-Kahachi sent after her through his disfiguring blue goggles.

CHAPTER VIII.

AFTER this episode Madame Izàn seemed to have more frequent fits of pensiveness, but through her pensiveness there shone a certain radiance, and her April-day moods were often just now illuminated with a sunny smile. She was so amiable—it is true, in rather remote fashion—towards Windeatt that his gloom was not quite explicable. As for the others, Herminia included, they were thoroughly enjoying Kioto, and it seemed to Julia Eugarde that her brother's too evident dissatisfaction with himself and some of his companions was the only discordant note in the general harmony.

'How can you be so ill-tempered?' she said. 'Nobody ought to be ill-tempered in Japan. It's an incongruity. Do you imagine that this sweet and smiling nation could, even in domestic privacy, permit itself the luxury of a good old row? Why, the open house-fronts and the rice-paper walls protest against the bare notion!'

'Are you quoting from your "Jottings," Ju?' inquired Windeatt sulkily.

'And if I am!' she returned unabashed. 'Why shouldn't my nicely-turned reflections have an airing before they go into print?'

They were on the platform of the Kiomidzu temple—that one built over the brow of the hill, whence jealous Japanese husbands used to hurl their faithless wives—and a certain vague association of ideas may have suggested the fierce and irrelevant remark Windeatt now made.

'I wish to Heaven that there was somebody to keep that courier fellow in his place!'

'Do you mean Yamasaki?' asked Julia with malicious innocence. 'I should not like Yamasaki to be suppressed ; he is so extremely amusing.'

'No ; you know I don't mean Yamasaki ; it's the other one who annoys me. I shall be obliged myself to put him in his place some day.'

'Well, I presume that he *is* in his place,' said Julia. 'He is paid two dollars a day for instilling Japanese knowledge into Madame Izàn, and I'm bound to say that he is faithful to his obligations, for he doesn't lose an opportunity for private instruction.'

'He is always hanging round,' grumbled Windeatt. 'One can never get in a word. I shan't stand it any longer.'

'Don't, then, Jack ; they've settled with Kencho to go on to Miyanoshita after this. Let them go, and you and I will take a trip on our own account. I really do want to write about the Ize temples, and Mrs. Bax declines the expedition ; she says she has had enough of temples.'

' No, thank you,' replied Windeatt ; ' I'm of Mrs. Bax's mind : I've got temple indigestion, too.'

But Julia Eugarde knew well enough that there would have been no question of temple indigestion with Windeatt here at the Kiomidzu, had he only been permitted to wander with Madame Izàn in and out of the shrines, through the camphor-groves, and among the moss-grown stone lanterns, and to talk sentiment to her, undisturbed by Kencho's haunting presence. For it was quite true that Kencho seemed to conceive it his duty to remain always within earshot of Madame Izàn, and though Windeatt had to own that she was graciously accessible to every commonplace atten-tion on his part, and ready enough to accept his escort, the guide was invariably just a little behind her elbow, and certainly in his English studies did not appear to have read the adage that ' Two is company, and three is none.' So Windeatt got very slight opportunity for any communication of a personal nature.

It was Madame Izàn's humour just now to want to know everything she could learn about Japan, and to be absorbed in its history, its romance, its heroes—were they not going to see the play of the ' Forty-seven Ronins' at the theatre that evening?—its Shoguns, and all the rest which Kencho could impart to her. And, as everybody knows, there is a good deal of history tacked on to the Kiomidzu. Kencho was only too eager to gratify his young mistress's desire for information, and so it had followed that Windeatt had found himself very much out in the cold, and was not overpleased with the sensation.

Apart from these aggravating conditions, no more suitable background for sentiment could be imagined than this old red-brown temple, set half-way up the mountain-side amid the forest greenery.

It is an enchanting place, Kiomidzu, with its cool dark cloisters and the great shrine, where Kwannon of divine compassion rears her gilded majesty amid clouds of incense, and round her the bowed forms of her priests chanting their deep-toned prayers to the beat of the gongs. And then there are the many other shrines, fragrant and mysterious, with their lighted tapers and lamps, and banners and lotus-blooms and golden-tongued gongs. And there are the outer courts, at their different levels connected by stone stairways, with their rows of lichen-stained lanterns and ancient monuments and gray pillars ; and the fountains, where water pours from dragons' mouths;

and the pilgrim altars, whose canopies are upheld by strange-shaped gods, and where thousands of votive flags wave against the dark-green firs. . . . How beautiful and fantastic it all is!

The clank-clank of the clogs sounded continuously as the worshippers stepped along the pavements. The working people came and went. Some poor woman with lined yellow face and blackened teeth would set down her bundle and umbrella, knock her head upon the ground, count her beads, and get up spiritually refreshed, to resume once more her umbrella and clogs and bundle, as well as the duties of life ; or else a farm labourer would pull at the straw rope, rattle the brass gong, clap his hands and call his god, and then go about his affairs the better fitted, no doubt, by his little prayer, to make a good bargain in the market-place. There is a funny mixture of piety and barter in the courts of the Kiomidzu —a red Buddha face to face with a vendor of cheap cigars, and a good tea-house business going on in front of the shrine of Goddess Kamnosube-ne-Kami, the friend of unhappy lovers.

Now, Windeatt had studied his guide-book, and, as his methods of courtship were not exactly subtle, he had determined that he, too, would try and propitiate the goddess by adding to the many fluttering scraps of paper which almost hid that mystic grating. And he had resolved that Madame Izàn, and Madame Izàn only, should be witness of the charm. Accordingly he had bribed Yamasaki, and had manœuvred that Herminia Bax and Julia the unsympathetic, should be conducted towards the tea-house, he and the lady of his choice remaining in the rear. There's no knowing what might have resulted from this strategy, and whether the impassioned declaration he contemplated might not have stirred Madame Izàn's pulses to a degree that would have altered the whole course of her destiny, were it not that, at the critical moment, Kencho, whom Windeatt had believed safely disposed of, stepped out from a side-chapel, and stood grim and impassively courteous, his eyes fixed on the Australian through their blue coverings, so that the lover's ardour turned to a most unloving fury, and that fateful strip of paper, instead of being affixed to the grating with thumb and forefinger, following the cabalistic directions, was torn to angry shreds which the breeze carried away.

The worst of it was that Madame Izàn seemed quite unconscious of these underworkings, and smiled impartially both on him and the offending guide. Being desirous of obtaining full particulars of Kamnosube-ne-Kami, she left Windeatt again with a maddening smile, and disappeared in company of Kencho into the obscurity of the great Hondo ; nor had she reappeared when Mrs. Eugarde and her brother joined Herminia Bax, who, in one of the open compartments of the tea-house, was under Yamasaki's guidance making experiments in Japanese food.

The tea-house overlooked the valley, the winding white roads, and the gray roofs of the dwellings among the trees. From one of these floated a baby's cry, which gave a touch of homeliness to the scene. The rice-paper partition of the next compartment was drawn, and within, a Japanese family squatted beside a repast of macaroni and other condiments which were shovelled out of tiny flat boxes on the matting, into lacquer bowls set about on wee tables. They were a merry set of persons, and laughed and chattered in the intervals of eating and smoking. Mrs. Bax had expressed the wish for a flat box on her own account, and Yamasaki forthwith produced a mess which turned out to be composed of pounded onion, radish, vermicelli, soy and little fishes, not altogether agreeable to Herminia's palate. She repented of her curiosity, and sentimentally reminded herself of Dr. Duppo's warning. Herminia had a tendency to become sentimental when she thought of Dr. Duppo. Yamasaki waited his opportunity to mix up the concoction deftly with a pair of chopsticks, and pitchforked it in a half-surreptitious fashion into his capacious mouth. But he affected to despise it, all the same, putting it down contemptuously with the remark, 'That only Japanese food. No good make fight Japanese soldier.'

'Yamasaki,' said Mrs. Eugarde, 'do you think Japan is going to fight Russia and become a great nation ?'

Yamasaki heaved himself up on his haunches, made play again with the chopsticks, and delivered himself in his quaint English :

'Some time. Suppose Russia by herself, Japan not frightened. Suppose France and Germany—that too much ; no try ; not ship enough. Japan wait ten year, perhaps. Then, no little war like China. Then all Japanese man fight. Beforetime Japanese soldier no good—very young peoples. Fourteen year ago, Japan quite savage ; difference very much. Every year more better. That China war for soldier practice. Every day, Japanese small man practise catch big man, kick up, take throat, learn gun ; Japan all right now ; very quick nation, order very much. Suppose no order, get drunk—no good. I not learn gun,' pursued Yamasaki. 'Never before. I wife, I child. But I pleased very. I go. I give my bloods for my State.'

Yamasaki's little brown face glowed all over with martial enthusiasm ; his tusks seemed to bristle, and he plied his chopsticks with an amazing energy. It was just then that Madame Izàn, with Kencho, came along, her arms full of photographs, and pins, and fans with Kiomidzu views, and such trifles, that she had been buying. And she was most sweet and winning, and made poor Windeatt's heart bound anew, and restored him again to happiness, by seating herself on the edge of the platform beside him, and showing him her photographs, and telling him that he would have to escort her down Teapot Hill, and take charge of the hundred-and-one teapots she meant to buy there and have packed and sent home as a present to Aunt Sophia.

'For, do you know, Mr. Windeatt,' she said, 'Aunt Sophia has two particular and pet economies —and they are, string and teapots. It was a capital crime to throw away the tiniest bit of string, and no matter whether you wanted one cup of tea or twenty, it all had to be brewed in the only teapot which the establishment provided, a great clumsy nickel thing which *felt*——' Madame Izàn's gesture with her fingers was eloquent. 'Of course, I couldn't see it, but it gave me the creeps. And when I asked Aunt Sophia if I mightn't have a little china pot just for our two selves, she would say I was a wicked, extravagant young woman, and deserved to live in China, where I might have as many teapots as I pleased. So now I am in China, or next-door to it, and actually walking down Teapot Hill—for I'm going to walk, and you must walk with me—I shall buy up all the monstrosities of teapots that I can find, and take my little revenge on Aunt Sophia by giving her the trouble of unpacking them.'

Windeatt lent himself enthusiastically to Madame Izàn's small scheme of good-natured malice, and as they went down Teapot Hill, the whole four, perhaps not including Kencho and Yamasaki, had a most amusing time over the purchase of these same monstrosities. Upon this occasion Kencho did not obtrude himself unpleasantly to Windeatt. Probably he thought there was no great danger to the fair lady, and not a too favourable opportunity for amorous declaration among the open booths of teapots that lined the way.

It happened to be a Matsuri, and the crowd was great, and little children fluttered about like swarms of butterflies in gay-coloured crapes and painted sashes. All the buildings were decorated with swaying lanterns and banners. Priests sat under their canopies beating gongs and waiting for alms, and all the 'go-downs' were on the alert for trade. Here was doll-land, and for the moment Madame Izàn forgot the more serious aspect of Japan. But that was recalled again at the Dai-Butsu Temple, which Mrs. Bax flatly refused to enter, and the grim monument to those thousands of human ears, the trophies of Hideyoshi's blood-stained fame. Then they wandered through the hall of that vast host of many-armed Buddhas—the god-market, as Windeatt called it, and he made an irreverent joke on the plethora of deities, to which, somehow, Madame Izàn did not respond as graciously as was her wont.

But what could be more tenderly poetic or inspiring than the lotus-pond seen in the dying daylight?—though, alas for Windeatt! here again was Kencho vigilantly attentive. And how strangely solemnizing seemed the gray walls of the temple enclosures, and the colossal gateways which they passed on the Maruyama, and the unearthly vibrations of those big bronze bells!

Three of the *Makara* young men turned up at the next table in the dining-room at Yaami's that evening, the melancholy Mr. Barradine making a fourth of the noisy party. He was on his way to the baths of Miyanoshita, whither Dr. Duppo had recommended him to betake himself.

'They say the hotel is cleanly, the air salubrious, and the baths agreeable, and that, as the kitchen adjoins the dining-room, you have a chance of saving yourself from the perpetration of any culinary atrocity,' he bleated resignedly. 'I shall remain at Miyanoshita till it is time for me to take the Empress boat. Now I shall retire to bed. No, thank you, Madame Izàn ; it is very kind of you to ask me to accompany you to the theatre, but I am not interested in the Japanese drama. As for these wild young men, they may go henceforth their own inartistic way. I took them to Icheda's curio store this morning, and they said they had never seen such a collection of rubbish.'

'The fact is, Madame Izàn, we are suffering untold agonies, and our minds need distraction,' said the Irrepressible Young Man, and he certainly did look a little more subdued than usual. 'We've been tattooed. Don't you try it; it hurts like red-hot pokers—that chap over there cried all through it. But we're lovely. Do look ;' and he pulled up his sleeve. 'The stork is a little inflated at present, but he'll tone down in a day or two.'

Kencho was waiting in the garden outside the dining-room. Maybe he had been studying the tourist crowd through the open windows and renewing recollections of festive evenings in Europe. Over his arm he carried Madame Izàn's wrap, which never upon these occasions did he forget, or any other small property which might

contribute to her comfort. It was a dainty feathered
thing, and he seemed to handle it with more
caressing love than he gave to Mrs. Bax's service-
able chuddah.   Down by the gateway Yamasaki
chaffered with the rickshaw-coolies.   Windeatt
would fain have guided Madame Izàn, but it
was Kencho who adroitly stepped forward and
helped her in, and tucked her round, and then
contrived that his own rickshaw should be within
hand's-touch of her, so that Windeatt was forced
to take a backward place in the procession.   To
be sure, Kencho had the advantage of speaking
Japanese and could give his own private instructions, while Windeatt was obliged to wait for
Yamasaki to interpret his desires.   So presently a
string of overgrown perambulators flew down the
steep incline, between the flaming cressets set
at intervals by the roadway and the myriads of
lanterns—elongated globes of light, the white ones
pale blurs, grotesquely cut into patterns by the
lettering upon them ; and others yellow and
vermilion and parti-coloured.   Everywhere they
swung and swayed—all over the tea-houses, the
booths and temples and trees, at the end of long
poles borne by squads of army schoolboys in
blue coats and scarlet hoods, who sang patriotic
songs as they marched along.   The lanterns flew
at the end of strings, like kites hovering over

clusters of gaily-attired children. There were arches of lanterns across the narrow streets; they crept beneath rickshaws like fat glow-worms, and wobbled with the jerky motion of the foot-people. Oh yes! to be whirled in a rickshaw on a feast-night through the streets of Kioto is to be an abnormally big baby rushing in a child's carriage through some glorified pantomime-land. Never, surely, had Madame Izàn's long-darkened eyes gazed upon so bewildering a scene.

They stopped on one of the bridges to survey it, and the moony radiance of two high electric lamps served only to enhance its fantasy. The lanterns were reflected in the shallow streams dividing the river's pebbly causeway. To and fro they bobbed as fan - figures moved in and out threading the booths set about with gaudy wares, and the booths where drums beat, and samisen and koto sounded. Every brown house on either side had its giant cylinder of light, inscribed with the sign of its calling in big strange lettering, besides all the many dozens of yellow and pink lanterns hung from eaves and lintels, and festooning the windows and balconies, where eccentric forms exhibited themselves. The whole place seemed one vast Will-o'-the wisp playground, only that the fireflies had upright bodies, most of them curiously variegated and with gorgeous middle-

bands, like the stripe of some tropical beetle
while their heads were big with shiny loop pro-
tuberances, and antennæ, as it were, of gold and
coral. And there, away back, the Maruyama hill
seemed one vast resplendence, for the green slope
was bejewelled with bonfires, and from a great
gilded flagstaff on the summit hung strings of
banners as from a gigantic maypole.

'Japanese people go up and make feasts; give
thanks for war,' devoutly explained Yamasaki,
who was uplifted by the fact of having impressed
these Europeans.

But Theatre Street was the one for which the
party was bound, and many tourists know the
long, narrow arcade—a confusion of lanterns and
banners and stalls and cheap shows—down which,
on a gala night, it is no very easy matter to make
one's way to the big building at the end, where,
under a row of electric lights, hangs the huge
illustrated programme of the evening's performance. Yamasaki had had conventional scruples
about this expedition, in which he had had no
particular part: for Kencho had been quite
anxious to arrange the affair, and had taken great
pains to secure a suitable box, and to cater as
luxuriously as might be for his two ladies.
Yamasaki was contemptuous.

'This only second-class theatre,' he said. 'No

first-class here. First-class at Tokyo. Ministers and high-class people go. Here, only common people.'

Mrs. Bax was deeply impressed by Yamasaki's high-class standard. Sometimes, when she admired a pretty Japanese woman, she would ask Yamasaki whether that were a high-class lady; but he would waive the question disdainfully aside : ' No, that not high-class lady ;' and it appeared that no high-class personages moved about in Kioto. Julia Eugarde gravely mooted the doubt as to whether they themselves were considered by Yamasaki high-class people, for he had been sad and silent when, in answer to his oft-repeated inquiries as to communications to or from the Legation, and tentative suggestion as to certain privileges and immunities possible only to ' Legation friends,' Windeatt had told him that the Legation might go to the devil, for all that it concerned his sister and himself. Yamasaki had retired abashed, but the next morning, with many deep bows, demanded an advance, on account of his railway-fare home from Tokyo, when Windeatt should have further need of his services. Only Julia's calm philosophy and Mrs. Bax's tearful entreaties had restrained Windeatt from despatching the guide there and then home to the bosom of his family. As it was, he hurled a bank-note

13

at Yamasaki, who was thereafter trustfully obse-
quious. Windeatt reflected that Herminia Bax's
preference for Yamasaki constituted a link between
the two parties which it was as well not to break.

To-night he welcomed the blessed chance which
removed Kencho from his post for a moment, and
enabled the Australian to fold Madame Izàn's
sensitive fingers securely within his coat-sleeve.
This young creature, in spite of her love of adventure, was always timid in a night crowd, when
the lights danced, and distances were incalculable,
and eyes and . brain were dazzled. Upon such
occasions, when he had the good fortune to be
her pilot, Windeatt's whole soul would glow and
expand in the ardour of his protective tenderness.
Now, as the stream bore them along, and an occa-
sional obstruction blocked their course, he had an
opportunity for some tender whisperings.

' If you only knew how happy it makes me to
be allowed to take care of you once more!'

She gave a faintly embarrassed laugh.

' But one doesn't really want any special taking
care of in Japan ; everybody is so amiable and
considerate, and sight-seeing is made so easy.'

' I wish,' went on Windeatt, ' that I could be
your guide instead of Kencho. For, certainly,'
he added, after a pause, a little irritated by her
silence, ' I don't see the use of all this retinue—

two couriers between us—who want to manage us entirely. I am sure we should do quite as well—in fact, feel freer and less in the globe-trotting category—if we had no guides at all. That's what I have been saying to Ju, and I fancy she agrees with me,' said the mendacious young man. 'You see, we have always Murray and Chamberlain and Hearn and Conder, and all the rest, if we only take the trouble to read them. And, then, the people at Yaami's are so obliging, and there are so many rickshaw-coolies who speak English. What do you think, Madame Izàn? Suppose we get rid of our guides, who are just tacked on to the Legation and judge us by Legation notions. And, you know, in all these foreign places, if you want to get into the real spirit of the country, you must avoid Legations and all that British snobbery. Suppose we start on our own hook? I'm quite prepared to undertake the job, if you will allow me to perform the functions of your courier.'

Again there was a little silence, which to an eager listener behind seemed breathless—indeed, to two eager listeners, for Herminia Bax was most curious to know what Izo would answer.

'Well, I don't know about that,' she said. 'I think I would much rather keep you as a friend. That was what we settled, wasn't it? I don't think you'd do as a courier.'

'And why not?' he asked, considerably piqued at her business-like way of considering the matter. 'Why not? There are plenty of books, and every tourist goes just on the beaten track. I can't see any great difficulty in getting at the ins and outs of Japan.'

'Don't you?' And she laughed again. 'Oh, but I know much better—now. Have you any idea how conceited you are? Could you tell me the true history of the Forty-seven Ronins ; no, you know you couldn't, though it's just as elementary here as the history of our Ali Baba and the Forty Thieves. And as for Hideyoshi the Shogun, you had to read him up in Murray. And you had never heard of the Lord Yozan, or of the great Saigo, the last of the Samurai, or of the Master Nichiren, or of any of those others Kencho tells me about. I delight in listening to Kencho: he doesn't talk "guide-book." Now, do you call this sort of thing getting at the ins and outs of Japan?' continued the young lady, with a fine scorn that fascinated and half amused her unseen auditors. 'Why, it's nothing but Gilbert and Sullivan—a burlesque, that's all. It's no more the true Japan, the grand Japan, the feudal Japan——'

And here she broke off suddenly, for one of those blocks occurred which separated the whole party, and Madame Izàn and Windeatt were stranded and alone in a surging crowd, breaking back from the theatre doors which they were approaching. Something had happened, but it was impossible to tell what. And yet it was a gentle, well-meaning mob, which would not for the world have done any wrong to inoffensive strangers, and was only turning back disappointed from its own national theatre, and making its own little grumblings at a change of programme in its own sweet language, which has no swear-words whatsoever.

But Madame Izàn did not know this, and was frightened and clung closely to Windeatt, and appealed to him in just such a fashion as turned the head of the young man from the Bush, who regarded all foreign nations, and especially any one distantly related to the heathen Chinee, abhorred of Australian policy, as fiends let loose for his particular aggravation.

'Oh, Mr. Windeatt,' cried Madame Izàn, 'I don't like this at all. I'm quite terrified. I wish Kencho hadn't left us to look after ourselves. Oh, Mr. Windeatt, my poor head is so worried, and my poor eyes see everything anyhow. Oh! do get me out of it, if you can.'

Then Windeatt, moved by his deep devotion and anxious at all hazards to allay her alarm, braced up his great body and—instead of merely shadowing her with his bulk, as he might have done, and waiting till the human eddy had widened out—pushed his strong frame forward, clearing a way by mere brute strength, and thus arousing angry murmurs amid the swarm of chattering little people. This cross complaining incensed the Australian, whose native contempt for yellow men got the better of him ; and as the mob grew angrier, he pushed more strenuously, and at last knocked two or three poor little Japs altogether off their balance. It was then that Madame Izàn might have seen, if she had not been too terrified to think about anything, an ebullition of the old barbarian element—that of the feudal Japan she had been talking about. The fierce looks and fiercer gestures startled her, and she called out involuntarily, in shrill appealing, ' Kencho!' Whereat there sounded another voice in return. Then a lull followed and a sudden break in the human block. Some more authoritative words that none of the Europeans could understand were pronounced in a voice that was Kencho's, and yet, somehow, did not seem like the voice of Kencho ; and then the guide himself appeared, his pale face —pale through its brownness outside the blue goggles—parting, as it were, the dense mass of men, as he darted to Madame Izàn's side, and, taking her arm from within that of Windeatt, pressed it close to his own heart.

' Sir,' he said, addressing the Australian, ' you

don't know how to deal with my people. Treat them courteously and they will be courteous. But offer them insult and, physically inferior as they may be, you will find that they can avenge it. Come, madame. Everything will be quite clear before you. You will see that the Japanese can respect a lady. It was merely that another piece has been substituted, and that many who were going to enter have changed their minds. The alteration,' he added, ' has been made for political reasons. Party spirit runs high; the populace does not approve of concessions to the Powers after a victorious war ; and it is considered unwise to rouse old Japan.'

The strength and dignity of this small man had a curious effect on Madame Izàn, which, thinking it over afterwards, she could hardly account for. All her tremors vanished, and with perfect content-ment she allowed Kencho to lead her out of the crowd, which made way before him, casting just one uneasy glance back towards Windeatt, whom she felt guiltily that she was leaving to his fate.

' He is quite safe,' said Kencho reassuringly ; ' he will follow us in a moment. I have ex-plained that he is not a Russian, for you under-stand that there is great ill-feeling against Russia here at present ; nor even an Englishman, but that he comes from a land of savages who deserve pity and toleration.'

'Oh dear me!' exclaimed Madame Izàn. 'Is
that how you look upon Australia? But I am a
savage, too.'

'You are quite different, and even were you a
Russian, madame, you would find that in Japan
you would be powerfully protected.'

His words and the tone in which they were
uttered struck strangely upon the Australian
woman's ear. She withdrew her arm, for they
were now in the long wooden corridor of the
theatre, and at a little distance she discerned
first Yamasaki's tusks protruding from his anxious
little brown visage, and then the familiar forms of
Herminia Bax and Mrs. Eugarde. Presently she
said to Kencho, as they were moving on to the
places assigned them, 'Why do you so dislike
Mr. Windeatt?'

The expression of the guide's face, as far as the
blue spectacles permitted it to be seen, troubled
her anew.

'Perhaps it is because he is always with you,'
exclaimed Kencho recklessly ; then corrected himself, speaking in a quieter tone : 'I am wrong. I
don't dislike Mr. Windeatt for any particular
reason: it is as I said, that he comes from a crude,
unpolished nation, which has no sympathy with
Japanese subtleties.'

'That is true,' replied Madame Izàn.

CHAPTER IX.

KENCHO stood respectfully behind the row of stools which, in consideration of European peculiarities, the management had provided ; while every now and then the tea-house attendant, subsidized for the evening, appeared with the customary refreshment and the customary obeisances. Windeatt, who had joined them in the corridor, sat next Madame Izàn, and no doubt had Kencho, like Yamasaki, betaken himself for short periods to more congenial society, the Australian would have emptied his heart of its bitterness and its wounded love. But the guide was there, and Windeatt remained tongue-tied, sitting gloomy and morose under the unpleasant consciousness that he had not cut an altogether heroic figure in the defence of his lady-love, and that for this time, at any rate, the heathen Jap had got the better of him. As for Madame Izàn, she, too, was silent and preoccupied, and the frightened look had come back to her face. She took no interest in the performance, which, in truth, to most of them seemed a grotesque and unnatural affair. No doubt there was justification of Yamasaki's contempt, for here was not Danjiro nor any other theatrical star, and Julia Eugarde and Mrs. Bax, who had studied up the ' Forty-seven Ronins,' and were disappointed at the change of piece, frankly confessed themselves bored, and unable to comprehend in the very least what was going on.

The whole thing seemed to these Europeans as unreal as a dream: the strange music; the fantastical figures of the actors and their uncouth gait, as they tripped to and from the stage by a long passage which ran level with the heads of the spectators, cheered or derided as they went; the vast auditorium, with its sunken pit; the matted pens where groups of men and women squatted and smoked and joked and ate, carrying on a sort of *vie intime*, to the accompaniment of much tea and of a kind of chorus sounding through merriment and applause — the thunk-thunk of tiny pipes against the small boxes of glowing charcoal with which each pen was furnished. Then the stage, with its revolving centre, on which at moments of crisis the heroes stepped, to disappear as in a whirligig; the posturing and grimacing with sword and umbrella; the queer decorations and the curious mixture of *bizarrerie* and realism. This was intensified by the flickering illumination shed on the actors' faces by candles in iron sconces, that were changed by mutes hither and thither as the performers crossed from right to left, and by the effect of a great electric ray streaming down from a hole high in the ceiling ; also by the thud of the stick heralding the rise of the curtain and the entrance of each principal performer, so that there arose in the minds of some of these foreigners alternating associations with Paris theatres and the backs of playing cards.

Madame Izàn had never been to any French theatres, but maybe her long darkness had stimulated rather than quenched the play of her imagination, and now an indescribable and melancholy sense of tragi-comicality and of travesty of the common emotions of life came over her—a feeling which, though she knew it not, was shared by that still and apparently self-contained man in the blue spectacles standing close behind her. Kencho, too, was in a dream.

As for the play, what was it all about? Nobody knew, unless it were Yamasaki. Here were two young women in trailing and extremely gorgeous kimonos and wonderful black wigs, having much paint and powder on their long oblique-eyed faces. They sat on their haunches and talked in high-pitched falsetto, and knocked their heads upon the floor, weeping between whiles into large pink-embroidered pocket - handkerchiefs. And there behind them, on a sort of tea-house daïs, divided into tiny compartments, were various groups of ladies and gentlemen engaged during the entire act in the silent making and drinking of tea. They seemed altogether indifferent and oblivious to the woes of the harrowed damsels, and so, too, was an elderly gentleman sitting apart absorbed in a book, till suddenly, for some reason inexplicable to the Europeans, he threw away his book, and in an access of rage drew his sword, leaped down and belaboured the damsels, who fled shrieking down the causeway the length of the pit, followed helter-skelter by the irate gentleman and all the rest of the *dramatis personæ*; and then a green curtain fell over the horizontally-striped one with the Emperor's chrysanthemums upon it, that had already been drawn incontinently several times, and they supposed that the act was ended.

'Never before I see green curtain happen,' remarked Yamasaki. 'That not been Daimio time. I suppose that European custom;' and he turned to question Kencho, and to hold with this grave person a short conversation in Japanese.

There was a chattering down below as of hundreds of parrots let loose, and which took the place of the samisen's twanging. Attendants handed round sweetmeats and oranges, and some of the audience clambered over partitions and disported themselves on the stage. The *Makara* young men came crowding into the box.

'And what do you think of that for tommyrot, Madame Izàn? And can you have patience, now, with those asses in London who write to the papers and say we don't know how to stage a play in England, or to act one, either, and that Henry Irving ought to come over to Japan to study his business? It's a fact, I assure you. I know one of them, have read his articles and heard him hold forth. Well, all I can say is: give me a good old music-hall and " Her golden hair " —or the " Mikado," if you must have genuine Japanese—and I certainly shan't ask leave to see a play in Kioto again.'

'Mrs. Bax!' exclaimed another of the tourist young men, 'you can't stand this sort of infliction any more than we can, I'm certain : though you are not suffering agonies from a dragon on your back and a stork below your elbow. I say, do persuade Madame Izàn, and let us clear out of the place and inspect the penny shows outside. There are any amount of them outside, and stunning good ones, too, I can tell. We saw a white snake that will give you the creeps, and there's a dwarf-devil who is simply ripping.'

Mrs. Bax was taken by the superior attractions

of the dwarf-devil and the white snake, so was
Mrs. Eugarde. Izo, when appealed to, awakened
out of her dream, and was eager to leave the
theatre ; while Windeatt was delighted to go anywhere or to do anything which might deliver him
from his wretched broodings, and give him the
chance of a word with Madame Izàn. So presently they all went down the steep wooden
staircase and along the narrow passage, and again
they were outside, in the noise and dazzlement of
Theatre Street. But it was much less crowded
now than when they had entered the theatre.

Windeatt pushed almost rudely past Kencho
Hiro-Kahachi ; but, then, it was not to be supposed
that the guide would under ordinary circumstances
presume to offer Madame Izàn his arm.

'Please !' Windeatt said beseechingly. 'If you
send me away, I shall think that you are angry
with me.' He ventured to take her unresisting
hand. 'I will promise not to get into rows :
though you must have seen that I didn't really
mean to knock the fellow down, and that it was
all out of my intense anxiety to get you away. I
am not naturally a belligerent person, except out
in the Never-Never Country.'

'But we are not in the Never-Never Country,
which I know all about, Mr. Windeatt ; for Uncle
O'Halloran used to describe it to me.'

'Well,' said Windeatt ruefully, 'I must say that I never felt so thoroughly bushed, anyhow, as when I'm talking to you here in Kioto.'

'I don't think that even in the Bush people knock each other down without having a very good reason for it,' replied Madame Izàn, evading the personal inference.

'And what better reason could anybody have than wanting to get you out of a nasty Chinese crowd?' cried Windeatt.

'This is not a nasty Chinese crowd. Japan isn't China,' objected Madame Izàn distantly.

'It's next door to it—you said so yourself on Teapot Hill,' returned Windeatt.

'I didn't mean it—not in that sense ; and you don't understand Japan and the Japanese, Mr. Windeatt, and it's no use arguing,' said Madame Izàn, remembering Kencho's strictures on the inhabitants of the Never-Never Country. Then unconsciously she quoted him : 'It's really impossible that you can enter into Japanese subtleties.'

'I've had enough of Japanese subtleties—in private life, at any rate,' said Windeatt ungraciously. 'Madame Izàn, I hate you to go down on your knees as you do before everything Japanese. It—it's un-British. But, as you say, there's no use arguing about it, especially when those same subtleties are jostling one very materially all the time. Look here : Yamasaki is ever so much better as a showman than your superior Kencho. Let him look after us two, and Kencho can take charge of Mrs. Bax and Ju. I beg your pardon '—he had suddenly discovered the guide's proximity—' I didn't know you were so close. There's Mrs. Eugarde waiting by the entrance.'

But Kencho firmly addressed himself to his mistress.

' Unless you desire it otherwise, madame, I think it will be best that I should take you into these places. They are not all of them quite fit for an English lady to enter.'

' Well, I should imagine that Yamasaki is as competent a judge of Japanese proprieties as you can be, Mr. Kencho,' retorted Windeatt, and felt ashamed of himself, for Kencho met his remark with a bow of exquisite politeness.

He make no other answer, but waited stock-still for Madame Izàn to issue her commands.

' Oh, Mr. Windeatt,' she said with slight hesita-tion, and Windeatt did not know how to interpret the little tremble in her voice, but was vain enough to construe it to his own advantage—' oh, thank you. I shall be very pleased to have your arm again, and I think I should like Mr. Kencho to keep by us—quite close by, please—and to decide what we are to see. I am sure that he must know best.'

'The snake comes first, Madame Izàn,' called out one of the *Makara* young men. 'We know all about it. This way—to the left. Do take my arm, Mrs. Bax.'

Thus it happened that there was no separation of the party this time, for the whole seven of them and their guides kept close together ; and, indeed, such an invasion by these foreigners of lofty stature and peculiar ways created no little flutter and diversion in certain places of cheap entertainment on that night of war rejoicings in Kioto. In fact, the victory over China in comparison faded for the moment into insignificance.

It was all very amusing, and delighted the tourist young men, who flung about sen, and even yen, pieces right royally. The white snake writhing in its oblong basket was truly an uncanny object ; and then there was a marionette representation, where white skeletons descended through a grating into the hands of a host of red devils, who sawed their heads, pounded them in mortars, impaled, racked, and otherwise ingeniously tormented them, which was most grim and suggestively horrible. It reminded Julia Eugarde of certain Florentine pictures of the Limbo of departed spirits, as well as of the frescoes outside the Temple of the Sacred Tooth, and she observed to Madame Izàn that the crude idea of purgatory seemed pretty much

14

the same in all ages and among all races ; whereat
Izo remembered Kencho's art theories and the
discourse of the priest at the Hongwanji, and
found fresh food for reflection.

And besides these peep-shows there was a
panorama of the storming of Port Arthur, which
aroused more martial enthusiasm in the breast of
Yamasaki ; and there was the dwarf, now rein-
forced by a female dwarf-demon, and by a chorus
of bigger demons in black satin kimonos embroidered with gold monsters, who sang behind
and played on the samisen and other instruments.
They stayed quite a long time at this show, where
they were brought blue cotton futons to sit upon,
and tea and pipes and charcoal boxes at which to
warm themselves. For the dwarfs were followed
by a Japanese Chevalier who sang, doubtless,
Oriental coster melodies, and changed his mask
and costume with a lightning rapidity ; and after
that there was conjuring, and actually a Japanese
parody on ' Her golden Hair,' which worked
the tourist young men up to a pitch of ecstasy,
and seemed for the moment to allay effectually the
gnawing torture of stork and dragon.

' Izo,' said Mrs. Bax, as later that night she
came into her friend's room arrayed in the wadded
kimono which she adopted as a dressing-gown,

and which went badly with her blue eyes, fair crimped hair, and freckled countenance—'Izo, I don't feel at all comfortable about Kencho. I've got quite an uncanny feeling about him. He is not what he seems.'

Madame Izàn had been brushing her long, dark locks, staring dreamily the while at her reflection in the glass. She started so violently at Herminia's remark that the brush dropped from her hand, and the ivory handle was broken in two. She picked up the pieces, and examined them with an expression of dismay that covered any other emotion which might have assailed her.

'There now, Herminia! You know I can't bear having my nerves shaken like that. How am I to get another brush?'

'Well, I suppose there are Englishwomen in Tokyo who use brushes,' returned Herminia unsympathetically. 'Now listen, Izo, and don't go off into a tantrum. You don't understand men as I do. Of course you haven't had the same experience. Well, it was that horrible white snake this evening which put the idea about Kencho into my head. . . . And the way you broke your brush——'

'I can't see the connection between men and my brush, and white snakes and Kencho,' returned Madame Izo.

'Well, if you take it that way, the back of the

brush and the snake are both white, and Kencho
is a man ; though, to be sure, one doesn't naturally
consider Japanese men—as men—at least, not in
Japan.'

'And why not in Japan?' asked Izo, speaking
with slow deliberation. 'It seems to me, Herminia, that here in Japan there is a reality, a
dignity, about men — who are men, and not
grimacing monkeys—a depth and a knowledge
which one had never thought of before. And if
you want to know who has made me feel that—
well, then, I don't mind telling you that it is
Kencho Hiro-Kahachi. I will tell you, too,
Herminia, the reason why you say he is not what
he seems. That is because he is what he *is*—a
gentleman, a learned, courteous and most simple
gentleman of the true Japan, the Japan of the
Samurais and the Daimios and all the old grand
people—and not what you imagine him, a common
courier person like Yamasaki. I will not have
you talk about him in that way, Herminia.'

'Izo!' Mrs. Bax ejaculated, completely taken
aback by the outburst, which was so unexpected
and so unlike Madame Izàn. 'Izo, what *do* you
mean? Oh, it can't be—it can't surely be that
you have fallen in love with Kencho?'

'I will not have you talk in that way,' indignantly repeated Madame Izàn. 'You are de-

grading yourself—and me. You are common, Herminia—vulgar—*impossible.*'

' Izo, Izo !' moaned poor Herminia, too astonished for the moment to be properly angry. ' I see what a terrible mistake I have made. Oh, I knew it wasn't right of me to let you go about as you do, and talk so familiarly to Kencho, whose head you must have turned. You can't realize, Izo, the effect your manner has on men, and how upsetting it is to all the ordinary notions of propriety. Then, too, making a jealousy between him and Mr. Windeatt—I've seen it ; I saw it plainly enough this evening, and that day at the temple when you went off for more than an hour alone with Kencho. And Mrs. Eugarde has seen it, too. Oh dear ! oh dear ! you'll get us into the most dreadful complications. I ought never to have agreed to all this mixing up together, and I ought to have trusted in my intuition about Kencho at the very first. What are intuitions given us for, if we are not to trust in them? I *felt* that Kencho had designs upon you—a man that won't look you in the face ! I don't believe in those goggles : his eyes are as right as mine ; I asked Yamasaki. And I can't get over the queer feeling I have about Kencho—the sort of feeling that Plato—wasn't it ?—I'm sure it was Plato— wrote about.. My poor dear Mr. Bax used to say

that kind of feeling should be taken as a warning—
he was a student of Plato—the feeling that you've
done the thing somehow before, and yet that
somehow you haven't done it. It's just one of
those mysteries one can't describe. But I had the
feeling about Kencho, and that was why I was so
particular in inquiring if he had any testimonials.
How should I know that the testimonial wasn't
forged? How do I know, even, that there is a
Minister of Justice in Japan? But I was all
alone; I had no one then to consult. And I
trusted in what Dr. Duppo said, and I thought
that if I did just give you your head——'

'Herminia!' Madame Izàn interrupted in
deepest wrath; and she rose to her splendid
height and gazed sternly down on the incongruous
little figure in the blue kimono. 'Herminia, is it
possible that you have dared to talk about *me* with
Dr. Duppo?'

'Oh, Izo! I didn't mean to tell you, for, of
course, you couldn't understand. A doctor is so
different from anybody else; and you must know,
Izo, with what a peculiar sentiment I must always
regard a P. and O. doctor. I don't know how to
express it—I might almost say a sentiment of
sanctity. You went with me, Izo, to the grave in
Hong Kong.'

'Yes, I did,' replied Madame Izàn grimly.
'And I don't like graves, or dead husbands, or

living ones, either, or P. and O. doctors. And if I did, Dr. Duppo isn't a husband—yet, at any rate; and he isn't dead in a Hong Kong grave. I wish he had been, before you insulted me by taking him into your confidence about my concerns.'

'Oh, how unkind you are, Izo—how unsympathetic!' Mrs. Bax's tears now flowed freely. 'And you mustn't think that I betrayed any secret; I only spoke generally. I was terribly perplexed; my responsibility weighed upon me, for Mrs. Eugarde had been speaking to me about her brother. And I told her—yes, I did tell her, Izo—that I must decline to pursue the subject any further, because I was bound by a promise to you not to discuss your private affairs with *anyone*.'

'Except Dr. Duppo!' scornfully interposed Madame Izàn.

'I spoke generally,' pleaded Mrs. Bax. 'It was on my own account that I consulted Dr. Duppo. I am very dependent upon sympathy; I can't help it—it's my nature; I don't know how to get on without it. I don't know how I should have got on on the *Makara* unless I had received consolation from Dr. Duppo. What he said was, "Don't you worry yourself, Mrs. Bax. Give her her head until you get to Tokyo, where you won't feel so lonely and deserted and apart from your own countrymen." For he——' Mrs. Bax faltered and blushed. 'I should not be at all surprised if we found Dr. Duppo at Tokyo when we got there ; it would be about time for the *Makara's* return voyage. And he might be there for some time. He—he was thinking of giving up the service, and settling—perhaps going back by an Empress boat. I did think it would be such a comfort and satisfaction to know that there *was* an English gentleman in this country of heathens whom one could depend upon, supposing that there were legal difficulties or troubles of any kind. I see plainly now—if it's only by the way Yamasaki looks at things—that we *ought* to have provided ourselves with letters to the British Legation. You can see for yourself how much more Japanese people think of you when you have Legation letters. If your uncle had been alive, he would have thought of that.'

'If my uncle had been alive—my dear, kind uncle, who only wished that justice should be done, and that my happiness should be secured in the best way possible,' said Izo, her voice breaking in an emotion that was quite unwonted in her— 'if he had been alive, he would be here now to protect and advise me and to save me—from you, Herminia—you and your folly and disloyalty !'

'Izo ! Oh, to say that to me, who have devoted myself to you !'

'Yes, you have, Herminia ; I'm not forgetting

it. You are the only woman friend I ever possessed, except my dead mother. And you were very kind to me in my dark days—I don't deny it, and I'm grateful to you for it. I dare say you thought that you were acting well by me in persuading me to—you know what. But that doesn't prevent you from being foolish, Herminia. It was your romantic folly that wrecked me ; and now—now you are adding on more folly— and disloyalty as well. I shall never forgive you, and I shall never trust you again.'

'Do you mean, Izo, that you wish me to leave you?' said Mrs. Bax with an injured dignity which struggled through her genuine heart-break. ' Do you mean that you intend us to part company, and that you will henceforth manage your affairs as best you can without me? Very well. It is you who are the rich woman and the mistress. I suppose that, in reality, I am nothing better than your paid companion. I believe that, in such case, a notice of three months of the termination of the engagement is customary ; it would, in- deed, be courteous. But I don't stand upon such formalities,' she added witheringly. ' And happily, though I may be poor in comparison with such wealth as yours, I have my independence, and it is a matter of no importance to me that I should be stranded thus in a strange land among heathen people. I have a sufficient competence to cover my expenses in Japan, and to take me home in comfort by the Empress line, as I had originally intended. I am ready, if you wish it, Izo, to bid you—good-bye.'

Mrs. Bax dissolved into sobs; and Madame Izàn, really touched, went up to the poor little soul, and laid her hand on her heaving shoulder.

'You know perfectly well, Herminia, that I never meant anything of the kind ; and it is you now who are cruel to talk about terminations of engagements, and three months' notice, and all that nonsense. How *could* there be any such ridiculous questions between you and me, and if you weren't utterly foolish, they would never come into your head.'

'You s-said that you never meant to trust me a-g-gain !' sobbed Herminia.

'That is quite true,' frankly replied Madame Izàn. 'I don't mean ever to trust you again with any secret that I don't want repeated to Dr. Duppo. But that needn't hinder us from being good friends. What I do want you to understand, Herminia— and I was thinking about it while I sat brushing my hair when you came in this evening—is that I am not in the very least the girl I was in my blind time five years back ; no, nor even the girl I was six months ago. For I've gained something just

lately that I never had before—is it a soul, do you
fancy, or a heart, or a sense of what a woman's
duty may be? Anyhow, I've altered even since
I landed in Japan. And I was thinking that in
future I must undertake my own responsibilities.
Why should you be responsible for me, you poor
little thing, who can't get on without consulting
Dr. Duppo, or anybody else who might come
handy? No. Here I am, twenty-six years of
age, a helpless baby no longer. My life is mine,
not yours; and I mean to manage it according to
my own lights. For I'm not blind now. I've
got my eyesight, and am every day becoming more
accustomed to it, and less afraid of knocking up
against a wall or tumbling down a precipice. And
my head is clear, and I can see the world—and men
and women in it—more as it all is, and less as I
fancied it should be. The feeling has come over
me here in Kioto that I've got to be prepared for
anything that may happen at Tokyo; and that life
isn't just dancing round and amusing one's self
and seeing sights, but that I must somehow work
things into a scheme for myself, so as to make the
best of it. Well, I am going to work things out
all alone; I shall not tell you as I go along what
conclusions I come to. You may think what you
please—you and Dr. Duppo, and Mr. Windeatt
and Mrs. Eugarde—and Yamasaki: for I have no

doubt that you would be very glad to consult Yamasaki, perhaps as to the steps necessary for winning the favour of first-class Legation people. But I am not going to ask advice of anybody— except, when the time comes, of one person.'

'Izo, you don't want to tell me that one person is—Kencho?'

Mrs. Bax had ceased sobbing while Izo's strange eloquence had poured forth, and now stood looking with bright wondering eyes at this stately and transformed young woman.

'I don't want to tell you anything whatever, returned Madame Izàn; 'but I will tell you that, though not Kencho, this person is one whom Kencho has made me feel differently about from what I felt when I started out to see the world.'

'Is it—is it—your husband?' asked Mrs. Bax in an awe-stricken voice.

But Madame Izàn turned away, and began preparing for the night in obstinate silence. Herminia waited, still staring and overwhelmed, and at last Izo condescended to go up and kiss her.

'There, that's for bye-bye, and the seal of oblivion likewise. Oh, the beautiful bell! I'd live in Japan just for the sake of the temple bells. Listen, Herminia! Do Buddhists have matins, and is that to call the priests? And how much sleep shall we two get before we start for Lake Biwa?'

CHAPTER X.

W.HILE Madame Izàn and Herminia Bax were
establishing an amicable divergence of opinion at
one end of the wing at Yaami's in which the
party had been installed, Julia Eugarde and John
Windeatt, in their part of the balcony running
along the building, were arriving at more harmonious conclusions. A late moon had arisen to
vie with the war illuminations, now more scattered
and dimmer than at the beginning, and the effect
of the pale orb as it shone over the sacred city
and great plain, in its slow mount above the girdle
of hills, had drawn Julia from her chamber, and
she had stumbled upon her brother, who was
leaning upon the railings smoking ruminatively.

'Moon-gazing, too?' she said.

'Is there a moon? Oh, I see,' he rejoined
absently. 'Let us sit down, Ju ; there are some
chairs somewhere. I'm abominably wakeful to-
night.'

'So am I. I've finished my weekly instalment
of " Jottings." '

'Oh, confound the "Jottings"! It is so absurd, your playing quill-driver.'

'Well, I don't know about that,' she objected amiably, placing herself in the basket-chair he had drawn up for her. 'It appears to me that, as a resource against boredom and ill-temper, my "Jottings" are to be commended. I assure you that I found them so at the Hongwanji, when you and Mrs. Bax were so cross and hungry, and also the other day at the Shogun's palace, while Herminia and you spent a good half-hour mournfully contemplating the gold-fish in the pond from the summer-house balcony, till it pleased Madame Izàn and Kencho to return from that mysterious Cha-no-yu ceremony in Yoshimitsu's tea-house.'

'Do you suppose they were drinking tea *all* the time?' jealously remarked Windeatt. 'And why weren't the rest of us invited?'

'Dear Jack, the rite of Cha-no-yu can only be performed by a limited number of votaries,' sententiously explained Mrs. Eugarde; 'and this particular high-priest of tea is a friend of Kencho's, and a highly aristocratic and first-class personage, Yamasaki informs me. No doubt he would consider it sacrilege to admit the common or garden tourist to such hallowed observances. Madame Izàn, by grace of Kencho, was specially favoured.'

'I should very much like to know,' pursued Windeatt acrimoniously, 'whether Kencho loses Madame Izàn on purpose.'

'Well, I must admit that view of the matter has occurred to me,' candidly observed Mrs. Eugarde. 'But I suppose that Kencho wouldn't lose Madame Izàn unless Madame Izàn did not object to being lost. And, you see, Mrs. Bax doesn't like Kencho, but clings to Yamasaki ; so it's natural, after all, that Kencho should consider his obligations limited to Madame Izàn, which seems satisfactory enough from his point of view. We, anyhow, have no right to claim his services.'

'I suggested to Madame Izàn this evening that she should send him away, and appoint me courier in his stead,' said Windeatt.

'And, of course, she promptly refused to entertain the suggestion. I can't say, Jack, that I think it was made at an opportune moment. You didn't exactly distinguish yourself in the line of diplomatic courier when you knocked down those two poor little Japs. We should have had a row if it hadn't been for Kencho. They took you and Madame Izàn for Russians, and were preparing to make themselves extremely disagreeable.'

'How do you know that ?'

'Oh, I've picked up a few words of Japanese.

I studied Theodosia Gotch's dictionary on the *Makara*. What has become of her, I wonder? . . . Well, you didn't succeed in dislodging Kencho?'

'No. She laughed at the notion—said I knew nothing about the real Japan, or about the Shoguns and Daimios and saints and all the rest of those old bounders Kencho stuffs her with. I can't understand the meaning of this extraordinary enthusiasm about Japan.'

Mrs. Eugarde was silent for a moment or two.

'It is clear, at any rate,' she said, 'that Australian squatters are not in it with Japanese Daimios. What do you mean to do, Jack?'

'I am going to challenge Fate and put all to the test,' he returned melodramatically, 'and that very soon. I believe she likes me, Ju—there was a moment on the *Makara*——' and he sighed and gave his great shoulders a shake as though rousing himself out of a dream. 'Yes, I really do think she likes me as much as she likes anyone. I believe that if it weren't for Kencho and his impertinent assiduities I could make some fair running.'

'I think,' said Mrs. Eugarde gravely, 'that before attempting to make running, as you call it, I'd find out for certain whether Madame Izàn is really married, and, if she is, where this mysterious husband has his abiding-place.'

'That's exactly what I mean to do. I'm glad we're agreed so far, Ju. You have been beastly unsympathetic since we landed. I mean to do it on the very first opportunity. Try to make one for me at Lake Biwa to-morrow.'

'I'll try,' she answered. 'But it's rather difficult on these expeditions.'

'Oh, I know that well enough,' said he. 'I should have spoken before this if I had had a chance. But how can I? You know what time we get in the evening—no nice balcony loungings like those at Hong Kong. Then, we don't meet till breakfast-time, and there's Kencho waiting outside with the wraps and counting every mouthful we eat through the windows. And how can you propose in a jinrikisha? And when you are out of the rickshaw, and have managed to shirk a temple and are enjoying the beauties of Nature, one of those little men with chrysanthemums on their caps turns up and bothers you about your passport, which gives Kencho a fresh innings. Then, you know how it is in the temples. Oh, Lord, how sick I am of temples! Some Buddha that is degenerate, or not degenerate! As if it mattered! And as if one wanted Kencho's opinions on the subject. Or else some hideous screen or kakemono that Hokusai or Hideyoshi painted.'

'Not Hideyoshi, Jack. He wasn't a painter.'

15

'Whatever he may have been, he *is* a most confounded nuisance ; and I don't intend to stand him any longer. I shall be thankful when we get to Miyanoshita. Yamasaki says there are no temples there, which is something to be thankful for. When are they going to Miyanoshita, Ju ? Have you heard ?'

'Mrs. Bax was talking about it yesterday. She thinks they will stop at Kioto another fortnight. You see, one has a great deal to do here yet. There's Osaka, and there's Nara, and there are the Rapids to be shot. I do think, Jack, as far as I can make out from the guide - book, that you might manage to give Kencho the slip, and lose yourself with Madame Izàn in the groves of Nara.'

'It will have to come off before that,' declared Windeatt resolutely. 'I can't stand the suspense. I shall challenge Fate to-morrow.'

And somehow, in the earlier part of the next day's expedition, it seemed as though Fate were going to smile on the young man's wishes. First, at the breakfast-table, it struck Windeatt that there was an indefinable difference in Madame Izàn's air and manner. She was paler than her wont, and looked timid and faintly distressed ; indeed, he noticed particularly just now that there had gone from her much of that exuberant vitality and goddess-irresponsibility which had so struck him in Hong Kong. The notion occurred to him that since that first meeting she had been gradually becoming more the woman, and turning back to his Undine theory concerning her, his sore soul took comfort in these signs of feminine weakness and perturbation. He fancied that she, too, in the watches of the night must have been reviewing the events of the last few weeks and making up her mind as to a certain course of conduct. Perhaps she was beginning to see that a man's heart is not the most convenient implement with which to play battledore and shuttlecock. Certainly, he said to himself, there was a sweet resolution in the tightening of her beautiful lips and a strange suggestion of high heroism in the set of her head and in the gaze of her brown eyes, which had, too, a tinge of sadness. She was rather silent, made no small jokes with Herminia, and did not issue little edicts for the day in her pretty imperious fashion. Nor did she make any show of interest in what they were going to see, or inquire as usual the result of Mrs. Eugarde's nightly study of Murray and Dresser and other Japanese authorities, which it was the habit of that literary lady to retail at breakfast for the benefit of lazier members of the party. But she smiled very graciously, and penitently, too, he fancied, upon him, and delivered over into his charge her little field-glasses, which was a tacit permission that he might consider himself her escort. Further, to his surprise and joy, she took no notice of Kencho, who waited in the garden with her wraps, but laid her hand on his—Windeatt's—arm to steady her steps down the uneven stairway, and allowed him to put her into her rickshaw and to fasten the apron over her dress.

But it was not very far they went now in the rickshaws, not farther than to the canal bank, where a boat was awaiting them—a sort of gondola which had a wooden canopy and paper lanterns wobbling from the roof, and an oarsman at the prow. They put themselves on the floor of the sampan on mats and cushions, Yamasaki and Kencho taking places further forward, and so glided along the narrow waterway. Now, through a plain bordered by green slopes which were patched with blossoming azaleas and the dark green of firs, with the crinkled roof of a pagoda here and there, or a barbaric gateway, showing through the serrated pine-tops ; now by a gray village, set in the hill-bend, or among bamboo thickets, or now between high banks gorgeous and perfumy with pink azaleas. There were many other sampans and barges, in some of them gay pleasure-parties making music with song and samisen. Windeatt wanted to get out and walk along the towing-path, hinting to Madame Izàn that there would be a fine opportunity for putting the Kodak to its uses. But she shook her head, and, silent and preoccupied, leaned back with half-closed eyes against the side of the sampan, her hat in her lap, and the wind playing at will among the classic coils of her hair, which Windeatt admired so much.

' I am afraid you tired yourself last night,' he said, bending nearer and arranging her cushions with the most tender solicitude.

' No,' she answered ; ' but I think that I should like to go on like this for ever and ever, just dreaming one's life away,' which seemed a strange sentiment for Madame Izàn to give forth.

Presently there appeared in front of them a cavernous mouth in the side of an azalea-clad hill which blocked the stream. The sampan darted in, and now its occupants were plunged into the Cimmerian gloom of that long underground canal which pierces the mountains between Kioto and Otsu. Yamasaki lighted the paper lamp which hung from the edge of the canopy, but it gave so feeble a glimmer as scarcely to make a luminous spot in the blackness—blackness above and beside, dense, noxious, sending out damp drippings and unwholesome exhalations, while below spread a more shining blackness of turgid water, with lurid gleams upon it as of suns in eclipse, made by the lantern reflections of moving craft. Slowly and phantasmally these glided by, each with its flickering light, blotted out every moment or so by the swaying form of a man at prow or stern, bending to and fro over his oar. Now a barge of merchandise appeared and disappeared, more redly illuminated, the naked figures of the rowers giving the suggestion of a demoniac crew ; and now a little ghost gondola, as it seemed. And how strange and unearthly sounded the wailing music from a pleasure-boat ! And had the samisen ever twanged so eerily as here, with its echoes given back from the brick walls and vibrating through the murk ? Yes ; it was rather a Stygian sort of business, and lasted the length of nearly three miles.

Madame Izàn's easily wrought imagination was impressed by it. She shivered and gave a little cry of alarm as the monster shape of a sampan laden with cylinders of rice, and its big red eye winking, loomed close to her elbow. Involuntarily her frightened hand groped out, and, as might that of a nervous child, yielded itself with comforting trust into the man's strong grasp which closed round it. She did not want to withdraw her hand, though, no doubt, she had scarcely expected it would be thus seized.

Not a word was spoken. How could Windeatt speak when Herminia and Julia Eugarde were within a few inches of them? But surely the longing and the devotion which expressed itself in that warm enfoldment—surging up in him and setting his pulses to a quick throb—must have thrilled through Madame Izàn ; and surely, too, it did not vex or appal her, for he could feel the fluttering of those bird-like fingers stilled as under a quiet contentment, and he knew that if she had been beset by any vague girl-tremors or disquieting emotions, this firm, caressing clasp was doing something towards their assuagement.

It might have been a quarter of an hour—a blissful quarter of an hour to Windeatt—that her hand rested thus in his. By-and-by, a small silver half-moon came in sight afar off at the end of the passage, and this widened a little till a soft dawn rose upon the night of the canal. Gently Madame Izàn took away her hand ; but was it before Julia Eugarde's sharp eyes had noticed the caress, or before another pair of eyes further down the boat had seen it as well? And did the other eyes observe also that Izo's withdrawal was not done angrily, but even with a kind of tender lingering—a suggestion of regret?

There is no excuse whatever to be made for Madame Izàn, beyond this, that, in her curious childlikeness, she did not realize the significance of what she had done. To Windeatt it seemed that the long pressure had established an understanding between them, and that now he might hope as audaciously as he pleased. She must know from it that he loved her, and, had she wished to rebuff him, it would have been easy for her to show her displeasure. But she had not done so, and he might draw his own inferences. Moreover, when they emerged into the broad daylight of the lake, and his eyes, full of daring entreaty, met hers, her brown orbs did not shoot out fires of wrath, but had in them a dreamy consciousness as of newly-awakened feeling, and lowered in maidenly manner, while a delicate blush suffused her cheek. All this was sufficient warrant for Windeatt's eager whisper to his sister as they alighted at the tea-house, where they were to have luncheon.

'Ju, you must try and manage my opportunity for me, somehow. It is a favourable moment. I am sure — at least, I hope — that she likes me a little.'

Mrs. Eugarde looked at him in some consternation, her ideas of propriety startled by this unexpected development. She had been so convinced that Izo was quite indifferent to her brother. But she was a sensible woman, and of Lady Macbeth's opinion, that, if things had to be done, it were better for them to be done without shilly - shallying. And then, besides, she had all the interest of the professional novelist in an impending crisis.

'All right,' she said ; 'I'll do my very best. But it's no use trying till we get to Miidera temple. I'll see if I can't pull it off there. I don't suppose it's possible at the tea-house.'

That was a sweet little house, all brown and scented, with a bewilderingly complicated doll's garden, and queer little balconies connected by cross-bridges. It seemed a most appropriate setting for a love scene, till the proudly tripping nesan ushered them into a room with a hideous striped Kidderminster carpet, and abominable chairs in rep, and a German-gilt chimney-glass, to which Yamasaki complacently called attention as furnished 'European way.' Then all the romance of the Japanese garden and of the dainty nesans was gone, and there was nothing to do but unpack the flat boxes and china pots, in which their luncheon was stowed, and to uncork the wine from Yaami's, in which proceedings Kencho took the lead with a strange grimness, and in absolute silence. Presently the nesans came back again with a smoking omelet and some coffee, and Kencho was about to withdraw. But the nesans did not want to go ; they were far too interested in these European women—in their bracelets and gewgaws, and the fashions of their dress, and, beyond all, in the beauty of Madame Izàn. They stroked her garments, and went round behind her chair to examine her hair, babbling softly to each other, and smiling artlessly at Kencho.

'Yuroshi!' they exclaimed, in an ecstasy of feminine delight. 'Yuroshi! ichi ban!'

And Izo, with corresponding simplicity, appealed also to Kencho : 'I wish you would explain to me why they always say "Yuroshi!" when they look at me,' she said.

Mrs. Eugarde laughed, and so did Herminia, more loudly. She had recovered from her depression of the previous evening, and looked upon the quarrel with her friend as wiped out by the forgiving good-night.

'Oh dear, Izo, you are too funny! Fancy your not having discovered by this time what "Yuroshi" means!'

'I meant to look, and forgot,' she answered. 'Please tell me, Mr. Kencho.'

The guide seemed to hesitate, and then said, in an odd, repressed voice, and with a slight and formal bow :

'It is an expression of admiration.'

Madame Izàn blushed, and, struck by his manner, looked at him, as if to ask what was the matter. But he moved to the door, again making the deferential gesture, which, with its blend of the Japanese, seemed a sort of shadow of Yamasaki's elaborate obeisance on entering and quitting the presence of his employers.

'Madame will probably be ready to set off for the great pine at Karasaki in about half an hour. I shall be here then to take orders,' he said, and departed.

Herminia, who announced herself as ravenous, spread out one of the sheets of rice-paper provided with the luncheon-boxes, remarking:

'Why don't we have rice-paper napkins in England?'

'Because there's no rice,' said Windeatt.

'Yamasaki,' irrelevantly exclaimed Herminia, arresting the little man in his progress towards the door, 'what makes Kencho so different from you other Japanese?'

Yamasaki was evidently not quite sure as to whether he ought to feel offended at this rough generalization. He screwed up his little eyes with a 'would an I could' expression, and answered stiffly :

'Mr. Kencho not same as commercial Japanese. Mr. Kencho, he very high-class learn—European education.   Mr. Kencho have high-class friends in Tokyo.   There, all European custom.'

'Well, I should really like to know what the mystery is about Mr. Kencho ; and so would you, I am sure, Mr. Windeatt, for I am certain there is a mystery.   No, you needn't look cross with me, Izo.   I suppose it is not exactly unlawful for me to wish to satisfy a natural curiosity.   Now, Yamasaki, if Mr. Kencho is so very high-class and has such high-class friends in Tokyo, why don't he earn his living in a more high-class way than going out as a guide to European tourists, whom he despises?   Now, you know he does despise us, Yamasaki.'

Yamasaki shook his head.   Perhaps he had already mooted to himself the problem, without finding any satisfactory solution thereto.   Perhaps he had suspicions which he did not want to disclose to Mrs. Bax, Kencho having an honourable claim as his own countryman, and Herminia not entirely representing to his mind the European equivalent of a first-class or otherwise 'Daimio' lady.   Perhaps he knew the truth, and was bound over to secrecy.   He politely evaded Mrs. Bax's second accusation, and, anyhow, there was no getting more out of Yamasaki.

Nor did Windeatt find an opportunity at the tea-house for putting the important question to

Madame Izàn. He was, however, consoled by observing that she avoided meeting his eyes, and that, when forced to do so, the same delicate flush which had been revealed by the glare of the lake after the obscurity of the canal again mantled her pale check. So he possessed his soul in what patience he had at command during the rickshaw course along the banks of Biwa, and their inspection of the Karasaki pine, which, as everybody knows, is one of the wonders of Japan. Afterwards, while Madame Izàn accomplished her usual purchases of local products, and Windeatt started the small boys diving for copper coins, Mrs. Eugarde, in part fulfilment of the mission with which her brother had charged her, made an excuse for drawing apart with Kencho.

The guide had been following Madame Izàn with his eyes, as she moved away by the side of Windeatt. It was always a little difficult to judge the expression of Kencho's face, so large an area of it did the blue goggles cover ; but Julia Eugarde, who had a professional aptitude in her notice of trifles, was struck by the drawn, pained curve of his mouth showing beneath his dark moustache, which, in contrast to his silvery hair, gave not a trace of gray.

'Mr. Kencho,' said Julia ; 'Mrs. Bax and Madame Izàn have got Yamasaki to look after them, and I wanted to ask you a question or two about the sights of Lake Biwa and the Miidera temple.'

Kencho gave her a startled glance, but made her his little formal bow. Mrs. Eugarde deliberately seated herself on one of the red-blanket-covered platforms by the Pilgrims' Pine, and motioned him to take a place by her.

' Mr. Kencho,' she began, ' Mount Hieyzan is a sacred mountain, isn't it, and the scene of all kinds of romantic stories? And isn't Lake Biwa famous in Japanese history? And I wanted to ask if there isn't a most delightful forest all round the Miidera temple—a fascinating place to wander in.'

Kencho dutifully launched into an account of the traditions of Hieyzan, at which Mrs. Eugarde chafed a little.

' Yes, of course—that is in Murray ; and I know about the castle of Hikone and the eight sights of Lake Biwa.'

' To see the eight famous sights of Lake Biwa, madame, time is needed. No doubt you, being a writer yourself, would feel an interest in the memorials of our famous novelist Murusaki Shikibu——'

' Yes, yes——'

' And the Miidera temple, where we are going?

Probably, too, you know all about Hidesato's bell, and Benkei who stole the bell?'

'Ah, that is very interesting; and I am certain madame would like to walk to the tower of Benkei's bell, and to explore the forest roundabout. In fact, I believe that my brother has been reading up Benkei on purpose to explain it all. And do you think, Mr. Kencho, that they would have any difficulty in finding their way to Benkei's tower, supposing they started there alone—without a guide, you know?'

Kencho did not answer for a moment; he was pondering, perhaps, the bearings of this innocent question.

'It is not a difficult path to find, madame.'

'Because, Mr. Kencho,' went on Julia boldly, 'you are always so careful, you know, of Madame Izàn—and quite rightly—that sometimes my brother, who made great friends with her on the *Makara*, where *he* used to be her escort in her deck walks, is apt to feel himself a little out in the cold, and to be just a wee bit cross. You must have noticed that.'

'Yes, I have noticed that Mr. Windeatt resents my presence in the performance of my duties to Madame Izàn.'

'Very silly, isn't it? but one has to make allowances for young people. Yes, he is put out

sometimes because of the few opportunities he
seems to get now—compared with the *Makara*
time—for talking in a confidential manner to
Madame Izàn. Two is company, anyhow—isn't
it, Mr. Kencho?—and three is not. And we shall
be parting company very soon now, and to-day
may be the last chance he will have of discussing
with Madame Izàn a—some private matter that
was opened between them on board the *Makara*.
And so '—Mrs. Eugarde faltered, a little disconcerted by the steady glare of Kencho's goggles and
by his absolute immobility—' and so, you see,
Mr. Kencho, I'm treating you like a friend, and
asking you to let him have the chance I've
promised to try and manage for him to-day.'

Kencho made another obeisance, which was
more elaborate in character and most distinctly
Japanese.

'I am under the orders of Madame Izàn, and,
subject to these, at Mrs. Eugarde's service.'

'But, Mr. Kencho, these are not Madame Izàn's
orders. How could she give orders on such a
matter to you?'

'To me!' Julia could not fail to remark an
underlying and curious bitterness in the guide's
tone. 'That is true. I am Madame Izàn's
servant.'

'Oh no, Mr. Kencho; I am certain that she

regards you as her friend. And, if you will allow
me, so do I. And this is just a friendly hint,
which you must look upon as a sort of secret
between you and me.'

' It shall be so considered.'

There was a silence, during which Kencho stared
out on the waters of the lake, and Mrs. Eugarde
appeared absorbed in the ascent of a pilgrim to the
shrine in the trunk of the great pine.

CHAPTER XI.

THAT was how it came about that Windeatt and Madame Izàn found themselves pacing quite alone together the sacred groves of Miidera, and deeply grateful did the Australian feel to his sister, who had accomplished for him this strategical feat.

And could there be an atmosphere more propitious to a favourable hearing of love avowals than this dreamy, scented atmosphere of Japan? or any background more harmonious than the forest of ancient pine and camphor trees that closed them round, with its picturesque pavilions and altars set here and there along the winding way, and its little avenues of venerable lanterns—votive offerings of the faithful, and all hoary with lichen or green with moss—which they were continually threading? Or could one have a view more inspiring and beautiful than those glints through the trees of Biwa's blue waters below, their surface dotted with the white sails of sampans, while along the slope the curved pagoda roofs and gray terraces, the strange gateways, and lacquer ornamentation of the temple, showed in patches among the greenery?

Madame Izàn loved Nature, and all fair sights and tender sounds, and when brought immediately under the influence of these, quickly recovered the childish gaiety which occasionally she lost, if worried by the affairs of ordinary life. Now she drew in deep relieved breaths of the perfumy air ; her dark eyes glowed, her head reared itself back in the old triumphant goddess fashion, and never did Venus of old smile more sweetly and enticingly upon her adorers. The smile turned Windeatt's head.

'Izo!' he cried ; and she turned with a start, the ardour of his gaze checking her inconsequent chatter, and arresting her in her buoyant climb up the steep track. She blushed, and gave a helpless look down through the mazes of foliage.

'I don't think we ought to be going on so fast, Mr. Windeatt. Where is everybody else? And I don't believe you have the least idea where the famous bell lives. Really, I shouldn't like to get lost on Mount Hieyzan.'

'You can't do that,' he said, 'with the temple down there for a sign-post ; and, besides, I'm looking after you.'

'But please don't forget that I refused your

obliging offer to engage yourself as my Japanese courier.'

' Well, I *am* your Japanese courier during this little act, anyhow,' he answered ; ' for the others, thank Heaven ! are safely got rid of for the moment. And I mean to make the most of my chance, Madame Izàn. It's the first you've given me of talking to you—seriously—since—since we were on the *Makara.*'

' It seems to me,' replied Madame Izàn, with a slightly embarrassed laugh, ' that I get a great deal of your conversation one way and another. Really, Mr. Windeatt, you are quite rude to Herminia, and you neglect Mrs. Eugarde shamefully, and all just because you are so kind in talking to me while we are on our expeditions together.'

' Oh ! with Kencho three steps behind, listening to every word I say ! No, thank you ; that's not the kind of talking I mean, and that I want. It's now or never, Izo ; and you've got to listen to me.'

She laughed again at his bantering imperiousness. He could see, with joy, that to this tall, stately, and rather wilful young woman there was something pleasant in the affectation on his part of mastery. And, in truth, as Izo shot a glance at him standing there by her side, big, self-confident, persuasive, and splendidly handsome, she would have been less than woman and more than goddess had he made no impression upon her heart. Greatly daring, he put out his hand and took hers in a warm, firm clasp, leading her up a broken flight of steps, through some scattered lanterns, to a drinking-fountain hung with pilgrims' banners, and with little heaps of pebbles all round it, which supplicants had tossed in test of a response to sundry and various petitions. Irreverently he cleared a place on the raised stone platform.

'Now, we are going to sit here for a little while, and talk as I want to talk,' he said, ' which doesn't mean banalities. Oh, Izo, my dearest——'

He still held her hand. She tried to take it away, but he was tenderly persistent.

'You let me hold it in the darkness of the canal with all the others close to us,' he urged. 'Why not here, where we are alone together?'

'It was so gloomy in the canal, I was frightened.'

'And involuntarily you stretched out to me for protection, because I, who care for you so much, seemed the natural person to give it. I knew that, and in the knowledge I was so happy. That was what I had wished and hoped for. And ever since, I have felt that we belong to each other. Oh, if I could only have made you under-

stand then how my whole heart thrilled to your
touch, and how '— his voice lowered—' how I
thought of that blessed moment in the fog on the
Makara when I had you close—as close as though
we were never more to be divided ; and how I
would have given everything for that to be true,
everything in the world.' Then, frightened at
his own temerity, he paused dumb-stricken for a
second.

'Everything in the world,' she repeated dreamily;
and it was as if she, too, were under the spell of
emotion. 'Everything in the world.'

'What is the world to me without you?' cried
the young man. 'If it hadn't been for the others,
I'd have taken you there in the canal, in the darkness and strangeness, and I'd have held you again
in my arms close—close, and I'd have given you
many, many kisses—dear kisses—Izo.'

And this venturesome young man did in very
fact now draw her to his breast and kiss her, not
too boldly or hotly, but at first much as he might
have kissed his sister after some great danger
shared together, or after a parting of long
years—most tenderly and most respectfully. And
perhaps it was because of that tender deference
that she did not spurn him in anger, but allowed
him to hold her thus, with her head against his
serge-clad shoulder and her cheek upturned, his

fair beard brushing it. She was not thinking of
Windeatt as her lover or as her possible husband—
indeed, she was a strange, sexless sort of creature,
this Izo, to whom men did not appeal after that
fashion—but as someone strong and comforting
and devoted—her best friend, that was how she
liked to put it, someone whose affection would
take away the feeling of loneliness and insecurity
she had had since her quarrel with Herminia, and
who would perhaps help and advise her in the
complicated and forlorn position she had put off
facing, with the same silly instinct as that which
makes an ostrich fancy itself unnoticed when its
head is buried in the sand, but which now, as
Tokyo loomed nearer and nearer on her horizon,
she would be obliged to meet on her own responsibility.

'You are very good to me,' she said with
grateful accents ; 'and, oh, Mr. Windeatt, I have
been so miserable! I don't know what has come
to me lately. I can't put things away now as I
did. I used to be able always to make myself
happy in the passing hour while the sun was
shining and the birds singing and life was beautiful. But now there seems a weight upon me, and
I haven't the power to shake it off. If I forget
for a little while, it comes back again. And last
night I felt so lonely, I cried half the night

through. Oh, I do want a friend! I've got no
one, neither man nor woman, upon whom I can
rely—no one since uncle died. Ah! Mr. Windeatt,
you did mean what you said, didn't you? And you
will be my friend, my real friend, my best friend?'

This was not the response Windeatt had hoped
for, and, infinitely as he was touched, it quenched
slightly the flame of his love. He had been
gazing down upon her lips—those Diana lips,
curved like a bow, so tempting to the young man
and yet so curiously virginal. He longed to press
his own upon them and drink in their sweetness
in long kisses ; but somehow, notwithstanding her
tender trust and the gladness, even, with which she
allowed him to enfold her by his embracing arms,
he felt instinctively the lack of any answering
thrill in her, and dared not obey his ardent im-
pulse.

'Izo,' he said, 'of course I am your friend—
your real and best friend. But I want to be something more besides—something much more than
a friend—something which means friendship and
everything sweeter and dearer as well.'

She trembled a little, and, for all her stately
proportions, he had the fancy of her as a startled
bird, fluttering with vague uneasiness, and yet with a
half-confidence, in the hold of some kindly captor.
Then, in an appealing manner, looking up at him

the while, as if to deprecate his wrath, she slowly
unwound, one by one, the fingers of his right hand
which were clasped round her left hand, and
smoothed them out on his knee ; and having
performed this action, she removed his other hand
from about her waist, and drew herself a little apart
from him.

'Why is that, Izo?' he asked sorrowfully.
'You did not seem to mind at first. Are you
angry with me for what I said?'

'I had forgotten,' she answered—'forgotten
that you are *you*, and that I am *I*, and that we are
not related to each other in the very least, and
have no right at all to be—to be on terms so
affectionate. I was thinking all the time of my
dear uncle O'Halloran, who was always so tender
to me. Often, while I was still in my blindness—
and of course afterwards—he would gather me up
beside him, as if I had been a little child, and
croon over me, and call me pet names, and stroke
my hair and hold my hand in his, as you were
doing a few moments ago.'

Windeatt did not relish the comparison, which
under the conditions seemed certainly comic
enough. He gave an irritated, perplexed little
laugh.

'I don't believe that you are a woman at all ;
and if you are a woman, and not a fay, there never

was one in the world like you. How can you put our relation on the same level as that in which you stood to your uncle O'Halloran? The thing is ludicrous. He might have been your father—and I——'

'You seem to me,' she answered simply, 'just what my brother might have been, if I had had a brother.'

'Oh no, indeed!' he exclaimed. 'That is not at all what I meant or what I wish. I was a stranger to you till we met in Hong Kong.'

'And Uncle O'Halloran was a stranger till he came quite suddenly and took me away from Aunt Sophia and from all my wretchedness.'

'But he was an old man — gray-haired — a patriarch. The instant you saw him, you must have felt quite differently towards him from what you might feel towards me.'

'Ah,' she said, 'you forget. I never *saw* uncle till a few months before he died.'

He was remorseful instantly.

'My poor darling! That's what is so pathetic about you. And that's what makes you so absolutely unlike all other women. But *now*, Izo— now, you understand life as it is, and you must see how dearly I love you—in quite another fashion. You must know that the great hope and longing of my heart is to win you for my wife.'

'But that is impossible,' she replied gravely.
' I have tried to make you realize the impossibility ;
but evidently you cannot, or will not, without my
telling you the whole truth. I had not wanted to
do that until I had got to Tokyo, where I shall
know better how I am situated.'

' Do you mean,' he cried, ' that you have reason
to believe your husband is alive?'

' I mean that he is alive.'

'So you are really a married woman ?'

' I never pretended that I was not. Only I did
not wish to talk about it. Am I not called
Madame Izàn ?'

' That is certainly true ; and I suppose that I
was an insane idiot to imagine, as I half did, that
you, a girl, were, for some private reason of your
own, masquerading under the style and dignity of
a married woman. This, or that you were a young
widow, separated from your husband at the church
door, which was, and is, the only theory I can
reconcile with you and the fact of your marriage.'

' Perhaps it is a true theory. It was — it is
rather like that,' she answered hesitatingly.

' I knew it. You are no more a married
woman, in the real sense, than those Japanese
babies down there ;' and he flung a pebble in the
direction of a far lower level, visible through a
rift in the foliage, a white road winding round the

hillside, where a company of Japanese children were flying kites. 'If there was a ceremony, you were in some way imposed upon, and it means nothing. I know it, and you know it too. Why, I have your word, and it was because of that I didn't believe Ju's assertions, which she founded on mysterious hints Mrs. Bax gave her. You told me yourself on the *Makara* that you were free, and that nobody in the world had any claim upon you.'

'I don't think I ought to have said that, though I believed then that I was free. And I am free in my sense, though not perhaps in yours. I am rich and dependent on nobody, and I can go where I please and do what I choose. For my husband would never claim nor control me against my will —even supposing that he had the power legally to do so.'

'Then, there's a doubt about the legality of it all?'

'Oh, I don't know — they say not — that isn't the question. If uncle had lived, everything would have been made clear. But he died just as we were going to start for England — died quite suddenly, and without having been able to go properly into the matter.'

'And your husband,' went on Windeatt, 'if he is your husband? Where is he? And what has getting to Tokyo to do with him? Are you

expecting to meet him there? Is he as they said
—somebody on board said it—is he in the Russian
Legation?'

'Oh no.'

'Is he at Tokyo?'

'Yes,' she answered gravely.

'Then, in Heaven's name, what is he doing
there, and what is his nationality?'

'He is a Japanese.'

'A Japanese! Good God!'

There was a silence. Windeatt stared down the
hill at the little kite-flyers in an angry horror, as
though they were responsible for the fact that
Madame Izàn's husband was of their race. He
took up a handful of the pilgrims' pebbles and
sent them, one by one, crashing against an ancient
stone lantern some few paces distant. Then he
turned almost with wrath to Madame Izàn :

'I can't stand this uncertainty. I've waited for
you to explain affairs, because I thought it rather
a caddish thing to harry you with questions. But
I must know the truth now. It is my right—the
right of a man who loves you honourably and
devotedly. I will not be played with and deceived
any longer. Tell me everything straight out, Izo.'

His masterfulness, as usual, had an effect upon
her which all his tenderness and his entreaties
failed to produce. She was, after all, a very weak

and impressionable young woman, and probably it would have been easy enough for Windeatt, had he been granted time and opportunity, to make her in love with him as he would have wished her to be in love.

'I did mean to tell you; and please do not be angry. You will forgive me when you know all about things, and will put the other thoughts out of your mind, as I wanted you to do. I never wished to deceive you. It is my friend that I wanted you to be always, and that I want you to be now—the man-counseller of whom I am, indeed, sorely in need.'

'That may not be quite so easy for me as you think,' he said grimly. 'You women have a queer knack of asking hard things from the men who love you. Well, I'll do my best to come up to your expectations, however it may all end. Only begin : let me have the whole tale.'

She did begin immediately, and with no beating round the bush. 'You know, for I told you,' she said, 'all about my blindness, and how I lived a lonely, neglected orphan with Aunt Sophia. If you had ever known Aunt Sophia, you would understand my eagerness to take any way of escape from her that was offered me. It really was a terrible life. I never realized how terrible till somebody did come and take me away from it.'

Windeatt gave an incoherent murmur of indignant sympathy.

'Well, then, you know about Herminia—how she lived next door, and made friends with me after the poisoning of my cat. I told you about that.'

'Yes, you told me about that.'

'Herminia was extremely romantic, as I see now. It was not long after Mr. Bax died. The dream of Herminia's life was to go out to Hong Kong and see his grave, and visit all the places he had sailed to and from. She loved the East, and especially China and Japan, for it was on this line of boats that Mr. Bax served. That seems odd, doesn't it? I do truly think that Herminia will end by marrying Dr. Duppo.'

Windeatt laughed impatiently. The loves of Herminia and Dr. Duppo were ludicrously outside the question.

'So,' pursued Izo, 'it was not at all surprising that, when a young Japanese gentleman came to lodge in the same house, she should be deeply interested in him.'

'A young Japanese gentleman!' repeated Windeatt.

'His name was Izàn Shirazaka.'

'Shirazaka!'

'Yes. Why? Do you know anything about him?'

'No, of course not ; but I saw something in the *Kobe Chronicle* about a Shirazaka having been ennobled by the Emperor the other day for services in connection with the Chinese War. He lent a ship, or built a railway, or presented a powder magazine, or something—I forget what. Anyhow, he is now Viscount Shirazaka, and I thought how funny it sounded. Is it possible,' he added, ' that you are Viscountess Shirazaka ?'

'Oh, how bitterly you speak ! What have I done to so offend you? I know nothing whatever about my—about Herminia's friend. He was always called Mr. Izàn ; that is not so difficult to pronounce. I had forgotten his other name till Herminia reminded me of it, and then I asked Kencho if he knew any Shirazakas.'

'And what did Kencho say?'

'That it is a well-known name in Japan, and much respected, and that the old Shirazaka is a wealthy man, and much in favour with the Emperor.'

'Well,' said Windeatt, ' it may not be the same family. And what does it matter? As well one Japanese as another. The whole thing must be illegal, and I don't intend to take it tragically at present, dear Izo. Tell me, what was this young man doing in England ?'

'Eating dinners,' she said, ' in order that he

might be a barrister, and learning English. He couldn't speak it *very* well when I knew him, and his accent made him at first rather difficult to understand. He used to make Herminia read to him, and then afterwards he would read aloud to us, as he improved in the language. He was studying the "Iliad" and the "Odyssey." I was very much interested in the history he told me and the Greek stories, but they bored Herminia. She used to knit socks and count her stitches all the time, and I am certain never listened in the least.'

' But you listened, and you fancied the man, and he fell in love with you,' said Windeatt bluntly. ' Did you like his looks, Izo?'

' I never saw him,' she answered. ' How could I have judged him by his looks? I never dreamed of such a thing as his caring for me, till one day Herminia told me——'

' Oh, Herminia told you !' wrathfully exclaimed Windeatt ; ' Herminia fixed the noose for your Japanese friend to tighten ! Poor little innocent, confiding thing ! It makes me wild to think of it. And yet Herminia had eyes ! What could her object have been? And what else did she tell you?'

' Herminia always said that he was quite good-looking, and had charming manners, and that he was not very different from any ordinary foreigner. She tola me that he had conceived the most romantic attachment for me; that he used to watch me out of his window, which looked upon the garden, the same as Herminia's; and that his heart bled at seeing the treatment to which I was subjected. Herminia said that he had the notion of me as a sort of captive Princess whom he was bound to deliver, and that he was ready to face any number of dragons and go through any dangers in order to carry me off. Certainly, Aunt Sophia was as bad as the worst dragon one ever read of.'

'Oh, you poor child! you poor, blind baby!'

'But I was not a child,' said she with dignity. 'I am a great deal older than I look. I was twenty-one, and that, as he explained to Herminia, was the whole point, for it made me a free agent, notwithstanding my blindness.'

'I see; he wasn't studying law for nothing,' remarked Windeatt grimly.

Madame Izàn did not reply. She seemed to be listening, her ears and attention strained: she had that alertness of all her other senses peculiar to the blind.

'I thought I heard Herminia's voice,' she said. 'Perhaps they are coming to look for us, and we have not yet found the tower of Benkei's bell.'

'Oh, how can you think of Benkei's bell, or of anything else,' cried Windeatt, 'with your whole

life at stake, and not yours only, but mine as
well? Izo, tell me honestly: when this Japanese
scoundrel persuaded you into marrying him, did
you understand in the very least what you were
consenting to?'

A blush came over her face. 'I didn't think of
anything,' she said slowly, 'except that I wanted
to escape from Aunt Sophia; and Japan seemed a
long way off, like a wonderful fairy-story. . . .
And he said that he loved me, and that he wished
to devote himself and everything that he had and
all that he could ever do to my service, which
seemed a strange and beautiful thing for a man to
feel, and a great offer for him to make to a poor
blind, lonely girl.'

'But did you care for him—the tiniest bit?
Did you have the faintest conception of what his
love and his magnificent offer of devotion really
meant?' She was silent. He came nearer to her.
'Were you very intimate with this man, my dear?
Did you respond to his protestations? Did he
sit with you and hold your hand, as I am doing?
And did his touch thrill you, as surely mine must
thrill you now?'

She faltered. 'I . . . How can I tell?'

'Izo,' the young man went on fervidly, 'I don't
believe it ever happened. It's all some dreadful
mistake. You are not this man's wife; you never

were his wife.   It would have been impossible for
him to dare—— Izo, did he really make love
to you ?   Did he ever hold you in his arms and
kiss you—like this, dear—like this?'

And, carried away by his passion, Windeatt
again wound his arms about her and pressed his
lips to hers.   Again, too, she seemed to yield
to the personal spell he undoubtedly at such
moments cast over her, and her resistance was
so feeble and faint as to be a permission.   But she
did at last determinedly withdraw herself, and his
arms dropped.

' Izo,' he whispered, ' after that, you *must* tell
me.   Did he kiss you—as I have kissed you?'

Her face grew crimson.   ' No,' she murmured,
' never—never !'

' Ah !' Windeatt's exclamation was exultant.
' Then I don't care what mummery he and Mrs.
Bax concocted.   I have the true claim.   He could
not have loved you in the way that I love you.'

' Perhaps,' she said very low ; ' I have thought
sometimes—quite lately—that he may have loved
me better.'

She got up as she spoke, and stood, her eyes
averted, and with a deep and girlish embarrassment on her face.   Windeatt rose, too.   He bit
his moustache, seeming strangely downcast and
disconcerted.

'Why do you say that?' he asked. 'You know it can't be true.'

She flashed a glance at him, but as quickly, her eyes were lowered again.

'He gave me up at once,' she said, 'when it was pointed out to him that it was for my good. He has held to his compact scrupulously, and has respected me.'

'Do you mean that *I* do not respect you?'

'No, no, it is all different. But I have felt of late that I did not do him justice. He treated me like a queen; it was as though he thought himself unworthy to touch my little finger. He was very quiet. Herminia said that his self-restraint was chivalrous. I did not understand it then. I have only understood what it might have meant since——'

'Since?' he said. 'Since when? Has it anything to do with me?'

'Yes; since I have known you.' She spoke with perfect simplicity, evidently not realizing that her words might bear an interpretation wounding to him.

'If you were a different kind of woman,' he said bitterly, 'I should feel that the cruellest thing you could have said to me. But I'd rather take it as meaning something pleasanter. Anyhow, I'm certain you didn't say it in unkindness.'

'No,' she answered, 'I did not say it in any unkindness.'

They stood quite near, and yet apart, the faces of both working with trouble and agitation, and the silence between them full of vague promptings and bewildering thoughts, when suddenly both started further asunder, and in his confusion one of the pilgrims' banners fluttering over the fountain struck Windeatt upon the eyes, and for the moment almost blinded him.

'Madame Izàn,' said a hoarse and curiously stern voice on the other side of the fountain, 'I am sent by Mrs. Bax to ask if you have found your way to the bell-tower.'

It was Kencho who spoke, and there was something in his manner and in the expression of his face—of all that was visible beneath his heavy moustache and round his spectacles—which made Madame Izàn blush more redly even than before, and filled her with uneasiness and shame. Could he have witnessed that wild caress she had allowed so unprotestingly, and for which she now, in an odd revulsion of feeling, well-nigh hated herself?

And, strange to say, the simile which Windeatt had applied to her occurred at this moment to the Japanese guide. Kencho, in his bitterness, told himself that Izobel Izàn stood nearer now to the finding of her soul than ever before in her

troublous sight-dimmed life. Yes, the Undine
was becoming human, but the Hildebrand who had
worked the transformation was, maybe, a con-
glomeration of two persons and the process a
mystery to which neither Kencho Hiro-Kahachi
nor John Windeatt held the key.

While Izo stammered something, she knew not
what, and waited abashed in her sweet agitation,
Windeatt recovered himself. He, too, attributed
the agitation to a wrong cause, but for him the
sight of it brought a feeling of intense elation, so
that he forgot the smart of his eye and his annoyance at Kencho's untimely interruption in his joy
at this evidence, as he interpreted it, that Izo loved
him.

'Mr. Kencho,' he said stiffly, 'will you be
good enough to tell Mrs. Bax that I will bring
Madame Izàn along presently if she doesn't mind
a delay of a few minutes? For you put yourself
into *my* charge, Madame Izàn,' he added, turning
eagerly to Izo; 'and I'm responsible for your
seeing the outside, anyhow, of Benkei's bell-tower;
we really mustn't leave without having done that.'

'You are close to the tower,' replied Kencho,
still in that rasping voice which smote depressingly
on Madame Izàn's ear. 'Mrs. Bax and Mrs.
Eugarde are there now waiting for you.'

And he strode off without further words.

Madame Izàn followed him at a little distance, taking no notice of Windeatt's effort to detain her.

'Izo!' he whispered, as he gained her side, 'there is still a great deal that you have to tell me. I beseech you, don't keep me in suspense. When shall we be alone together again, so that I may hear it?

'I don't know,' she answered helplessly.

'But I *must* hear it. Whether you really meant it or not, you have given me the right to know the whole truth. I cannot and will not believe that you were lawfully married to that Japanese villain.'

'Don't,' she exclaimed, wincing; 'it hurts me to hear you speak of him like that. He wasn't a villain, though I have tried to believe everything bad of him, and though I have hated him. Oh, you don't know how at times I have hated the very thought of him.'

Her words were as balm to Windeatt's heart.

'You love me, Izo: you will confess that you love me?'

She gazed at him with a perplexed, almost frightened, expression. 'I don't know,' she said.

'You *must* love me,' he persisted; 'you have proved it. Dear, if you didn't love me, you'd have been angry with me—for what I did.'

'I don't know,' she repeated.

And he laughed in exasperation at the parrot phrase. 'Oh, if you weren't just your bewitching, incomprehensible self, I feel inclined to lift you up and carry you away, as the black fellows carry off the lubras in Australia, and I'd kiss you as though you were a great baby who wanted to be coaxed into knowing its own mind. Don't play the coquette with me, Izo. I'm only a rough Bushman, and I don't understand subtleties.'

No more did she, that was evident. And at the instant, there flashed across her Kencho's remark, that Mr. Windeatt did not comprehend Japanese subtleties.

'I'm only saying what is true,' she answered. 'I haven't any wish to deceive you. I don't know why you should make so much fuss about— about *that*.' She blushed again. 'You give me a feeling of having done something wrong and improper, and I didn't mean it like that. It all seemed—outside of me, somehow.' She spoke slowly and hesitatingly, as if groping her way through a mental labyrinth. 'I feel that I must shut my eyes, or be alone in the dark to understand. There's no good in running away from things. I've been trying to do that for ever so long, but it's of no use. Please, don't remind me any more of—of *that !*'

'But you will tell me the remainder of your

story,' he urged. 'You'll tell me how that abominable marriage came about—if it really did happen, which I can't fully believe. You'll let me advise you and act for you. And if the whole thing is, as I suspect, a fraud and a mistake, and you are free to choose once more according to the dictates of your own heart, then you will let your heart speak, Izo—you'll choose *me*, you'll marry *me* ?'

'Marry *you* !' she said in a low, dismayed voice, as though that were a practical outcome of the situation which she had never contemplated. 'Oh, but I don't want to marry. I hate marrying. I have had enough of marrying.'

Windeatt groaned within himself. Had ever other ardent lover, he thought, been at the mercy of a creature so wilful, capricious, and fay-like, so illogical, so unpractical, and yet withal so full of wrong-headed common-sense?

But just then they came to a halt before Benkei's lichen-covered tower; and there was the rest of the party grouped by the Brobdingnagian soup-sauce-pan, which had contained that brawny priest's unpoetic reward for the rape of the Biwa mermaids' thank-offering to Hidesato, of legendary fame. Mrs. Bax was looking cross, and wanted European tea, but she did not dare to reproach Madame Izan too loudly. Mrs. Eugarde, on the other hand, had the serene complacency of one who has fulfilled honourable obligations. She had given her brother his opportunity ; and if he had not taken due advantage of it—well, that was his look-out, not hers. She was, on the whole, not particularly anxious to be drawn into amatory complications which might result in a divorce suit, and Madame Izàn, sweet, charming, and ill-used by fate as she might be, was just a little doubtful as a sister-in-law.

Julia searched Windeatt's face, but could not find a satisfactory translation of the mingled emotions it expressed. Nor did the countenance of Madame Izàn afford clearer indications of the position of affairs. In fact, after prolonged scrutiny of all three, it was upon the demeanour of Kencho the guide that she founded certain melancholy vaticinations.

CHAPTER XII.

THE narrow little *table d'hôte* room at Yaami's, with its pale French wall-paper and long windows, and its rows of little tables set as in any ordinary English restaurant, was noisy and crowded that evening. There had been a new importation of travellers, and the tourist young men of the *Makara* were at Kioto again, and, as the smart of the tattoing was now considerably alleviated, their spirits had risen accordingly. They were planning all sorts of diversions and excursions before moving on to join Mr. Barradine and Captain Kelsey at Miyanoshita, one of these being a Japanese dinner with geishas and maikos and the best of everything, to which they now invited Madame Izàn and Mrs. Bax and the two Australians. After that, as they too expressed their intention of shooting the Rapids, there was nothing for it but to ask them to join the Katsura Gawa expedition that had been arranged for the morrow.

All these plannings and the recital of the young men's adventure in Nara, and their irreverent comments on the No dance and other matters strictly Japanese, made talk and laughter, and furnished a cover to the evident embarrassment and preoccupation of Madame Izàn and her Australian adorer. Windeatt was wondering to himself when she would vouchsafe to continue that strange story of which he had as yet only had the prelude ; and his soul burned with impatience to get particulars of the marriage, in which, notwithstanding her statement, he could not bring himself to believe, and with indignation against the designing scoundrel, as he termed him, who had inveigled Izo in her youth and innocence.   He hoped that in some way or other he might manage a private conference before she retired for the night, and was on the alert for signs of her disappearance. There was no question to-night of taking jinrikishas down to the town, except for the tourist young men, who started off after coffee to see the war illuminations that were still going on.   Japan, when it is her season for rejoicing, knows how to rejoice thoroughly. Kencho, as was his wont, appeared after dinner to ask for orders, and was dismissed, not by Madame Izàn, but by Mrs. Bax.   Windeatt bade his sister interview Yamasaki, while he, having perceived the flutter of Madame Izàn's white serge dress, and noticing the swing of her stately figure as she passed over the bridge connecting the wing in which they slept with the main building of Yaami's, rushed unceremoniously in her wake. He arrested her as she paused, attracted by the tinkling of a samisen in the bath-house opposite, to watch the silhouette upon the paper shutters of a fan-figure within.

'I am not going to let you lie down to-night without telling me the rest of that story,' he said abruptly. 'I shall go mad, or do something altogether desperate, if I'm kept any longer in suspense. I insist upon knowing whether you are free or not for me to woo you as my wife.'

'And if I am not free,' she said, 'will you go away and leave me to my fate?'

'No,' he answered determinedly; 'I will not go away. I shall never give up hope. I don't believe that a marriage contracted under such conditions as those I imagine could possibly be legal according to the law of England, even if it were so according to the law of Japan.'

'I know that the marriage was legal according to the law of Japan,' she answered. 'There were certain formalities—I did not understand about them at the time, but Uncle O'Halloran told me afterwards that they had been complied with. It was necessary to have the consent of the Japanese

Minister in London, and that he—Izàn—had taken care to obtain.'

'Japanese law is not English law,' returned Windeatt, 'and I don't care twopence about it. I want to know the exact facts of the case, and then I shall be in a better position to judge. Come with me to a quieter place, Izo, where we can talk safely.'

She moved on to the balcony, but seemed to hesitate, and would not, as he wished, sit down in the long cane chair he had once before pulled forward for his sister. Just now Mrs. Eugarde's voice was heard in the opposite veranda, along which she was walking with Mrs. Bax.

'Well, I have my notes to write up,' Julia was saying, 'and I shall bid you good-night.'

'And I am going to bed, for I've had a very tiring day,' said Mrs. Bax. 'I conclude that Izo has taken herself to her room.'

She sauntered across, stopping also to listen to the samisen ; while Mrs. Eugarde, whose quick eyes had noticed the pair on the balcony, entered her bedroom by a door facing towards the court. Mrs. Bax was either not so observant or had no scruples, for she crossed straight in the direction of Windeatt and her friend. They were standing by the railings, Izo's gaze fixed on the lights of Kioto, the Australian watching her face in despairing impatience.

'Izo, I'm going to bed,' said Mrs. Bax.

'Very well, Herminia.'

'I think you'd better come, too. I don't see that you'll do any good standing here talking to Mr. Windeatt. I should have thought you'd said all you wanted to say the time we were waiting up at that temple. I'm perfectly sick of temples. It's a comfort to think that to-morrow, anyhow, we're going to have Rapids and not temples, though I'm not at all sure that I shall go on the Rapids. Those young men were saying that the boats are very apt to upset, and that you're as likely as not to be drowned. I don't want to be drowned. . . . Izo, are you coming to bed ?'

'Yes, Herminia.'

Izo made an irresolute and weary movement, but Windeatt stepped forward with an air of fierce intention.

'No, Mrs. Bax. I'm not going to let her go to bed—not until she has told me whether she is free or not to marry me.'

'Gracious !'—Mrs. Bax gave a little scream—'I must say that you Australians do come straight to the point, when you've found out a thing.'

'It seems to me that I've been a long time beating about the bush, without being certain of my find,' said Windeatt. 'But when an Australian has once pegged out his claim, he isn't going to allow it to be "jumped" away from him without knowing the exact reason why. I fought a fight over the Wee-Waa, and went to law about it and got my claim. And I am prepared to fight for the woman I love, and go to law for her, too, if necessary ; for I mean to win her, if she is to be won.'

Mrs. Bax's blue eyes glowed sympathetically, and her little figure expanded in a small gasp of admiration. This kind of love-making appealed to all her romantic instincts.

' I'm sure you deserve to win her, for you go at it like a man,' she said, ' and if I could help you —why, you know I would.'

' Just as you helped the other man,' put in Windeatt sardonically. At this moment he was considerably incensed with Mrs. Bax.

' Well, he was just as determined as you are,' said Mrs. Bax, unabashed, ' and he talked beautifully, though he was a Japanese. I suppose you know he was a Japanese?'

Windeatt nodded.

' And I couldn't help feeling for him,' Mrs. Bax went on.

' No doubt he was a plausible scoundrel!' said Windeatt.

' Herminia,' interrupted Madame Izàn, ' tell him that—my husband—wasn't a scoundrel. He was a Japanese gentleman.'

'And since when,' cried Windeatt, losing himself in his wrathful passion, 'have you learned to feel such a sympathy with Japanese gentlemen?'

'Oh, you are jealous of Kencho,' put in Mrs. Bax. 'I told Izo so; and the idea is too ridiculous. I thought better of you than that. And, Mr. Windeatt, you'll excuse my saying so, but aren't you just a little rough and ready in the Bush?—in your dealings with ladies, I mean.'

'I beg your pardon,' exclaimed Windeatt humbly; 'I deserve that rebuke. But you must make allowance for a chap tortured beyond endurance, and kept in the dark.'

'Do you want me to go away? Is she going to tell you?' asked Mrs. Bax.

'If she does not tell me, I beg that you will do so.'

'Do you want me to go away?' asked Mrs. Bax again.

'No, Herminia; stay, and tell him, if you please,' exclaimed Madame Izàn. '*You* are responsible for it all : *you* arranged the marriage ; you persuaded me to my undoing!'

Mrs. Bax sank upon the end of the deck-chair, and, with her handkerchief to her eyes, bewailed herself with tears. 'You hear her, Mr. Windeatt. She is trying to drive me from her. That's how she went on last night. And it's all your doing— yours and Kencho's. I wish we had never seen

Kencho! Izo and I never quarrelled before.
Mr. O'Halloran himself said I wasn't to blame.
Would he have kept me with Izo all through that
time of the operation and afterwards if he had
considered me an unfit person to be with her?
And I that have sacrificed the best years of my
life. . . . It's no use trying to stop me, Izo ;
I've got feelings as well as other people. And
you don't realize—indeed you don't—what I've
sacrificed for your sake. It was only the other
day I refused—I said I couldn't even think of
marrying till our Japanese trip was over and I
knew that you didn't want me any longer. . . .
And, after my devotion, to be scorned and flouted
and upbraided! I can't stand it, Izo—no, I
c-can't! As soon as we get to Tokyo I shall
leave you, though—my—my—heart will break.'
Mrs. Bax's sobs here became overpowering, and
Izo was visibly affected by her grief.

' I'm very sorry, Herminia ; I did not mean to
upbraid you. What I meant was, that you can
tell him much better than I can all the circumstances of my marriage. It was you who arranged
it, and in whose advice I trusted.'

' And did I advise for my own advantage?'
cried Mrs. Bax, lowering her handkerchief with
a tragic air. ' Was it not out of love and pity
for a blind, penniless, and neglected—worse than

18—2

neglected—cruelly ill-used orphan that I did it? I did it to secure a home for her, Mr. Windeatt, and if you could understand the sort of woman her aunt was, you would understand, too, how it was that every soul round compassionated poor Izo, and longed to do something to help her find a different sort of protector. Why, I shudder to think of the fate she might have had, but for me and Izàn and her uncle O'Halloran turning up in the nick of time to save her.'

'I inferred that Mr. O'Halloran had turned up a little too late to save her,' remarked Windeatt now, with more regret than sarcasm in his voice.

'That is true,' admitted Mrs. Bax, melted by his sadness. 'I hadn't thought of it in that light. Of course, if he had come a week earlier the marriage would not have taken place. But how should I know that he would fall down like that from the clouds, out of an Australian gold-mine—though Izo does jeer at me for being romantic—and that he'd take Izo away from her husband, so to speak, at the church door!'

'At the church door?' repeated Windeatt.

'That was the understanding, and you will allow that it was quite an honourable one. Izo is quite right, and Mr. Izàn was a real Japanese gentleman. He did not wish to take advantage of the circumstances or to place Izo in an embarrassing position, which would have been the case if he had carried her off at once. He was to leave England very shortly, and in the meantime was expecting a large sum of money, and he had cabled to his father about his marriage, and preferred that the last step should be quite open and aboveboard, and that he should claim Izo from her aunt with no suspicion of their having lived together in a clandestine fashion. You see,' continued Mrs. Bax, ' there were reasons for hurrying the marriage, and for having a secret ceremony. Izo's aunt happened to be away just at that time, and so, naturally, it was more easy to arrange matters. For that old Gorgon always makes me think of the person with the hundred eyes or the hundred arms —like those Buddhas in the god-market that we went to see. If she had been anywhere handy, you'd have had to be pretty cute for her not to know what you were doing every minute of the day. Wasn't that so, Izo?'

Izo took no notice of the appeal ; and Windeatt writhed under Mrs. Bax's discursiveness, regretting that she did not possess the Australian virtue she had commended, of getting straight to the point.

' Please go on,' he said.

' Well, now, I'll tell you the whole occurrence right off, Mr. Windeatt. Mr. Izàn lodged in the same house with me, which was a boarding-house West Kensington way, next door to Izo's aunt. He was a very nice young man, who was studying law, and not at all bad-looking for a Japanese, though I never could afterwards persuade Izo ot that. Of course, he had high cheek-bones, and his eyes slanted a bit ; but I have seen bilious men who were quite as yellow, and Scotch people with equally high cheek-bones—and that was not considered a disadvantage to them. Besides, in regard to his eyes, which I own were slanting, and his being a Japanese, how was I to dream then that Izo would ever be cured of her blindness? And it really seemed to me, since she couldn't see him, that it made very little difference whether she married a Japanese or any other foreigner, provided he had no disagreeable heathen habits, and ate his food like a Christian, and was kind to her. Mr. Izàn wasn't in the least like a heathen ; and as for sitting on his shins, and eating rice with chopsticks, you simply couldn't have imagined it of him ; he was quite English in all his ideas and ways of eating. We always had late dinner at the boarding-house ; it was a most genteel establishment, and nobody was received into it without references—Mr. Izàn had a reference from the Japanese Minister and from an English banker, and you couldn't have anything more respectable than that. You see, even here, what

is thought of being connected with the Legation!'
In moments of excitement or reminiscence Mrs.
Bax occasionally fell back upon the associations
of Suburbia. 'Oh, I assure you the boarders
were most genteel. I shouldn't have felt comfortable in introducing Izàn to Izo, when he confided to me his desperate attachment, if proper
inquiries had not been made. . . . Where are you
going, Izo?'

For Madame Izàn, wincing, perhaps, at the
allusions to her blindness, perhaps at the train of
painful recollections Mrs. Bax's words aroused, had
made a sudden movement towards the French
window of her room. She stopped and turned
at Mrs. Bax's question.

'I don't think that I want to hear all this,
Herminia. You can tell him. You know as
much about it as I do. Make him understand——'
She paused, and added: 'I should like him to
understand that Mr. Izàn acted honourably.'

Windeatt went close to her, and, taking her
hand, kissed it in very respectful fashion.

'For my part, I can quite understand your pre-
ferring not to be present at Mrs. Bax's explanation,'
he said. 'I thank you deeply for having permitted it ; and you will let me say that I admire
your generosity.'

To his surprise, she burst into sudden tears.

Checking them after a moment or two, she exclaimed:

'Oh, it isn't that. It is that I see now I did not do him justice. I never understood him till I came here. At that time, in the midst of all the shock and wonder at the thought of getting back my sight, my marriage seemed somehow a secondary thing. My mind was all confused; and then Uncle O'Halloran was so kind, and seemed to be so sorry for me, and to want so much that I should see. It was a terrible disappointment to him, what I had done, though he was just in his way of looking at it, and blamed himself for having left me so long without trying to find out whether I was happy and taken care of. . . . But later on, when he talked to me about it all, he made me feel that I had done something very dreadful indeed, and that I had married a kind of monster. He told me the Japanese were a cross between South Sea Islanders and Chinamen. And he had also brought a South Sea Island servant over with him, so that you can imagine the shock I got when I saw this man for the first time. As for Chinamen, he often told me stories of them on the diggings, and of how the Government out there had been obliged to pass a law to prevent Chinamen from coming to the country, they did so much harm and were such dreadful people. And though he said Mr. Izàn was a good specimen of his nation, still, I could not dissociate him from uncle's description of the others. Once at Wiesbaden, after I got back my sight, we happened to see a horrible-looking Malay—he was some sort of Prince who was taking the waters. He had great thick lips, and a skin almost black, and eyes that filled me with dread and horror. I pictured my husband like that, and shuddered. Then I determined to put him out of my mind, and never to let myself acknowledge his existence till I was actually forced to do so. For, oh! when I began to see the world and all its beauty, and the Greek statues in the galleries, and the clean, brave, handsome Englishmen—I do think so much of splendour of form and colour; I cannot help it— well, it seemed to me that I had tied myself to something which was scarcely human; and nothing would reconcile me to my fate, except uncle's assurance that he would do everything he could to break my marriage. But he died—he died just when he was about to consult lawyers, and before anything at all had been settled. . . . Now can you understand?'

She had been speaking in rapid jerks, with little agitated pauses here and there, half sobbing the while. Windeatt's heart was moved by the deepest and most chivalric compassion and sympathy, so that for the moment he almost forgot his own hopes and his own bitterness, in the desire to spare her pain.

'Yes, indeed I see it all as far as you are concerned,' he said ; 'and my heart aches for you in your youth and inexperience and your terrible affliction. Dear Izo, I think it is well that you should leave Mrs. Bax and me to beat out the matter by ourselves. All this is unnecessarily agitating for you. Do you now go to your rest and try to sleep away the memory of our trouble—for to-night, at any rate. To-morrow we shall all be clearer and fresher, and a day in the open air will put us into better gear for tackling this miserable complication. But I'm not afraid, my dear. It is right that you should be freed, and you shall be freed, from that unjust bond.'

As he spoke, Windeatt looked like a new St. George in his bigness and fairness, with the ardour of true love animating his features, and making his eyes glow with something better than the mere selfish desire to secure for his own happiness the woman of his fancy. Yet though she was impressed by his manner, his tender solicitude, and enthusiastic confidence in her right to liberty, Izo evinced no enthusiasm herself, seeming still dissatisfied, frightened and reluctant. She made two or three hesitating steps, half turning and stopping

to say, before she disappeared within the Venetian
windows:

'Yes, I suppose I had better go. I've said all
I could. Herminia can do the rest. Only please
remember, Herminia—and Mr. Windeatt, too—
that I wish justice to be done to Mr. Izàn. I
wish it made clear that he was a Japanese gentleman, and that——' She waited a moment, and
added deliberately: 'I now see that this means a
great deal.'

'The fact is, Izo, that your head has been
turned by Kencho's stories about the Shoguns and
Daimios and saints, and the rest of what Mr. Windeatt calls those old feudal bounders,' said
Mrs. Bax crossly. 'Talk of *me* being romantic!
Why, you are a hundred times more romantic
yourself. You have let Kencho persuade you that
the Japanese are a nation of heroes, instead of being,
as they are, no better than savages.'

'Savages!' indignantly cried Madame Izàn.

'Yes, like the ancient Britons and the Druids
and the Crusaders and the people who strewed
grass on their floors and ate out of one dish. I
can't see much difference between that sort of thing
and living on bare matting, with not a chair or a
table about. What is feeding on raw fish, and
stalking round with nothing on, but being a
savage? Do you call it behaving like a gentleman

to take your bath in the street, and to walk out to it carrying every stitch of your clothing on your arm?'

'Herminia!' retorted Madame Izàn, coming back again in the heat of her protest, 'I have heard you say yourself that it is better for the poor people to take their bath in the street than to take none at all. Besides, I'm not talking of common Japanese people—we have got common, half-civilized people in Whitechapel, I believe—I am talking about Japanese gentlemen.'

'And I,' said Mrs. Bax with asperity, 'am talking about Japan as I find it, and not as Kencho describes it to me.'

'Herminia,' went on Madame Izàn, 'you change your opinions very often and very quickly. When I first knew you, you cared a great deal for Japan and the Japanese, and the East generally; and you would have been much offended if I had spoken of the people your husband was fond of as savages. That was when you were friends with Mr. Izàn, and looked at things from his point of view. Afterwards you got to see them as Uncle O'Halloran wished you to see them. You veered round altogether, and were ashamed of your enthusiasm. Oh yes, Herminia; I remember it quite well, and you know that what I say is true. Now it is Mr. Windeatt who has got your sympathy. I am

not insinuating anything against you,' she added,
turning a grateful look towards the Australian.
' You are very kind to me, and I feel very much
obliged to you for caring so much for me. Only
please remember that I wish justice done to
Mr. Izàn.'

When she had gone at last, Mrs. Bax gave
another deep gasp, this time half in exasperation,
half in relief.

' Well, of all the changeable, illogical, incomprehensible girls!' she exclaimed. ' To hear her now
you would fancy that it was I who had been all the
time abusing Izàn, and keeping him away from
her. When it's the truth, Mr. Windeatt, that
I've defended him by the hour together, and tried
to convince Izo that he was not such a monstrosity
as her uncle made out, and that it wasn't fair to
shunt him straight off into the rubbish-heap, as she
wanted to do. She absolutely declined to entertain the idea of him as her husband.'

' Mrs. Bax,' said Windeatt, ' are you sure that
he is her husband?'

' Really and truly, Mr. Windeatt, I don't think
there's any doubt. Mr. O'Halloran did get a legal
opinion, and it said that Izo's blindness had nothing
whatever to do with the matter; and that if she
knew what she was about, and had consented
willingly to the marriage, it was a good one.

Izàn was studying law, too, and he must have known what he was doing. He got the consent of the Japanese Embassy, which he said was necessary ; and I am sure that the license was all regular, and the ceremony a proper one. You see, Izo was of age. The clergyman of the parish married them ; and there's the entry in the register of her parish church, with my name and the clerk's for witnesses.'

Windeatt gave an angry groan.

'You mustn't blame me too much, Mr. Windeatt,' pleaded Mrs. Bax, becoming lachry-mose again. 'Of course, I see now that it was a mistake ; but at the time it seemed the only chance of rescuing Izo from a life of brawl and misery and dependence, or very likely beggary. Her aunt wouldn't have done anything for her. She had a son of her own, and a lot of grandchildren ; and she was always grumbling at being burdened with the expense of feeding and clothing poor Izo, and threatening to place her in an asylum for blind in-capables, which would have been the same sort of thing as sending her to the workhouse. And there was Izàn—and really, for a Japanese, he was almost good-looking, and not in the least objectionable—madly in love with her, ready to lay down his life for her, and with a father very well off, and in a good position in his own country. He explained all that to me, and gave me his word of honour that, as soon as circumstances permitted, he would make a handsome settlement upon her. I don't know how they manage these things in Japan, but that was what he assured me. Besides, 1 did not intend to desert Izo. I had made up my mind to go out with them to Japan, and satisfy myself as to her prospects ; it had always been my dream, ever since Mr. Bax died at Hong Kong, to visit the East. I should have seen for myself, and if she hadn't been comfortable, I would have brought her back to England and shared my last crust with her. Oh, I assure you I quite felt, and was pre-pared to undertake, the responsibility at any cost or sacrifice. And that is why Izo's ungrateful reproaches are so lacerating to my feelings.' And again she wept gently.

'I am certain, Mrs. Bax, that you meant every-thing for the best.'

'I did—I did. And though Izo accuses me now of having overpersuaded her, it wasn't a question of persuading in the least. She would have done anything then that anybody she liked had sug-gested to her. Since she has got back her sight she has developed pretty strong views and opinions of her own, but when she was blind a little child might have led her. In fact, in some ways she was no more than a baby herself. Her one thought

was to get away from the taunts and humiliations
and blows—yes, blows—which her aunt showered
upon her. When Mr. O'Halloran learned that,
even he, angry as he was, exonerated me.'

'Did she care for the man?' asked Windeatt
impatiently ; 'did she *know* him? Did she realize
at all that she was *marrying* him?'

'Well, I am not sure that she did,' candidly
answered Mrs. Bax. 'In one sense she knew
that she was *marrying* him, and settling herself
for her whole life—I told her that, but I don't
know whether she took it in. As for caring about
him, if you have never *seen* a man since you were
a baby, it must be difficult to form a correct idea
of what he is like, mustn't it? Then, as you can
understand, there were obstacles in the way of
their meeting. On those occasions I was generally
present, which naturally put a little restriction on
the love-making. Not that Izàn was effusive. I
don't think the Japanese are, do you? Now I
come to think of it, I have never seen two Japanese
kissing each other, and somebody told me that they
don't kiss. I meant to ask Yamasaki about it, but
found it a little embarrassing to approach the subject. It seemed Izàn's idea to make love through
me. He found me sympathetic ; most men who
are in love do find me sympathetic. I can't help
being touched by a man's devotion, whether it's

towards myself or another woman. I dare say you have observed, Mr. Windeatt, that I'm sympathetic? And Izàn's devotion to Izo was something quite out of the common. He hardly dared to tell her that he loved her; he worshipped her from a distance. I didn't see how I could explain things to Izo; I thought it best to leave that to Izàn. What he wanted was to get her safely his own, and then to live on his knees before her. But really, as you ask me, on the whole, if you had counted up the hours they spent in each other's company, it wouldn't have amounted to much, and I don't see, however, that it made much difference. Izàn's courtship wasn't an ordinary courtship. It was beautiful to see an adoration like that. It put me in mind of the days of my own brief wedded happiness.'

Mrs. Bax kept silence for a minute, lost in retrospect.

'Go on,' said Windeatt. 'She was married in the parish church, you said.'

'Yes, everything quite regular, as I told you. When the ceremony was concluded, we three had lunch together in a private room at a pastry-cook's; Izo tasted champagne for the first time in her life, and we had plum-cake with almond icing, which I took back with me and kept in my room, for it wouldn't have done for Izo to have it, on account of the aunt, who would have made things unpleasant. But we used to eat the cake when she came across to me, and I made tea with the spirit-lamp up in my room. It seemed hard that Izàn shouldn't have a morsel of his own wedding-cake in the company of his bride, but it wouldn't have been considered proper in the establishment if I had asked him to my bedroom. Well, we went on that way for a week, I getting together an outfit for Izo, and Izàn making his arrangements for the voyage, when, lo'—Mrs. Bax halted dramatically—'lo and behold! suddenly Uncle O'Halloran falls down upon us, as if it had been a bomb bursting, just like the lost uncle in a novel, you know. He had got hold of a gold-mine, as you have done, Mr. Windeatt. It's a strange coincidence, isn't it? He said he meant to adopt Izo as his heiress, and was full of a case of blindness the same as hers, which had been cured by a celebrated German oculist, and wanted to take her right off to Wiesbaden and have an operation performed. He was a very determined man, was Mr. O'Halloran, and he said that if money could buy European science, and European science could give back his niece her eyes, she should see before she was twenty-five, for he'd scour Europe and America for the purpose.'

'And what did Izo think of this?'

' Why, she was simply enchanted at the thought of getting back her sight. She had looked upon that as one looks upon going to heaven. The idea of seeing the sun and the sea and people and animals and flowers made her wild with excitement. She took to her uncle directly. I will say that, rough diamond as he was, he couldn't have been tenderer to an angel or his own daughter than he was to Izo. He was quite prepared, once he had taken a fancy to her, to repay the kindness some of us had shown the poor girl a hundredfold into our bosoms. But he and the aunt had a deadly row. He wasn't going to be humbugged by her, and it didn't take him long to see how the land lay. In less than an hour he had carried Izo off in a four-wheeled cab to a hotel in the Strand, where she told him quite casually—for she didn't seem to think it of much importance—that she was a married woman.'

' And I bet that then Mr. O'Halloran used quaint language,' said Windeatt.

' Yes, he did,' answered Mrs. Bax. ' It was awful. Never before in my life had I been sworn at by a gentleman, for Mr. Bax was peculiarly choice in his manner of expressing himself.'

' O'Halloran started in Australia as a bullock-driver,' explained Windeatt. ' He never lost the habit of objurgatory speech, but he always paid up handsomely when his temper got the better of him with his men, and apologized like a gentleman to his equals.'

'He apologized and paid up handsomely as well to me,' said Mrs. Bax. 'And no doubt he would not have forgiven me so quickly if he hadn't sworn at me first. Oh yes, he apologized and asked me to come and live with Izo as her companion, which I at once agreed to do. Then he sent for Mr. Izàn, and they had an interview at the hotel.'

'I should like to have heard what he said to him,' remarked Windeatt.

'I was not present at the interview,' returned Mrs. Bax. 'But I believe that Izàn gave Mr. O'Halloran proof of the legality of the marriage. There was no fraud or compulsion, you see.'

'I call it—*damnable* fraud,' growled Windeatt between his teeth.

'Mr. O'Halloran sent for Izo and me; but things were peaceable when we came down. It was in that sitting-room at the Adelphi hotel that Izo saw her husband for the last time. Oh, what am I saying?' Mrs. Bax laughed hysterically. 'Of course she didn't *see* him; she has never seen him. It was I that saw him, and I can tell you that he made me feel sorry for him, Mr. Windeatt. Poor Izàn! his cup of happiness was dashed away from his lips. I think that even Mr. O'Halloran was sorry for him, though he had such a prejudice against Chinese and Easterns generally. Well, Izàn spoke to Izo, and told her that her uncle had put the position before him and had appealed to his honour and his own sense of what was fair to her. He acknowledged that he had done her a wrong in marrying her in that offhand way, but he said that he had thought of her more than of himself, and that he could not have foreseen the alteration in her circumstances and the chance she now had of getting back her sight and of being able to choose a husband with full knowledge and under the advantages her uncle's wealth would give her. He really spoke very nicely, poor Izàn! and I think his calmness was only assumed to hide his despair and agony. He released her from her promise to go back with him to Japan, and told her that he had agreed to her uncle's demand that she should be left entirely unmolested by him for three years, or as long a time, within reasonable limits, as might be required to give the oculists a chance of restoring her sight. He gave his word of honour that he would not write to her or attempt to see her, but this he declared should only be on the understanding that she was recognised as his wife and called by his name, and that whether blind or seeing she should be under

solemn engagement to meet him in his own
country at the end of the term, and that he in his
turn should be granted the opportunity to win her
affections and plead his own cause, and then he
said she should be at liberty to decide for herself
whether or not she would live with him as his
wife.   Now, I hope Izo will allow that I have put
things in such a way as to do justice to Mr. Izàn.
I do call that acting like a gentleman, don't you,
Mr. Windeatt?' she concluded impartially.

' It would have been quite impossible for him
under the circumstances to act in any other way,'
replied Windeatt.

' Well, I don't know. He might have armed
himself with the majesty of the law,' said Herminia,
who enjoyed a fine phrase.

' I don't think the majesty of the law would
have been of much use to him if O'Halloran had
done what he clearly ought to have done, and
taken immediate steps to break such an iniquitous
marriage.   I am certain that no English jury
would have upheld it.'

' I remember Dr. Duppo showing me a kind of
prickly creeper at Nagasaki that he said was
sometimes called " lawyers," because when the
thorns caught you, it was so difficult to get away
from them,' sapiently observed Mrs. Bax.

' I know that plant,' said Windeatt ; ' it grows,

too, in Australia.   But tell me, how did Izo take the farewell speech and confession?'

'Well, she didn't seem much moved by it, not half as much affected as I was.   You can't think what an odd, undeveloped girl she was, Mr. Windeatt, at that time.   I used to think sometimes that she was only half grown up.   Or else she was so accustomed to scoldings and cataclysms, that she took everything as coming in the day's work.   Besides, it wasn't till after she had her sight that she got such a feeling of horror and repulsion about her husband.   All she said in answer to him was, "Yes, Mr. Izàn, I should like very much to come out by-and-by to your country, and only think how glorious it will be when I can see Fuji-san for myself!"   For he used continually to describe Fuji—the mountain, you know—to us. I fancy his home was somewhere near it, and I heard him say to her that she reminded him in her beauty and purity, and because of the reverence in which he held her, of his beloved and sacred Fuji-san.   It was a pretty, poetic idea, wasn't it, and appropriate too?'

'I shall be better able to judge of its appropriateness when I have seen Mount Fuji,' said Windeatt grudgingly.

'Now I am really at the end of the story,' said Mrs. Bax.   'What a pity it is that your sister,

Mrs. Eugarde, couldn't make a book out of it! Time, too, for me to finish. It's awfully late, and the hotel is in darkness. Izàn did another pretty thing, Mr. Windeatt, though it seemed rather ridiculous in that stuffy Adelphi hotel. He said to Izo: "I hold you to your promise. There in my country, my beautiful country—which for your sake I would even renounce, but which, I hope, you too may learn to love — there you shall come to me of your own accord, and together we will gaze on Fuji-san, or I will give you your freedom and we shall be parted for ever." And then he said something in Japanese ; and now I'm coming to the pretty thing he did. He prostrated himself on the ground before her, just as they do here on occasions of great ceremony, and afterwards got up and went away without another word. And that's the last I know of Izo's husband, Mr. Windeatt. Tell her, please, that I did do him justice. He has kept his word of honour, and has never in these years written to her, or in any way reminded her of his existence ; and now she is keeping hers, and is out in Japan. At Tokyo those two have to meet, and I am wondering what will come of the meeting, and just whereabouts *you* will be placed in this scene. I wrote to him for her ; and that's the arrangement. Now you know all about it,' wound up Mrs. Bax, as she rose from her chair;

'and if either or both of us are going to shoot those Rapids to - morrow, it seems to me that we had better prepare for danger and calm our nerves by getting as much sleep as we can to-night.'

CHAPTER XIII.

THE Japanese night must surely distil nepenthe, for, to look the next morning at the small company of tourists which set forth so blithely from Yaami's, one would certainly never have guessed at those agitating emotions which, during the previous day and evening, had racked the bosoms of two, if not three, of the party. This not including Herminia Bax, though, as a matter of fact, Mrs. Bax's delicate freckled face — the bloom of it faded, and reddish-violet rims circling the dulled blue eyes—gave more marked indication of ravaged feelings and sleepless hours than did the countenance of either Windeatt or Madame Izàn. Nobody looked closely at Kencho; and, indeed, he, on his part, was apparently engrossed in preparation for the excursion, and his chief anxiety seemed to be that the *Makara* young gentlemen, who had enjoyed a late night in Kioto, should not cause a delay in the embarkation upon the Rapids, planned for before mid-day, as, if the hour of starting were postponed, double fees would be exacted by the rowers. Yamasaki shrugged his shoulders, and grinned upon this representation. He had come to the conclusion that an Australian millionaire must necessarily be above such parsimonious considerations. But Herminia, who in her leaner days had been trained to frugality, commended Kencho—a very unusual thing in her—for his thoughtfulness in the matter.

Madame Izàn had arisen from three hours' placid slumber, a goddess refreshed, for ' Melancolia ' belongs to the Middle Ages, and is not enshrined among the Olympians, who were, on the whole, an irresponsible, laughter-loving set. Windeatt, too, was three-parts Greek to one of medieval, and had strung himself up almost to hilarity. Mrs. Eugarde, as always, presented a cheerful embodiment of common-sense, and Herminia Bax was unnaturally gay. Anyhow, there seemed to be a tacit understanding among them that for this day, at least, tragedy should be shunted. Perhaps it happened opportunely that the *Makara* young men were of the party. Who could be emotionally tremendous with the Irrepressible Tourist humming music-hall ditties and chaffing his coolies, as the rickshaws bowled along between gray-coped temple walls and among yellowing cornfields and groves of dwarf bamboos till the great Kioto plain was left behind, and with many a 'Hoi! hoi!' and much streaming perspiration, the runners climbed to hillier regions?

There, round the sacred city, rose the mountains veiled in their mystic haze. . . . And now the slopes were green and pink with maple and azalea, and the wisteria was in bloom on the trellises. Oh, the tender dreaminess of that scented air! The locusts made a soft whirring on every tree and shrub; down in the dry river-bed, cobwebby wisps of muslin were drawn, which the bleachers assiduously sprinkled, giving a laugh every now and then at the moon-faced children who were flying kites. Sweet, clean, Nature-blessed creatures are they, those Japanese babies! Betimes, there would be a halt at a tea-house, and the serving out thimblefuls of pale tea, and doll-plates of sweet, square, crumbly wafers; afterwards, on again, among the cherry-orchards, the gray villages, and the roadside shrines guarded by architraved gateways.

Yes, on such a dream-day, with the earth-imps laughing at conventions and old Pan defying wigged judges, what is there for care-laden humans to do but throw off Mrs. Grundy's burdens and join the nymphs and fawns in innocent frolic? Of what consequence could it really be, under these conditions, that an unmeaning recitation of a certain formula holding good in the law-courts threatened to interfere with the happy purposes of a love-intoxicated young man, and to confuse and complicate the new stirrings of a maiden's awakening heart?

Some perception of this dawning consciousness in Madame Izàn was beginning to force itself upon poor Herminia. It added greatly to her own perplexities, torn as she was between sympathy for Windeatt the near, and remorse in regard to those righteous claims of Izàn the distant, and she was wondering in a half-terrified way whether this strange enthusiasm for things Japanese, which Kencho had inspired, might not, after all, lead to a more conventional termination of Izo's romance than she had ever anticipated.

It was a three hours' spin through a vast landscape garden, where, as Mrs. Bax put it, the mountains seemed ' placed,' and the forests designed in ' decorative patches.' Then, in a tea-house by the river, there came luncheon, which the *Makara* young men turned into a boisterous feast, washing down their cold chicken with many draughts of Kirin beer. After that, the whole party, runners, rickshaws and all, was shipped into queer flat-bottomed boats, awned over, and manned by sailors in blue sacks and mushroom hats of basketwork, who were armed with oars and poles. For a while, they were gliding along at the bottom of a great green trough, with a curving rim, where the tops of the banks were wavily outlined against the sky. There was nothing else, only the steep, smooth sides of the trough, splashed here and there with azalea, and the irregular edges, with the vast blue dome above and the still water below.

Presently the water was still no longer, but boiled, and bubbled, and foamed, and now the oars ceased their monotonous squeak in the row-locks. The men in mushroom hats brandished their poles, gripping them tightly as they stood grim and alert, warily steering in and out of the huge red - brown rocks which bristled up, the waters roaring and bellowing round them. The boat sprang, and bumped, and plunged, and darted downward, and the muscles of the boatmen's arms swelled into knots as they handled their poles. Every moment it seemed as though the boat would be dashed to pieces upon the boulders which lay pell-mell in that chaotic flood. Windeatt jeered a little at the mildness of the excitement, compared with the reports that he had heard ; but his Australian blood was up, and he enjoyed it thoroughly. So did the *Makara* young men. They were in the foremost boat with Mrs. Bax and Yamasaki, and their yells of delight almost drowned Herminia's feeble plaint :

'Oh, Izo, I'm so frightened ! I should never

have come if I had known that it rained here last night. You know the guide - book says it's dangerous when there's rain. Oh, do let me out! —do tell them that I'd rather walk! Indeed I would rather walk.'

But Madame Izàn only laughed in response to Herminia's pitiful appeals. She was not frightened —no, indeed! She didn't want to be landed with a jinrikisha and a coolie, as Herminia petitioned. Her lithe shape swayed to and fro to the frenzied dartings of the boat; her face and hair were wet with spray; her eyes danced and dilated; and both Windeatt and Kencho thought, after their different ways of thinking, that they had never seen any being so glorious and beautiful. These two, with Julia Eugarde, were in the boat also, Kencho balancing himself on a cross-bar, and the rickshaws and runners forward.

'Now I'm seeing — and living, too!' cried Madame Izàn. 'Oh, it's splendid, it's magnificent! How can you be so silly, Herminia? Splendid, splendid!' she repeated, as, after the second of the Rapids had been shot, the boat settled into docility again. Izo's excitement subsided in a long-spent breath, her tense muscles relaxing, as the boat floated upon a still little lake, into which the river had suddenly widened.

But these smooth stretches were only intervals

in the tumult of the waters. Not far from Arishi-yama came another exciting shoot, and it was then that the accident which hastened dramatic action in this history took place.

How, nobody ever exactly knew. A culvert had burst in the night, swelling the cataract at this point ; a pole slipped on a slimy rock ; a boatman missed his footing—it was one or all of these things. Kencho, as the punt heeled, started up and seized the pole which the boatman had dropped. Then came a moment of wild confusion. The guide staggered, overbalanced himself in his effort to steer the craft, and fell sheer into the torrent. Madame Izàn, with a scream, rose impetuously ; there was a horrible bump, and before anybody could quite realize what was happening, all of them were struggling in the waves. The boatmen —luckily not unused to this kind of occurrence, and being as fish returning downstream—kept their wits as well as their limbs in working order. And luckily, too, the catastrophe happened at the end of the Rapids, where some bristling fangs edged the fall into stiller water. Past the fangs there was not so much danger, and Windeatt and Julia Eugarde, escaping the jagged rocks above the drop, were swept harmlessly down into the smoother stream. Windeatt had had experience of flooded creeks in Australia, and was a good swimmer. He struck out, supporting his sister, and reached the bank almost as soon as the boatman and coolie who were making for his assistance. They seized Julia and dragged her out. But now, with dismay, Windeatt saw that Madame Izàn had not been so fortunate. He would have plunged towards her, but that at that moment he perceived her in the safe keeping of another boatman, who now appeared with her in his arms from behind a nasty tooth of rock, and was bearing her landwards. Kencho had fared worse, for it was he who in the first instance had enfolded her from harm, and his body had made itself a buffer between his mistress and the threatening danger. Even when his own head had struck against the boulder, and his brain had reeled and become a blank, he still held her as in a vice, her safety his last conscious thought. Windeatt was too deeply concerned about Madame Izàn to do more than assure himself that the guide was being upheld into safety by two stalwart Jap runners. He turned to the lady of his love, and, as they laid her on the bank, ascertained with joy that she was not even stunned, only bruised and dripping, and for a few minutes so dazed as hardly to grasp the fact that she had been in danger. Izo's splendid vitality seemed, indeed, unquenchable, and she was in better condition than Mrs. Eugarde, who did not at once recover consciousness. Presently, however, Julia, too, opened her eyes and murmured some incoherent words, and by that time those in the foremost boat, having seen the disaster, had landed, and Herminia, in advance, was running wildly towards the drowned-looking group.

'Oh, Izo!' she cried, 'did I not say that it was dangerous? Izo, are you alive? . . . Oh, I knew something dreadful was going to happen. I had a presentiment of it. . . . Speak to me, dear Izo, and tell me that you are safe.'

'She is all right, Mrs. Bax,' replied Windeatt cheerfully. 'Everybody is all right, thank goodness, unless it's Kencho, poor chap! . . . Seems as if he had got a nasty cut. . . . Oh, I say! . . . By Jove!'

Windeatt's long-drawn exclamation ended in a funny kind of whistle. He cast a glance of half-humorous horror and amazement at Mrs. Bax. But she was too much occupied in wringing the wet out of Izo's skirts to appreciate its significance. Madame Izàn did not respond gratefully to the attention, but pushed Herminia pettishly away and rose to her feet. She made some tottering steps forward, her alarmed eyes fixed upon the inert form of a man which the Japanese coolies were carrying over the rocks, and which they laid upon the grassy slope close to where she stood.

It was this sight which had called forth Windeatt's startled exclamation and was accountable now for the pained perplexity on Madame Izàn's countenance. The man's face was bleeding from a cut on the forehead, his clothes were torn and mudstained, while small rivulets dropped from his garments to the ground. But what strange transformation was this? The clothes were the clothes of Kencho, so was the form. Yet could that be the face of Kencho?

For it was no longer the face of a middle-aged man. The iron-gray hair was gone. It had floated down the current and might have been seen, had anyone cared to look, considerably below the Rapids on its way to Arishiyama. Instead of those gray locks, curly black rings clung to a youthful forehead, rings that were clotted and stained, where the blood had flowed from a nastylooking cut above the temple. The goggles also had gone, sunk to the bottom of the river, no doubt, or broken to pieces on the rocks, and Kencho's eyes lay closed in their orbits, like those of a sleeping Buddha, beneath dark level brows, which the unsightly glasses had formerly hidden. The absence of those disfiguring spectacles seemed somehow to have altered the shape of the nose and the whole character of the face, which now revealed itself as that of an intellectual and comparatively young Japanese gentleman—a face which, in its rigid unconsciousness, showed well-featured, impressive, and even handsome, after the style of the East, and with a distinction independent of race, all its own.

Herminia Bax, when her eyes rested upon this pale, impassive face, gave one piercing shriek and flung her arm round Madame Izàn, drawing her from the spot on which lay the inanimate form.

'Come away!' she cried. 'Izo, you must come this instant. It isn't fit that you should be looking at him. Oh!' she went on, in despair at Izo's immovability. 'Do tell her it isn't fit; do take her away!'

Windeatt was at a loss to understand the cause of Mrs. Bax's agitation.

'Oh! the poor chap isn't dead, Mrs. Bax—nor likely to die. Here's our *Makara* friend, who's a sort of doctor—ain't you, old man? He'll bring him round in no time. That's not what has flabbergasted me. I'm a bit of a doctor myself. But why in Heaven's name is he masquerading like this?'

'Yes, yes, that's the puzzle. Just you tell Madame Izàn we'll bring him to his senses all right, and then Mr. Kencho will have to explain himself,' said the Irrepressible Young Man, who was bubbling inwardly with curiosity and amusement. He had his hand on Kencho's heart, and was examining the cut with professional nicety. He had been a medical student before his unexpected accession to a fortune gave him means of gratifying a long-cherished desire to go round the world.

'It's a rum go, ain't it?' he went on. 'Got plenty of hair, hasn't he? Wonder what he wanted with a wig. Well, he has lost his wig, any way, for good and all.' The young man, with Mrs. Eugarde's help, was trying to force some brandy between Kencho's locked lips. 'That's good. He's coming to. Now, don't you bother about him, Mrs. Eugarde. But do, ladies, look after yourselves. Give us the other brandy flask, old chap; oh, you've got some, have you? Well, now look here, Mrs. Bax and Mrs. Eugarde, and all of you: get off as quickly as you can to the tea-house, and change your things. Have a sup of this at once, and drink some more piping hot as soon as you are indoors. If you don't you'll be catching cold or going into hysterics. Mrs. Bax is half-way to hysterics already. Where's Yamasaki?'

Yamasaki, looking extremely like a soused monkey, was discovered squeezing the river out of his coat-tails, but otherwise none the worse for his ducking. Kencho seemed the only one who had come to serious grief, for all the other little Japs had bobbed up out of the water, smiling and uninjured. It was decided that the medical young man should look after Kencho, Windeatt and the second tourist remaining, while the rest of the party, under Yamasaki's charge, got into the first boat, and were rowed to Arishiyama. Mrs. Eugarde, who had recovered her usual calm, had meanwhile dosed the sobbing Herminia with brandy, and administered some to herself. Madame Izàn impatiently pushed away the dose offered her. She did not seem able to think of anything but the condition of Kencho.

'It was in saving me,' she said, half aloud ; ' he thought of me, not of himself.' Then she turned wildly to Windeatt. ' What does it all mean ? Why is he so changed ? Why is his hair not gray ? Or is it that I am seeing wrong ?'

'Oh, you are seeing right enough, Madame Izàn,' replied Windeatt gruffly. ' You are only seeing what all the rest of us see. The fellow is an impostor—that's what it means ; and the sooner the authorities—the British authorities, I mean—are informed of that fact, the better. How does anyone know that he didn't mean to run away with Madame Izàn's jewel-box, which he always hugs so carefully ? As soon as we get back to Kioto, I will go to our Consul and tell him all about it.'

'No, Jack,' put in Mrs. Eugarde softly, 'you'll do nothing of the kind. And you mustn't be thinking stupid things about Kencho. It's ridiculous to suppose that he wanted to run away with any jewels. Come, my dear,' she said very kindly, taking Madame Izàn's hand in hers ; ' you must leave the poor fellow now with the men. Mrs. Bax is quite right : you can't do him any good at present. Besides, if we don't hurry up,' added this practical person, 'some of us, anyhow, will most assuredly be laid up with bronchitis.'

Madame Izàn, with the air of a frightened child, suffered Mrs. Eugarde to lead her away. She looked utterly bewildered, and said not a word till they had reached the tea - house at Arishiyama, which, fortunately, was not far distant.

Here the news of the disaster had already arrived. At the entrance, awaiting the dripping excursionists, were the proprietor, the proprietress, and the whole troop of nesans. Sympathy breathed in every honorific phrase with which the distinguished travellers were greeted. It was manifest in each profound obeisance—forehead upon the floor ; in each mellifluous ejaculation of the nesans, each infantile gesture, and in all the bobbings and trippings to and fro, and the general clutter of these wing-sleeved, sweet-faced creatures.

They convoyed the ladies up a flight of steep wooden steps to the back of the tea-house, where, behind rice-paper screens, Madame Izàn, Julia Eugarde, and Herminia Bax—the last dry, but unresisting—were divested of their garments and put into wadded cotton kimonos, while the wet clothes were taken out to be dried.

An old woman with very black teeth, carrying a tray of flat cakes and sticky sweets, came in. After Mrs. Eugarde had bought some crumbly cakes, and made a feint of nibbling them, the old woman squatted on the matting and pulled out her pipe and smoked. ' Yuroshi nasai !' she cried, in an ecstasy of admiration, as she contemplated Madame Izàn and Herminia Bax. Each wore a large - flowered kimono, but Madame Izàn's only reached to the ankles, showing a pale pinkish strip above her tabis, to hide which she had to duck, Japanese fashion, in her embarrassment. The nesans, too, were ecstatic and loud in their praises of the blonde Herminia. ' Verai clean !' they stammered, pointing to Mrs. Bax's blanched cheeks. For Herminia seemed upset in a manner out of all proportion to the cause of shock—far more upset, outwardly, than was Madame Izàn, who, at least, had suffered the severer physical shock of immersion in icy - cold water. But whatever might be Izo's inward perturbations, it was seldom that she did not contrive to maintain a fairly composed demeanour. Herminia's countenance was now of a sickly pallor ; she shivered in nervous tremor, and spoke in an inconsequent way, giving queer little gasps, as though she were trying to swallow an emotion which she found it extremely difficult to dispose of. In fact, she behaved very much as though she had seen a ghost.

'I'm all anyhow!' she exclaimed, pointing to her kimono, and bursting into a quavering peal of laughter. 'Why did I let them put this on? *I*'m sure I don't know. I wasn't wet. *Was* I wet? *I* didn't tumble into the river. I didn't want to change. And why am I shaking like this?'

'You've caught cold, perhaps ; and you're suffering from nervous agitation,' said Mrs. Eugarde. 'You must have some hot tea at once, and more brandy. . . . Tea! . . . Oh, what is tea? Where is my dictionary?'

'Tea. . . . Yes, yes! . . . Hot tea, immediately,' cried Mrs. Bax, still laughing.

The nesan prostrated herself, but was uncomprehending. Pantomimic explanation only made Herminia more hysterical.

'Don't be a goose! Cha—o cha! Here it is,' said Mrs. Eugarde, having consulted her vocabulary.

'O cha!' The nesan beamed compliance, and

tripped off. Herminia gasped again. Madame Izàn stood like a statue, regardless of the shortness of her kimono. Then presently the nesan tripped back with the tea, and Mrs. Eugarde dosed Herminia, who began to babble.

'Don't ever tell me again that there's nothing in intuitions. . . . I knew something was going to happen. . . . I knew it on board the *Makara*. . . . I told Dr. Duppo so . . . and now it has come true . . . and what am I to do? I really don't know what I ought to do. . . . It's a most terribly embarrassing position. Oh, I wish Dr. Duppo was here to advise me!' she added, in a murmur, with a furtive glance towards Madame Izàn, who was staring into vacancy, and paying no attention whatever to her friend's distress.

'Well, I must say that I think our combined intellects ought to be capable of tackling this situation, without assistance from Dr. Duppo,' dryly remarked Julia. 'For my own part, if you care for my opinion, this metamorphosis scene appears to me quite the most appropriate wind-up to the Kioto act that dramatic ingenuity could have devised. To be sure, that isn't saying much for dramatic ingenuity, but I've never known playwrights work much outside the conventional lines. Managers always feel safest when they're not asking a great deal from the comprehension of the British public. The worst of a real-life drama is,' she went on, 'that there are such undramatic pauses in its action. Now, if I were stage - managing this business, I'd walk Kencho down as soon as his cut is bound up with sticking-plaster, and put him into the centre, with all the rest of us grouped ready for a curtain. I wouldn't fool round any longer.'

Mrs. Bax glared in astonishment at the lady of professional instincts.

'My goodness gracious!' she cried. 'How have *you* got to know anything about it? I never told you. . . . No, Izo may accuse me as she likes; but I solemnly swear I never told you.'

'Make your mind easy, dear soul; I'll uphold your integrity,' answered Julia. 'But, you see, one doesn't write novels for nothing. I had a very shrewd suspicion before that venerable wig and those abominable goggles were swallowed by the Rapids. I hope you'll excuse my remarking that, from my point of view, it all seems dreadfully elementary—rather the hot-poker and butter-slide sort of thing, you know. In matter of copy I gain absolutely nothing. And really, dear Mrs. Bax, considering your previous acquaintance with the man, I am surprised that you didn't see through that disguise at once.'

'It's more than five years ago—and I never

could remember faces ; and my poor husband, who was a very clever man, always said that I was more intuitive than logical,' faltered Mrs. Bax.

'Well, he may have been right there ; but intuition doesn't seem to have done much for you here, any way,' said Mrs. Eugarde. 'As for Japanese subtleties, I can't compliment Mr. Kencho upon his personal application of Eastern methods.'

Just then there was a discreet tap upon the frame of the rice-paper screen, and at Mrs. Eugarde's 'Come in,' the tea-house proprietor presented himself, deeply bowing, somewhat in the attitude of 'I Curios' of Yaami's, and accosted the excursionists.

'Honourable ladies, river-gazing condescend,' translated Julia, with the aid of her vocabulary. Whereupon Yamasaki advanced with butting obeisance, his hands upon his knees, transformed once more into a Japanese. The screen flew back, and the rice-paper box lay all open to the landscape. They saw a broad shallow stream, the beak-prowed sampans gliding along it, and beyond, the hillside in its variegated green of pine and maple, dotted about with sylvan tea-houses. Out on the balcony stood a fair-haired and broad-shouldered giant in a very inadequate kimono. He turned to confront Madame Izàn, who had come forth mechanically from her retirement.

The giant twirled his moustache awkwardly, and she blushed rosy-red, retreating again, as she dropped a sort of curtsey to hide her ankles. Truly, there was something excessively comical in the aspect of these Westerners masquerading in Japanese garb. The *Makara* young men burst into a peal of laughter, in which Mrs. Bax hysterically joined, and which was faintly echoed by Julia Eugarde.

And now poor Madame Izàn lost completely the self-control she had tried so valiantly to maintain. The old expression of bewildered appeal came into her face, and the tears to her eyes.

'Oh, how can you be so heartless?' she cried, sinking down upon a heap of futons that the tea-house keeper had set in default of a sufficient number of chairs. 'How can you laugh like that, when maybe there's somebody dying—drowned and bleeding because he saved my life? . . . I can't bear it! . . . It's horrible!'

'No, no! We've doctored him back into right form,' exclaimed the *Makara* young man, his laughter silenced.

'I assure you that there's no occasion for you to agitate yourself,' said Windeatt, torn between jealousy, admiration, and tender compassion for her distress. 'Kencho was walking about when we left him, and exceedingly alive.'

'It was nothing but a skin-cut—only wanted sticking-plaster,' said the *Makara* young man.

'Mr. Kencho send—tell ladies no trouble,' explained Yamasaki. 'He quite well—very sorry. He now open eyes and make talk. Mr. Kencho only like drunk man—suppose too much saki. Head very quick joined. Ladies go can Kioto. Mr. Kencho come little while after.'

'Yes, it's really all right, Madame Izàn,' pursued the *Makara* young man, who had been touched also by her tears. 'Of course, it's quite natural, and very kind, I'm sure, that you should feel anxious. There's no doubt Kencho did save you from a bad bruising. If we'd been higher up the Rapids, why, I dare say we should all have been drowned —all of you, I mean. It was downright plucky of Kencho. But don't you worry any more ; there's no harm done. And I say, Mrs. Bax '— for Izo's chest still heaved ominously—' by Jove ! you look a jolly sight more shaken than Kencho himself. Look here : don't you think it would amuse Madame Izàn to take a squint through those paper things into the next compartment? There's a regular jollification going on — the sweetest set of tea-house girls, squatting on their heels, and smoking, and winking, and ogling us like anything. They saw us peeping round the corner at them from the balcony. Give the screen a shove, Yamasaki ; *they* won't mind. Say something in Japanese—the honorific language, you know. Now they're beginning to sing ; perhaps it's a geisha party. And—oh, I say ! Great Scot ! If that's not the mission lady's accordion—well ! I'll walk to Yaami's in a kimono ! What a lark if we were to catch her and send her after old Barradine to Miyanoshita !'

Sure enough, when Yamasaki threw apart the rice-paper partition—having made a circuitous and more courteous assault on the next compartment by way of the balcony—he disclosed a scene in which Miss Theodosia Gotch made, if not the most attractive, certainly the most important figure. There, in a kind of semicircle, had gathered a group of gaily - dressed mousmés — or perhaps tea-house girls, since to these was Miss Gotch's avowed mission—their pretty little figures bent, as they pecked daintily with chopsticks at flat boxes of vermicelli or some such dainty mess, the ends of their obis—bright orange and vermilion and pink—standing out like wings, and giving them more than ever the appearance of a covey of dragon-flies, while the bristling coral pins in their sleek heads heightened the comparison. The vermicelli-pecking they varied with the swallowing of thimblefuls of tea and with tiny pulls at their wee pipes, the bowls of which they clicked after each pull against the rim of the charcoal-heater, making a queer metallic accompaniment to their hilarious babble. Certainly, if securing salvation were their main object, they made themselves very merry over the operation. A little above them, on a raised recess, Miss Theodosia Gotch squatted like some strange and uncouth goddess. She had discarded her black satin dress with the beaded Medicis collar for a kimono of sober brown and a sombre-hued obi, though her coarse iron-gray hair frizzled back from her big knobbly forehead, and was coiled in European fashion as of old. Her dark eyes beamed benevolently, and her massive jaw relaxed as she gave forth, to the wail of her concertina, the 'Do, re, mi, fa' in deep falsetto—that same scale practice which had so disturbed Mr. Barradine's afternoon siesta. Her Bible stuck out of the folds of her obi, and the Japanese dictionary, as in *Makara* days, reposed upon her lap.

When Miss Gotch perceived Windeatt and the rest, she uttered a cry and dropped her accordion, and there was a fluttering among the dragon-flies as she made an elephantine leap from the daïs into the other compartment, and shook hands all round with her old travelling companions.

There followed a good deal of questioning on the part of Miss Gotch, and of information, delivered chiefly by the *Makara* young men and Julia Eugarde, concerning the sight-seeings of the Kioto party and their recent misadventure. Herminia Bax was much too discomposed to enter into any relevant explanations, and Madame Izàn, who had never been conversational with the mission-lady, sat apart absolutely silent, and apparently not listening to what was going on. Presently she was mysteriously beckoned to by a nesan, and went off behind the screens at the back to get into her dried garments. Herminia, after a moment or two of indecision and an enigmatic gesture in Mrs. Eugarde's direction, turned to follow her friend. Mrs. Eugarde interpreted the gesture in her mind, and with a little laugh whispered, as Herminia was departing:

' I'd get it over if I were you ; I'd tell her straight away. And I do presume that we should feel less ridiculous in our own clothes, if it's settled that we are to group for a " curtain," as I suggested.'

Herminia responded with an hysterical murmur.

' Oh, I couldn't—I couldn't indeed ! . . . I'll tell her to-night, when we get to Kioto.'

' Tell her what?' asked Miss Gotch when she and Julia were alone. ' Has anything happened to Madame Izàn ? and has her husband turned up yet ? If it has to be broken to her, you had really better employ me. I don't think much of Mrs. Bax's discretion, and I'm used to that sort of thing. Do say—has her husband turned up?'

'I can at least state that I have not been officially informed of the fact,' replied Julia.

'Well, if I can be of any use, I'm staying to-morrow in Kioto,' said Miss Gotch. 'I'll come immediately if you should be landed in a difficulty, and feel strange in foreign parts. I may say that I've already pretty well learned my way about in Japan.'

Julia thanked her, but observed that she hoped they were getting out of a difficulty instead of falling into one.

'I'd never trust a man,' said Miss Gotch. 'Of course, you are thinking of your brother. It was as plain as a pikestaff what he was after. Just you take my advice, and separate those two. It's Madame Izàn I'm anxious about; your brother isn't a blind baby. And that Mrs. Bax is such a fool. I'm interested in Madame Izàn—always have been, though she don't like me. And I imagine that, if there is a difficulty, she's the one that will suffer from it.'

Julia Eugarde gracefully evaded the point with further thanks, promising to avail herself of Miss Gotch's services should there be any news 'to be broken.' 'And now tell me about your own prospects,' she went on. 'I see that you are carrying out the plan of campaign you proposed to yourself on board the steamer, so I conclude that the mission authorities approve of your accordion as part of the artillery of salvation.'

Miss Gotch coloured slightly.

'To tell the truth,' she answered, ' they weren't altogether encouraging about my accordion practice at the mission-house. In fact, I was a good deal hurt at my reception, and found that to some extent there had been a misconception in regard to my joining the staff. They never met me at all that day when you left the *Makara*. However, it's all over now, and I'm going to another station. Fortunately, I had brought a personal letter of introduction to the Bishop from the wife of a great Law Lord—I believe I mentioned him to you in connection with a case of a mixed marriage that I was interested in. That gave me an opportunity of explaining my position and my views in regard to abandoned Eastern women, and tne Bishop has been good enough to allow me to make a kind of tour with a converted Japanese laay, right along to Tokyo, stopping as I please on the way. This was with the idea of my gaining knowledge of the country, and of its people and language, and I am able at the same time to perfect myself in my music.'

'And do you find it answer?' asked Julia. 'I hope that you are getting as satisfactory results as you anticipated.'

'Oh, one can't expect to accomplish serious conversions before mastering the language of a country,' said Miss Gotch. 'But I'm preparing the ground for seed, and shall come back this way, I hope, and sow my grain. I'm very hopeful—extremely hopeful. . . . But I mustn't leave my girls too long to themselves,' pursued the mission, lady, turning a wary eye on the *Makara* young men, who were flirting with the mousmés in the next compartment. 'My Japanese friend is down below, and I shall deliver my charges and come back for a little further chat, if there's time before you start.'

'I must be changing into my own clothes again,' said Mrs. Eugarde. 'I suppose that Jack has gone off to do the same thing.'

The *Makara* young men volunteered to find Windeatt, and see after the jinrikishas. Mrs. Eugarde went off in the wake of a nesan, and Miss Gotch took her place among the disturbed dragon-flies, while Yamasaki drew the sliding panels together once more.

CHAPTER XIV.

NOBODY saw the *Makara* young men again. They trundled off in their rickshaws to Kioto, and Mrs. Eugarde wondered if they, too, had scented a dramatic dénouement, concluding, however, that their departure was of no consequence, as their presence was not indispensable for due effect of the 'curtain.' The fact was that they had made their own private arrangements for an evening's entertainment at Kioto, and the ex-doctor had a lurking fear that Madame Izàn might detain him in attendance upon Kencho, an unnecessary professional obligation that he had no wish to undertake.

The rice-paper compartment was empty when Madame Izàn, robed once more in British blue serge, came back and seated herself forlornly, waiting till Herminia and Mrs. Eugarde should be re-clad in their own garments. But she was too greatly disturbed mentally to be able to wait in quietude. She got up, walking nervously to and fro, and presently clapped her hands, which brought an obliging nesan literally head foremost to her feet.

'I want Kencho—guide—Mr. Kencho Hiro-Kahachi,' she stammered, and attempted some halting Japanese phrases in further explanation. But the nesan had no need of fuller enlightenment, for someone else spoke to her in Japanese from the balcony; and with an obeisance she tripped off, making signs to Madame Izàn that her behest was already fulfilled.

'I am here, madame,' said Kencho's deep voice; and in her bewilderment Izo turned in the wrong direction, and then back again, and saw a man in Japanese dress who was Kencho, and yet not Kencho, standing before her.

His attitude was one of proud humility. She could see that he was moved to the roots of his being, yet struggled to appear calm. Now, as she looked at him earnestly, a painful flush spread over his olive face, which before had been startling in its pallor. The flush faded as quickly as it had come, intensifying still more the pallor; and his eyes, larger, more hollowed in their orbits, and less obliquely set than those of most of his countrymen, glowed on her with mournful fervour. She had never seen those eyes before, and their expression affected her in a way that surprised herself. One of his arms was in a sling, and his head was bandaged. Perhaps it was the white bandage which gave him that ghastly look, and his eyes that peculiar brightness. He seemed altogether so shaken, so ill, and so unlike his former impassive self, that she could scarcely believe the evidence of his voice, and even now doubted if he were indeed Kencho. He saw her hesitation, and cut short the trembling words she began to speak :

'I . . . can't . . . I don't know——'

'Madame,' he said, hardly less tremulously, 'I have to beg your forgiveness—to express my deep regret for this unfortunate accident. . . . But I do not dare. . . . I know that you can never forgive me. . . .'

'Accident !' she exclaimed. 'It is not that— not the upsetting of the boat. That is not what you mean. . . .'

'I hope,' he said more calmly, 'that you were not hurt in any way, or too much terrified.'

'*You* saved me from being hurt.' She blushed, and faltered anew : 'Oh yes, I know, Mr. Kencho, that you have kept me from harm, not thinking of the risk to yourself.'

'Before Heaven,' he answered solemnly, 'I have not thought of myself.'

'I know it. . . . And I thank you. . . . But you meant something else than the accident— something for which you want my forgiveness.

Well, it is granted. Only tell me : why—why did you disguise yourself like that? You must have had a reason. I will not believe that it was anything but an honourable one.'

'Ah !' he cried ecstatically. 'You do trust in my honour?'

'I trust in the honour you have talked to me about,' she answered softly—'in the honour of a Japanese gentleman. But your reason must have been a strong one, Mr. Kencho, for deceiving us all.'

'Yes, it was a strong reason, one that you might understand and excuse, perhaps, and that yet you might never find it in your heart to pardon.' His emotion was becoming uncontrollable. 'Madame, if we were in any less public place, if we could be alone and you would listen, I could fling myself down before you, and pour out my very soul to you. And you would hear me ! True and noble as your nature is, you would pity me, and that woman's nature would plead in my behalf. You could not remain unmoved if once you realized, as you have never yet done, the fulness of my—my devotion for you.'

'As I have never yet done!' she said, gazing at him with wild eyes, in which a faint comprehension dawned. . 'Oh, what does it mean? ... Tell me ... tell me.'

'Not now—not here. My dream had been.—

my longing — to tell you the dearest secret of my soul, when, for the first time together, we should look on the beautiful Fuji-san — emblem to me of you, in your grace and loveliness, and of the love I would peril almost that soul to win. Oh, if we were but alone together now, as we were that day in the temple court. Did I not make you feel then that we Japanese know how to worship an ideal, and to honour a woman, even as the brave men of old honoured righteousness and the good of their country—yes, and could love a woman as I love you, though you are higher than the stars above me? But all that dream has been destroyed to-day. How can I speak? See, it is impossible!' He stopped, for at that moment, as though the 'curtain' Mrs. Eugarde had jestingly planned were being stage-managed to completion, there entered by separate openings, and almost simultaneously, Windeatt from the balcony on one side, and Mrs. Bax, followed by Julia, on the other. It had been Herminia's shrill cry of dismay and compunction that had checked Kencho's impassioned utterance.

Mrs. Eugarde hung back.

'Let them have it out,' she whispered, detaining Herminia ; 'Jack is on the war-path. You won't stop him.'

Windeatt strode to Madame Izàn's side as though he, and he alone, had the right to protect her against what he conceived to be the insolent love-making of a rascally adventurer.

'You hound!' he cried, losing all command of himself in his jealous fury. 'You scheming impostor! I have heard your impertinent speech, and if we were in any other company, I'd kick you down your own Japanese stairs. You will have to answer to me for this insult to a lady who has done you the honour to employ you as her guide, but who, now that she sees you unmasked, will, I am certain, dismiss you at once from her service.'

'Oh, Jack, Jack, you idiot!' murmured Julia Eugarde.

The Japanese man went more pallid than ever, and as he, too, braced himself in a spasm of rage, his hand instinctively sought the place where in ancient days the sword of his saumurai ancestors might have been girded. Thus the rivals confronted each other—the big, fair, blustering Australian and the small, dark Eastern, whose face might have been carved in wood but for the blazing eyes that shone out of it, and yet who, in spite of the taunts hurled at him, never relaxed his grim courtesy.

'Sir,' he said to Windeatt, 'I do not forget that we are in the presence of ladies. And before them I ask *who* has given you the right to resent what may appear in your ignorant eyes an insult to this lady whom, as you say, I have the honour to serve?'

And as he spoke, Julia reluctantly admitted to herself that, of the two, the Eastern had the advantage.

'Oh, you great blundering Jack!' she said under her breath. 'There are certainly some things that you have lost in the Bush.'

'My right!' exclaimed Windeatt fiercely. 'How dare you question it?' Then, recalled to himself, he turned to Madame Izàn, his whole face changing and becoming shy and appealing. 'Will you not let me say that I have the right to punish this intolerable presumption? You have given me the right. . . . You will not deny it.'

But Madame Izàn made him no answer. She stood statue-like, resembling rather now, in her slow-coming and anguished perception of the real state of affairs, a distraught Niobe or forsaken Ariadne than the triumphant Artemis to whom they had formerly likened her.

'You have not forgotten Miidera?' Windeatt whispered, not so low but that Herminia and the guilty Julia, who had connived at that compromising interview on the sacred slope of Hieyezan, heard what he said, and Herminia ventured to steal a little nearer, and, while she shot a smile of sympathetic encouragement at Windeatt, took in her own Izo's unresponsive hand.

Kencho also heard the words and understood. He, too, remembered Miidera, and perhaps he had seen more there on Hieyezan than any of them knew. The muscles about his mouth twitched involuntarily, and all his heart was in his eyes as he watched to see how Madame Izàn bore the allusion. The meaning and the sting it had for her were evident. A blush, as of outraged maidenhood, reddened her cheeks ; her eyes filled with tears, and unconsciously she made that pathetic blind movement which showed always that she was frightened, and uncertain of her mental footing. It was cruel, she felt, of Windeatt to remind her of Miidera ; the recollection was embarrassing. How could she ever forget that he had held her in his arms and had pressed unrebuked kisses upon her lips, whispering vows of which her tacit acceptance implied, she was now aware, so much more than she had then realized? Yet now, when Windeatt, as if in proud vindication of the right he claimed, took her helplessly uplifted hand and held it clasped, she made no effort to withdraw it. She swayed between the two, neither of whom she trusted—friend and lover—turning from each, and all the time trying to avoid the persistent gaze of that other lover, who was an even greater mystery and pain, while her expression was as that of a trapped bird, searching vainly whither it may flee for escape from its captors.

Another, and unobserved, witness of this strange scene noted the look and gesture, and Miss Theodosia Gotch—for it was the mission-lady come back to say her farewells — declared to herself that there should be offered to Madame Izàn, at any rate, a means of temporary flight from the difficulties and perplexities, the false friends, and true and false lovers, that surrounded her. Perhaps this rough soul-saving old maid divined the situation more truly, and had a fuller sympathy and compassion for poor Izo, than many of those with better pretensions to knowledge. Windeatt certainly read Madame Izàn's emotion wrongly, interpreting it, after his wont, in the way he wished, and Kencho, too, was wrong in his interpretation, and, with a miserable recollection of the Miidera episode, told himself that Windeatt might indeed have full reason for his confidence. The glad tenderness in Windeatt's face maddened him, and he was tortured beyond endurance, and felt that he *must* speak, when Madame Izàn herself passionately broke forth :

'I did not know what I was doing at Miidera. I tried to make you understand the truth, and

that I couldn't give any promise—till after—
after Tokyo. Oh, Mr. Windeatt, you took advantage of a poor girl who has never had much
experience of the world, and whose only thought
and wish were then to be free. I did not mean
to give you any right. That was all I cared about
—to be free—to be free !'

It was the last words which pierced like knives
through Kencho's heart. He stifled a hoarse
exclamation, holding himself in again, as Windeatt
turned to Madame Izàn in self-exculpation.

'You know that I would not for worlds vex
or harry you ; you know that the right I ask
is that I may help you to fight for your freedom
—that I may rescue you from the clutches of a
scoundrel.'

Then Kencho could contain himself no longer.
Again Julia Eugarde admired the dignity with
which this small Japanese man comported himself.
He bent down before Madame Izàn with a most
touching and profound reverence, as though
begging her pardon for the blunt avowal he was
forced to make. Gently taking the hand Herminia,
with a scared look into the guide's face, now released, he kept it for a moment or two against his
forehead, then laid it back by her side.

'I had not meant to tell you now,' he said
simply. 'I had meant first to win, if I could,

your respect and affection, and then to reveal
myself in my own way. But things have gone
against me, and this stupid accident has forestalled
my plans. If you do not already guess the truth,
you must know it presently ; for though Mrs.
Bax has said nothing, she cannot fail to recognise
me. I am Izàn Shirazaka! It is for you to tell
me that you wish for your freedom, and I will
give it to you in the only way that is possible.'

'Izàn Shirazaka!' Although she had expected
this, had known that it was coming, all the
blood left Madame Izàn's face, and she repeated
the words mechanically, as though she hardly took
in their meaning. At the same moment, under
stress of the surprise, Windeatt relinquished the
other hand. It seemed to him, too, in spite of
his surprise, that he might have known this from
the beginning. So Izo stood unsupported. And
yet it seemed to her that she had simply gone
back to her old blindness in these last weeks, and
that there never should have been any manner
of doubt in her mind as to the fact that this man
was her husband.

'It's not my fault, Izo,' broke in Herminia.
'I know that you think I have behaved badly, and
you have lost confidence in me completely, but I
really cannot tell why or how I could have acted
differently. I'm prepared to be blamed by every-

one—that's always the way when one has done one's best—and I must say that I think it is most cruel and inconsiderate and ungrateful '—here Herminia's pocket-handkerchief came to the fore—'when all I have done has been to show sympathy. . . . And perhaps, after all, now you will admit, all of you, that there was something in my intuition about Kencho. And as to his being Izàn himself, I solemnly declare to you that I had no more idea of it, till he came out of those Rapids without his wig, than if I had never seen him in my life before. I suppose you will think me a fool for not knowing him, but I can't help it.'

'I don't know that it's so surprising,' said Izan with a sad little laugh. 'With this object in view, I have been taking lessons in the art of make-up and facial control from the great Danjiro himself. But that isn't of any consequence, and it isn't here, Mrs. Bax, that I can plead excuses for breaking my implied engagement not to meet you till your arrival in Tokyo.'

He turned to Madame Izàn, who stood still, dazed and again speechless, and the deep note of feeling came into his voice, while it was certainly with great difficulty now that he kept his lips from giving that betraying twitch.

'All the rest,' he said, 'is between you and me ;

and by-and-by, when you have been able to think the whole matter out, you will meet me face to face and tell me your decision. You shall be free if you wish—yes, I will make you free. I only ask you to think well, and to be true to yourself. Do not let others bias you. I would implore you, if it were possible, to remove yourself from all the present influences, and to give me a fair chance. But it's not possible, and I don't ask even that. You have told me that you trust in my honour ; it is enough. I trust in yours, and I place my honour—my life—in your hands.'

'You are going away?' she said ; and something in the manner of her speaking those simple words and in the look of her face caused the man's heart to thrill again with a trembling hope.

'Yes, I am going away,' he answered. 'What else is there for me to do? I am no longer Kencho the guide. The position is false—impossible. I am going that you may make your choice, undeterred by me. You must now know which of us two men you love, or, at least, care for best ; you must know which counts for most with you—Miidera, or that ceremony in the church in London, which I believe I have the power to make meaningless.'

'Oh,' cried Mrs. Bax, 'do tell me how it's possible to get over that! Mr. O'Halloran did

so want to know, but he died ; and there came a
lawyer's letter, which said it all depended upon
whether Izo was of sound contracting mind ; I
remember the very words. But how were we to
know what they meant ?'

' Later on,' he answered, ' I will write to you,
and will send you the opinion on the question of
our foremost Japanese counsel, who, like myself,
is a barrister of the Middle Temple. You can
place it before Madame Izàn and her Australian
friends. Mrs. Eugarde, I have the honour to
wish you good-bye.'

Julia held out her hand and warmly shook
that of the Japanese. ' Good-bye, Mr. Izàn—or
Shirazaka ought we to call you? I sympathize
with you from my heart, and I wish you well,
though I suppose, if I'm doing that, I'm wishing
my brother ill.'

' Thank you,' he answered, and then he shook
hands with Mrs. Bax. ' You are wrong,' he said,
seeing that she hardly liked to meet his eyes. ' I
don't blame you. But make it all as easy for her
as you can, and leave her to herself. There are
some things which I think she might have been
spared.' Afterwards he turned to Windeatt, who
was moodily gazing out on the broad flood below
Arishiyama. ' I leave you alone in the field,
Mr. Windeatt.'

Windeatt gave a discomfited little laugh like that of a schoolboy who has been worsted in a fight and does not like to own it. There was a little flutter at the moment, caused by the entrance of Yamasaki, bowing his information that at last rickshaws had been found to replace those broken on the rocks in the Rapids, and that all was ready for a start to Kioto. Also of Miss Gotch, who came forward, frankly admitting that she had played eavesdropper, and requesting that she might be allowed to join the party as far as Yaami's, the converted Japanese lady having taken over the troupe of mousmés.

'And I'm going to dine at Yaami's,' announced Miss Gotch ; 'and I want to have a little talk with Madame Izàn.'

The small commotion gave Windeatt an opportunity he felt half inclined to take, of turning on his heel and ignoring Madame Izàn's husband as he would have ignored a foe with whom he was as yet unable to cross swords. But native generosity conquered in his breast, for, after all, they fight like gentlemen in the Bush.

'I wish to apologize to you,' he said, 'for the expressions I used a little while ago. I spoke under an entire misapprehension, and was in the wrong. I beg that you will accept my apology.'

Izàn bowed with his formal Japanese courtesy.

'And I, on my part, Mr. Windeatt, offer you my apologies and regrets for any offence that my manner may have given to you. No doubt there has been cause.'

Windeatt laughed again in melancholy, half-humorous discomposure.

'I fancy the offence was excusable on both sides,' he said. 'Rather like the wind-up of a farce, this, isn't it? But, if you don't mind, I think I would prefer not to shake hands. You see, I mean to take your wife from you, if by her own will and any legal possibility I can get hold of her. Though we are rough-and-ready out West, anyhow, we do things on the square.'

'I understand,' replied Izàn. 'Like you, I prefer not to shake hands. We shall see which man wins.'

That was how Mrs. Eugarde's 'curtain' went off, without any stage-management from her, or from Herminia Bax either. Poor Herminia was sadly subdued. She felt that somehow Izàn had had the best of things, and that somehow, too, she had been convicted of disloyalty, though she didn't exactly know why. The moral bearings of the case were far too muddled in her mind. Finally she ended by laying the blame on Mr. O'Halloran, whose prejudices against Mongolians and Easterns generally had, she felt, upset the balance of her reasoning faculties, and blurred her impressions of Izàn as a boarder in the genteel establishment at West Kensington. Her sympathies, which a little while before had been all for Windeatt, began now to veer round. It would be such a comfort to see Izo established as a properly and openly married woman. There could be no doubt that, as Kencho the guide, Izàn had made himself agreeable to her, and had practically wooed her over again. No doubt was there also that Izàn's manners were strictly European, and even Mr. O'Halloran, were he alive, Herminia felt sure, would hesitate to class the future Viscount Shirazaka with the heathen Chinee detested of the Australian Legislature.

During the rickshaw ride back Herminia interrogated Yamasaki on the subject of hereditary titles in Japan, and on the elder Shirazaka's position at the Imperial Court. It seemed to Mrs. Bax that to be a Viscountess would be a grand thing, even if it were only to be a Japanese Viscountess— better, on the whole, perhaps, than to be the wife of an Australian millionaire. And, besides, how did she know that Windeatt was really a millionaire? Most likely he was nothing but an ordinarily rich man, with a small share in the Wee-Waa Mine, and Australian gold-mines are proverbially uncertain quantities. No ; on the

whole, Herminia concluded that Viscountess Shirazaka sounded better than Mrs. John Windeatt.

Then Dr. Duppo had told her that divorces,
and annulments of marriage, and so forth, were
always disagreeable and troublesome affairs, and
not always certain to come off. He had quoted a
case in which a South African savage—or something of the sort ; Mrs. Bax could not quite
remember the facts—had been proved the legal
wife of an English gentleman, though the marriage
ceremony had been no more sacred in character
than the exchange of a woman for a few heifers or
some beads. Then, too, there were Herminia's
own private and personal arrangements to be considered. Oh, how she sighed during the ride
home for Dr. Duppo's manly support and consolation! And, by the oddest coincidence, what
should greet her upon her arrival at Yaami's but
a letter with the Yokohama postmark in Dr.
Duppo's handwriting, the perusal of which had
such an effect upon Mrs. Bax that she did not
appear at the *table d'hôte*, but shut herself up in
her room, with the door locked between it and
the chamber of Madame Izàn. Was she not
mindful of Shirazaka's injunction—she must call
him Shirazaka now—to leave Izo to herself?
Herminia spent the best hours of the night in
re-reading the letter, and in writing an extremely

emotional reply—a reply which settled all senti-mental difficulties and tergiversations for her in the future, and provided her with an infallible guide and protector for, it was to be presumed, the remainder of her existence.

Those same hours, or part of them, were em-ployed by Miss Theodosia Gotch in the con-version, not to say the abduction, of Madame Izàn. Had Mrs. Bax been less busily occupied over her letter, she might have heard through the partition, and above the murmurs of Theodosia Gotch's somewhat strident voice, sounds betokening a hurried packing and stealthy removal of light baggage. If she did, she paid no heed to them ; and when her wearied head was at last laid upon the pillow, all was still on the other side of the wall. It was fairly late the next morning when, disturbed at hearing of Madame Izàn's absence from the breakfast-table, Mrs. Bax knocked re-peatedly at her friend's door, to find on entering that the bed had not been slept in, that the trunks and effects generally were in disorder, and that some bags and a small portmanteau were missing. Madame Izàn had likewise disappeared, and there was a letter addressed to Mrs. Bax on the table.

'She has eloped with her own husband !' gasped Herminia.

But this was not the case, as she found on reading Madame Izàn's letter, which ran thus:

'MY DEAR HERMINIA,

'I hope that you will not think me unkind in leaving you so suddenly, but I know that you will be quite safe with our friends and Yamasaki, and I am taking the advice of Miss Gotch, whom I am sorry I did not appreciate as I ought to have done on board the *Makara*; for I find her now most sensible and helpful, and well disposed towards me. We neither of us feel that it would be comfortable, or right, for me to stay on with you all after what took place yesterday ; and, besides, I want to be by myself for a little while—as I think my husband wished also—in order that I may think things out properly.

'I am a little afraid of all the fuss there might be over saying good-bye, so, as Miss Gotch has asked me to stay with her for the present—till we all meet again at Tokyo, or, at any rate, till something is settled about my future—I have decided to accept her offer, and we both think it wiser to start off quietly to-night or early to-morrow morning, without saying a word to anybody.

'Will you please explain all this to Mrs. Eugarde, who, I think, will understand and approve, and give my kind regards to Mr. Windeatt? I am leaving you circular notes, and will write again in a few days. I believe that we are going first to Nagoya, and then to Kama-Kura, where the big statue is that we all wanted to see. But I hope you won't trouble to come after me, as I should not like it, or let my going interfere in any way with other people's plans. I dare say that, after all, you wouldn't dislike the Ise temples so much as you seemed to think you would.

' Your affectionate

' Izo.'

Mrs. Bax threw this letter like a bombshell at Windeatt and his sister, and dissolved into floods of tears, broken by hysterical upbraidings of Madame Izàn, who she said had deserted and betrayed her, notwithstanding the sacrifice of her— Mrs. Bax's—life on the altar of friendship. In the course of her bewailings she announced the fact of her engagement to Dr. Duppo, which Mrs. Eugarde at once said simplified matters a good deal, and which she made the subject of her heartiest congratulations. Julia Eugarde took an entirely optimistic view of the whole situation. She used temperate arguments to draw her brother out of his mood of wrathful consternation, extolled Miss Gotch as, for the occasion, the god out of the machine, and praised Madame Izàn for having taken just the sort of initiative which would under the circumstances have occurred to a really nice woman.

'Of course, Jack,' she said, 'after the brutally crude way in which things were managed yesterday —and I blame you for that, and not poor Izàn, or Shirazaka, or whatever he calls himself—it would have been too embarrassing for her to carry on the old tourist relations with us. This was really the only proper thing for her to do, and I'm very glad she has done it.'

Julia did her best to persuade her brother into the Ise expedition ; but he, like Herminia Bax, declined any more temples, and the idea had to be given up. Windeatt was determined not to let himself be whirled off in a jinrikisha beyond reach of treaty ports, British Consuls, railways and tele-graph-wires. How was he to be certain that Izàn Shirazaka was not in league with the Japanese Spy Department—he had been given to understand that Japan was in advance of all civilized nations in the efficiency of her Secret Police service—and was it not likely enough that some hideous plot against Australian life and liberty, and against the safety of Madame Izàn, was being concocted ? No, he would not leave his beloved to the mercy of his treacherous rival, even though that rival might be her lawful husband. He would be near and ready to respond to her faintest call.

It was in vain that Julia told him he was a fool, and that to follow Madame Izàn to Kama-Kura would be a breach of the laws of good taste. He affirmed that Izàn had committed a worse breach of good taste in disguising himself as Kencho the guide, and that, moreover, all was fair in love and war. And was not the Dai-Butsu a notable statue —the shrine of all tourists—and had he not as good a right to gaze upon it as any English or American or Australian globe-trotter? Anyhow, it was at last arranged that Miyanoshita, which is only a short journey from Kama-Kura, should be accepted as a compromise; and thither, under guidance of Yamasaki, these three pilgrims, of whom two might certainly be called passionate, duly started.

In the meantime there had come a letter to Mrs. Bax from Izàn Shirazaka, enclosing a digest of the opinion of Mr. Ohosumiya, of Tokyo and Yokohama and the Middle Temple, Barrister-at-Law.

Mr. Ohosumiya was of opinion that the marriage between Izobel O'Halloran and Izàn Shirazaka was valid both in English and Japanese law. In English law the only argument against its *primá-facie* validity lay in the question whether, at the time of its taking place, the lady had been under no outside compulsion, and of sound contracting mind——

'There, I told you that was what they said,' put in Herminia—'of sound contracting mind!'

It would be for the jury to decide, in any attempt to prove the marriage void, if she did knowingly and willingly contract. In Mr. Ohosumiya's view of the case, blindness constituted no element of importance, nor did he consider the circumstances laid before him as justifying such contention.

The dissolution of a Japanese marriage, Mr. Ohosumiya averred, presents no serious difficulty, and may be done by the mutual consent of the parties involved, it not being the Japanese custom to make of such matters a legal question, but referring them for settlement to the family council. Mr. Ohosumiya went on to explain that there still prevails in Japan a law similar to that among the old Romans in reference to domestic relations. This Mrs. Eugarde thought very interesting, and she made notes of the barrister's information for the benefit of the British public in her 'Round the World Jottings.'

It would appear that conjugal unions and separations are not hedged round with all the difficulties and restrictions of a Western civilization, the formalities to be gone through for the contracting or dissolution of any Japanese marriage consisting merely in the entering or striking off the names of the persons concerned in the rolls of their respective families, such rolls being kept by Japanese law.

'What an artistic nation is here!' wrote Julia Eugarde later. 'The essence of true art, it is agreed, lies in simplicity, and for these people, life in all its complex relations is a fine art, to be moulded into a harmonious whole, so that to them even marriage is shorn of its revolting commonplace intricacies, and may be annihilated without violation of a delicate tranquillity. No jarring revelations; no scandalous newspaper reports : the dignified deliberations of a family council, and all is done. It is not necessary for a Japanese to become naturalized in Texas in order to readjust his marital sympathies.'

It will be observed that Mrs. Eugarde's literary style had something of the journalistic quality, which was no doubt natural enough. The dissolution of the English marriage, however, Mr. Ohosumiya went on, would be a more complicated affair. In ordinary procedure towards such end, the Japanese husband would obtain a divorce granted by Japanese customary law, and would thereafter marry again. Proceedings in a divorce action in the London courts might then be commenced on the part of the English wife. They would involve, probably, a commission issued by the London courts to take evidence in Japan, an expensive and dilatory business. Such commission, on returning to London, might be used as evidence, and the evidence so obtained of first, a Japanese divorce, and second, remarriage of the respondent, would certainly be followed by a *decree nisi*, made absolute after the lapse of six months.

That was the substance of it all. The indefatigable novelist began forthwith to plan a romance upon the lines of Mr. Ohosumiya's communication, and for the moment, the exciting consideration that she would be breaking ground practically new in fiction turned Julia's thoughts from Madame Izàn's position, and the manner in which it might affect her brother's future.

The emotional Herminia, however, showed a surprising readiness in seizing the points of the situation. It may have been that she had already skirted it with Dr. Duppo. Clearly, this had been the meaning of Izàn Shirazaka's magnanimous offer to give Izo her freedom. To accomplish that end he was prepared to sacrifice his predilections in favour of Western womanhood, and to take a wife from among his own charming compatriots, a soft, confiding, biddable little mousmé, whom he might divorce also if he so pleased, later on, under the compliant jurisdiction of another family council.

So far, so good. But — and again it was Herminia Bax who aired the appalling supposition —what about the Queen's Proctor? She had caught the phrase from newspaper reports, which she was fond of reading—or was it Dr. Duppo who had suggested it? Neither she nor Julia had any but vague notions as to the peculiar functions of this mysterious official; nor was Windeatt much better informed. But they comforted themselves with the reflection that Izàn, being learned in English law—not to speak of Ohosumiya—must have contemplated the ghastly possibility of such intervention, and was duly armed against it. Or was he fully aware of the danger, and was his seeming generosity nothing but a blind in order that he might the better secure his own end—the capture of Madame Izàn?

CHAPTER XV.

EVERYTHING 'happens' in Japan, if one only chooses to wait a little while. It is an artistic deity that presides over these blest isles, and this benign divinity had somehow arranged that on one particular day Fuji-san should show herself as she so rarely does—unveiled, virgin, glorious, her snow-streaked cone rising clear in its purity, the exquisite outline reflected in a duplicate perfectness upon the blue waters of Lake Hakone.

'Fuji-san!' cried the coolies, waiting by their rickshaws below the tea-house.

'Fuji-san!' called the gardener, waving his hand to his dear mountain, so that the strangers might understand that this was no ordinary sight, but the best that Japan could offer her visitors— the gardener who tended the dwarf trees, which were so old—so old—and dusted the stone lanterns down in the grassy plat beneath the balcony.

'Fuji-san!' echoed the nesans, ecstatically rushing forward to point out their sacred mountain to two new-comers, who nevertheless were dressed in Japanese kimonos, and who were standing in one of the open compartments within the tea-house.

The elder of these two ladies was Theodosia Gotch ; the other—tall and straight and a little embarrassed by her unwonted costume, and very beautiful with the soft gray-blue folds of the kimono—that one which had been made for her in Kioto under Kencho's direction—showing the lines of her lithe figure, and giving to them a new nobleness, and with her brocaded obi tied, not in mousmé fashion, but in that of a Japanese matron —was Madame Izàn. And just then there entered a man in European dress, with a grave, anxious face and sad, eager eyes—a face which was not European, but was, in fact, that of Izàn Shirazaka, who had come, by appointment with the mission-lady, to hear his fate from his wife's lips. And the answer that Izo gave him was to step forward, blushing, yet radiant, with a little graceful-awkward twist of her draperies and an unaccustomed shuffle of her feet in their shapeless tabis, while, without speaking, she extended one arm, from which the matron's sleeve of her kimono fell backward, towards the propitious and ever· beloved Fuji-san.

BILLING AND SONS, PRINTERS, GUILDFORD

www.ingramcontent.com/pod-product-compliance
Lightning Source LLC
Chambersburg PA
CBHW021748110726
47902CB00006B/1440